THE WELL

A.J. WHITTEN

GRAPHIA

Houghton Mifflin Harcourt

Boston   New York   2009

For information about permission to reproduce selections from this book,
write to Permissions, Houghton Mifflin Harcourt Publishing Company,
215 Park Avenue South, New York, New York 10003.

Graphia and the Graphia logo are registered trademarks of
Houghton Mifflin Harcourt Publishing Company.

www.hmhbooks.com

The text of this book is set in Adobe Garamond Pro.

Library of Congress Cataloging-in-Publication Data
Whitten, A. J.
The well / by A. J. Whitten.
p. cm.
Summary: Fourteen-year-old Cooper must face a monster trapped for
two centuries in a well near his stepfather's Maine vineyard or risk everything
that he holds dear, including his girlfriend, Megan.
ISBN 978-0-547-23229-4
[1. Monsters—Fiction. 2. Supernatural—Fiction. 3. Mothers and sons—
Fiction. 4. Stepfathers—Fiction. 5. Brothers—Fiction. 6. Schools—
Fiction. 7. Maine—Fiction.] I. Title.
PZ7.W617829Wel 2009
[Fic]—dc22
2009007973

ISBN 978-0-547-23229-4

Manufactured in the United States of America
DOM 10 9 8 7 6 5 4 3 2 1

PROLOGUE

The boy would be his.

It was only a matter of time.

And then he could walk the earth again. See the sun. Breathe fresh, sweet air, not this fetid exhale of the dead.

He had waited so long for the life-giving blood that would resurrect his body. Turn him from a pathetic, scrabbling creature into something that resembled a human again. Take away the torture of his existence and allow him out of this darkness. How long since he had seen the light?

Centuries.

Two torturous centuries, the length of his sentence. But soon that wait would be over.

He lived in the depths of hell, in a hole where no one looked. He suffered, crawling through the muck, the wet, across stones that scraped what remained of his body, shredding his skin, tearing his nails. He had learned to adapt, like a creature in the wild.

So he could wait. Wait to be fed.

She would bring the boy to him. Today. He could almost smell the boy's blood. Taste his flesh. Feel the life that would pour into him, resurrect him.

Soon. He would be whole.

And then—

And then he would get his revenge.

CHAPTER 1

Dying in the movies always looks cool. The hero gets a big sendoff with flames and some hot chick. Behind him, a stack of bullet-stoked gangbangers' bodies are piled up in crushed SUVs. Everyone cries. Fade to black.

Dying that way rocks.

But the way I was going to die would suck. Stuck in the bottom of a well. No way out, no hope of anyone ever finding me. While some beast-creature-monster-thing waited in the corner for me to give up.

So it could eat me alive.

Oh my God.

I screamed for help, but it was a waste of time. Who could hear me this far down? Not even me, not anymore. My voice had pretty much deserted me.

Just like she had.

If I died—I couldn't think the word *when,* because that totally wigged me out—they wouldn't write movies about me. Cuz no one would stay past the opening credits. My fourteen years on earth had been that boring.

Until now.

I started shivering. I was cold; I ached all over. But more, I was scared. Scared all the way into my bones. My blood was popsicle juice—thick, freezing.

How long had I been here? Twenty minutes? An hour? Two? It seemed as if I'd spent my entire stupid life down here, covered in slime, wet, terrified out of my freakin' mind.

Worse, I had nowhere to go to get away from that . . . that *thing.* Whatever the hell it was. A rat? Yeah, I told myself, it had to be a rat. Or a raccoon that had fallen in, gotten stuck like me, in the bottom of a damp, moss- and mold-encrusted well. The light at the top as far away as Mars.

But you know what was worse? And yeah, there were worse things than being stuck in a hole while some monster lurked in the shadows.

Like being there because you were shoved down the well by someone who was supposed to love you.

That sucked ten times more.

My fingers felt like raw hamburger from scraping against the rounded, slippery bricks of the walls. But the well still held me tight. Twenty feet down. Maybe more. It was hard to tell.

There was no other way out, not unless I could pull a Superman and fly up. But I wasn't any kind of a hero, just a not-so-built high school freshman who'd been cut from the football team last week because my own father wouldn't give me a passing grade in English.

I heard a huff-huff. Almost like a laugh. Holy crap. Not again. I hugged the wall.

It was back.

That thing that lived in a dark space, maybe a tunnel, carved in the back of the well. I didn't know what it was. And I didn't *want* to know. I might have been fourteen and thought I was immortal when I was standing on firm ground, but when you're stuck in a two-inch skanky puddle in a well with some *thing* a few feet away, I don't care who you are— you're ready to piss your pants like a three-year-old girl.

It huffed again, and then something scraped against the floor. A scritch-scratch.

That was a rat. Yeah, a rat, with really long claws.

Or at least, I *prayed* it was a rat.

But no, there it was again, louder now, too loud to be a rodent. I shrank away from the sound, but where was I going to go? I had six feet of space, six feet of darkness filled with slippery, slimy wet that stuck to my clothes, my hands, like glue, but I scrabbled back all the same, away from that *scritch-scratch, scritch-scratch,* patiently coming closer to me, one clawing, scraping step at a time.

Oh God.

More huffing, as if it were smoking a huge cigar or it had an anteater nose and was inhaling my scent. Did rats eat people?

If it was a big enough rat, I bet it would. Then why hadn't this one come after me yet? What was it waiting for? Was it waiting until it sensed I'd finally given up? Or waiting until it was sure no one was ever coming back for me?

Oh God, oh God, oh God.

Get me out of here. I'll do my homework, clean my room, be nice to my brother, my stepfather—hell, everyone, all the time. Just please make someone notice I'm missing.

Please.

I pressed against the wall. The stones scratched a pattern of hard lines into my back. The water beneath my Vans sloshed against my socks, slippery, thick as—

God, thick as blood. But it wasn't blood. No way, wasn't blood. Every horror movie I'd ever seen raced through my mind.

Scritch-scratch.

Closer now.

Bile rose in my throat, the puke thick, burning on the rewind. I spewed chunks.

"Help!" But all that came out was a croaking whisper. Up above, I heard the barking of Whipple, my dog. Little terrier yips, useless against the well, the creature.

Who'd hear him this far from civilization? We were in the woods, for God's sake, not in the mall. Dog kept on barking his head off. Thought he was Lassie or something. "Whipple," I whispered, calling him even though he couldn't hear me. Like a hope-aholic, I reached up the stone wall. My hands grasped for leverage, for a nook, anything to grab, to latch on to within the cold, damp bricks. I found nothing but more of that gluey, slimy moss and crevices too thin to gain a foothold.

I was going to die. Alone down here. And no one would ever find me.

I started to cry. I didn't care if boys weren't supposed to cry. My guts twisted, and I had to punch a fist tight into my solar plexus to keep whatever was left of my lunch from riding back up the throat elevator.

Scritch-scratch. The breathing heavier, thicker. Filled with the smell of rotten eggs and dead animals. I gagged.

Oh, God. Oh, God. Oh, Jesus God. I swiped at the sweat and tears on my face. The slimy moss stuck to my cheeks, holding on like spider webs. It wouldn't let go. Was going to stay with me forever. Would be there if they found me, if they ever found my body—

Buck up—stop crying. Be a man.

Trying to go somewhere?

The words came not from a person's voice, but in my head. And even weirder, not in my own voice. In another voice, one that was deep and gravelly. The voice of . . .

The thing. Holy freakin' crap.

The dog kept barking, the sound of his yipping going in and out like a radio station that wouldn't stay tuned. Was he looking for help? Running in circles? Chasing a stupid rabbit?

Scritch-scratch. I'm coming closer.

More breathing, more of that smell, like a stink bomb released right under my nose. I grabbed at the walls again, but whatever sticky slime was on them wasn't enough to hold me.

I closed my eyes, thought of Megan, tried to smell her shampoo, picture the deep pools of her blue eyes. But I couldn't. It was as if trying to conjure her up in this foul place only made the whole situation worse—

And this was bad enough already.

Oh, Cooper . . .

Holy freakin' mother. Did that thing just say . . . my *name?* The rest of my lunch came hurling forward.

Someone, anyone—I didn't care if it was Harvey the

Clown on Channel 33—please notice I was gone. But who? Who would think to come this far back in the woods?

And look in the well, of all places?

Then Whipple stopped barking. Terror filled every blank spot inside me. The last thoughts of hope ran away.

No one was coming. Who was I kidding? *She* wasn't coming back to get me either, and that thing—

The thing's breathing got louder, the huffing increasing in volume, bouncing off the walls, heat multiplying in the small space, coming at me like a mortuary fan filled with the scent of formaldehyde and rot, and then the breath was on my neck, making my tiny hairs stand at attention. I was scrabbling against the wall, knowing it was useless, knowing the thing was going to get me, eat me, have me for dinner—

"Grab the rope, you idiot. I'm not going to climb down there and get you myself. God, you're such a moron."

I looked up at the circle of light above my head and saw my older brother, Faulkner. Thank God. He looked about as excited as a senior citizen at a Green Day concert, holding a thick rope and waiting for me to grab it.

I chanced a glance over my shoulder. The huffing had stopped, the darkest shadows now just shadows again, not inky pools of doom. Had I imagined it? Made the whole thing up, out of fear?

Yeah. I must have, I told myself, because it was easier than believing the truth. What could live in a well, anyway?

Yeah, it was nothing. So don't be scared. Stay awhile, Cooper.

I didn't hear that. Didn't hear a thing.

My hands trembled when I grabbed on to the rope, my palms so sweaty it took two tries before I had a solid enough grip. My Vans slipped against the well's walls. Faulkner cursed three times as he hauled me out of there, calling me stupid in English *and* Spanish.

Showoff. He's in Spanish III and thinks he's going to Spain after graduation, so he runs around spouting, *"¿Cómo estás? ¿Dónde está la puerta?"* and crap like that, like he's freakin' Juan Valdez. Our father thinks it shows he's got genius material. I think it's a sign of dementia.

But he was the one on the other end of the rope, pulling me away from that thing, so I kept my *"¿Hermano loco?"* thoughts to myself. I decided I didn't mind the Spanish so much right now anyway.

"How the hell did you end up down there?" Faulkner asked when I reached the top. He didn't offer me a hand, just stepped back and left me to scramble over the edge on my own. Hey, at least he'd come with the rope.

I brushed my pants off, but it was a wasted gesture. The slime stuck, a black-green glue with eau de decay. I watched a show about this death farm once, where these forensic guys left pigs and dead bodies outside in old cars and watched them rot, measuring the maggots on them to tell how fast a body would go from fat and fleshy to ashes and dust. About two weeks in, things got really hairy and nasty.

That was what my pants smelled like. What the well stank of. If I could have, I would have stripped off my Levi's and "Hamlet Had Issues" T-shirt—an early and ironic birthday present from my professor father—right there and burned them, but I didn't think Faulkner wanted to see me in my Hanes briefs.

"What happened?" Faulkner asked. He picked up his pace to match mine, hauling butt out of the woods that surrounded the well and that served as a natural keep-out fence around the Jumel Vineyards to our east. The well sat in the center of the thick forest of trees, surrounded by its own little grapevine of these rare, pale champagne grapes. Our stepfather, who owned the vineyard, said those vines had been there since, like, the dawn of time. Then some smart Jumel dude bought the land for a song in, like, 1800-something and made gazillions. Didn't matter to me. I couldn't put enough distance between me and that Jumel history.

"You wouldn't believe me if I told you." I was his younger brother. He never believed me about anything anyway.

"Try me," Faulkner demanded.

I thought for a moment about what logical explanation

there might be for my ending up at the bottom of the well. "I tripped," I finally said.

Faulkner snorted. "Idiot. You tripped and fell down a well? What are you, five?"

"Just shut up." The slime was up and down my scraped-up hands, just as stuck as it was on my pants. I was going to need one serious shower. Maybe a pressure washer.

A flurry of leaves came rushing at us in a tiny cyclone, and my heart kicked up. I took three steps back, everything inside my gut rising to choke up my throat. Oh God, it had gotten out of the well.

It was coming after me.

The smell. I could smell it.

Hear it. Panting. Breathing. Running.

And then it was on me, it—

Was the dog. The stupid dog, leaping on my chest, his tiny body of fur one massive projectile of mammal love. "Whipple, you idiot." I went to hug the dog to me, but he leaped off just as fast as he'd jumped on.

He let out a whimper, his tail ducking between his legs. He scrambled back three steps, then dropped his nose to the ground and poked it forward, like a kid about to get busted for having Marlboros in his room. Whipple took one quick sniff of the green streaks on my Vans, then whimpered again and lay down, his head on his paws, his eyes wide and scared.

Did dogs get scared of slime?

"What's wrong with him?" Faulkner asked.

"I don't know." I shrugged, as if I didn't care. But there was something. Something in that slime.

Something I didn't want to know.

"That dog's acting psycho," Faulkner said. "First he runs off yesterday and stays gone all night, and he, like, never does that. Now he's . . . strange. Like he inhaled gas or something."

"Leave him alone." I turned toward the house. Pretending nothing had happened. Easier than admitting something had.

Faulkner and I walked back to the house, the leaves floating up around our shoes, so ordinary, so real, almost as though I had imagined that time in the well. But I hadn't, and I knew it. I could still smell the thing on me. Could still see the long, ugly red scratches—like claw marks—on my arms and hands from the fall and from scraping against the stone walls. Feel the throbbing ache in my legs, my feet, my hands, from landing on the bottom.

I shuddered and shook my head, pushing the thoughts away.

Pushing away what had really happened. Because I didn't

want to believe it. Yeah, so what if I wanted to hold on to a fantasy? Call me a baby; sue me for trying to be a kid a little longer. I kept telling myself the whole thing was one big-ass accident. That no one would purposely shove me down with that—

That *thing*.

No. It didn't happen.

Not like that. I'd pissed her off, that was all. It had been a fight, a misunderstanding.

Not on purpose at all.

"Are you going to tell me?" Faulkner said.

"Tell you what?"

"What the hell happened?"

"Will you let it go?"

Faulkner stopped and grabbed my arm, spinning me so hard that I collided with his chest, leaving a smear of dirt on his Hollister tee. I stumbled back. Faulkner, I noticed, was a mess. His short brown hair stuck out like tumbleweed, as if he'd been running his hand through it, messing with his careful gel job, and his face was splotchy with color. He wasn't cool, far from it. "Tell me, Cooper. Before I rip your head off."

"What is your problem?"

"You are, you freak."

I rolled my eyes and started walking again. If he hadn't

just saved my life, I'd hate him. No, I did hate him. I always had. Faulkner had been put on this earth ahead of me to torture me. We'd gotten along for about five minutes when he was nine and I was six. I'd gotten a train set for Christmas that he wanted to play with, too. We'd set it up, raced our Lionel HOs, and actually had fun—

Until he slammed his engine into mine, knocking my train off the tracks. A war broke out, the tracks got cracked in the scuffle, and we never played together again.

"Thanks," I said.

"Whatev." Faulkner shrugged, as if his being there today had been no big deal.

"What made you come out there? With a rope, too?"

He didn't say anything for a minute, just walked. In the forest ringing the outskirts of the vineyard, the wind whistled through the nearly bare trees. Here and there, birds called to one another, their songs almost lonely and desperate. I hated fall. Hated winter more. It was all so . . . dead. Quiet and still. Not that I was one of those happy spring kind of people, but I wasn't big on watching things fade, curl up, and die.

Not unless they were English assignments or creatures that lived in abandoned wells. Those I could do without.

"I know you're lying about tripping." Faulkner drew in a breath. "I saw her."

The world around us went silent.

I swallowed hard and kept walking, hoping if I ignored what he'd said he'd pretend he'd never spoken the words. I watched my sneakers pulverize the signs of fall, reds and oranges and yellows crushing to dust beneath size nines. "You didn't see anything."

"Don't lie to me, Cooper. I can't go back in the house if she's going to toss me down that well next. What's going on?"

I didn't say anything for a long time. We left the boundaries of the woods, then stepped onto a lawn so perfect, the grass was probably afraid to bend in case it disappointed my stepfather. An HGTV fantasyland of flowers and shrubs surrounded us, all part of the carefully maintained Sam Jumel image. Not a detail overlooked. There were days when I fantasized about doing a little garden chain-saw massacre, just to see the look on my stepfather's face.

But it wouldn't be worth the hell I'd be left living with, and I already had enough crap on my plate. More than enough—the kind a kid shouldn't have to deal with.

"Tell me, Cooper," Faulkner said, his voice rising into a pitch a choir leader would have loved.

I let out a breath and inhaled one that still smelled like the well, like death warmed over a barbecue. "Don't worry, Faulkner. I don't think you're the one she wants."

"How do you know that?"

I wheeled around and faced him, feeling a lot older right in that moment than fourteen. Older, in fact, than Faulkner, whose voice had taken on a little boy kind of sound. The kind that said, "Please don't destroy my perfect sitcom world with this attempted murder crap."

I knew the feeling.

"I just know." I didn't, not really, but Faulkner looked about as freaked out as I felt. Maybe if I told him the truth, he could even help me. "Because . . ." I drew in another breath, then confronted the truth that no son wants to tackle, the gut-twisting, soul-sucking truth that was smacking me in the face. Ignoring it had landed me at the bottom of the well with something that had briefly considered me an appetizer. "Because this isn't the first time Mom has tried to kill me."

CHAPTER 2

I made it as far as the washing machine.

She found me in the basement next to the Maytag, standing in my underwear, with the dirty clothes in one hand, the other hand reaching for the metal lid. "Cooper. What are you doing?"

I froze. Cursed. Goose bumps danced up my spine and my guts twisted like a pretzel. It wasn't just that I was a teenage boy caught doing laundry. In an ordinary home, that would be suspicious. Ordinary mothers would suspect stealing, snorting coke, hosting orgies in the afternoon, or something equally illegal or weird, like the world suddenly coming to an end. But this wasn't an ordinary house and she was no ordinary mother. I had to grip the edge of the washer before I could force a word past my lips. "Nothing."

She reached past me and I could smell her perfume, the

one she'd worn for as long as I could remember. Something that reminded me of fruit. I forgot the name of it, but it came in a red box and cost, like, sixty bucks. I remember because my stepfather had bought some last Christmas and groaned about how he could have gotten a chain saw or a leaf blower for that amount of money. Even though he could well afford two hundred boxes of the stuff. My stepfather came from generations of wealth, worked two days a week as an OB/GYN, owned a vineyard that practically poured money into his pockets, yet was as tight with his money as a lunch lady with seconds on pizza day. In the year and a half they'd been married, I'd never understood what my mother saw in him, other than maybe a checkbook. Faulkner and I worked on staying out of his way and counting down the days until we turned eighteen.

My mother's arm brushed against my shoulder. Her perfume no longer smelled like her, or like my childhood.

It smelled like fear.

Everything inside me turned to ice. A part of me didn't want to believe it. That stupid part that kept believing in accidents and chalking the whole thing up to one intense case of PMS.

"Cooper, you can't do that."

I waited. Waited for her to yank me out of there with some excuse about looking for the dog, lying to me about him being lost, and then when we got near the well, she'd grab me again by the back of the neck and drag me to the edge, and before I could think, react, dig in my heels, stop her, she would throw me down, down into that deep dark hole.

And this time, this time, I wouldn't get out.

But no, I told myself, remembering to breathe, to hold on to control, this time Faulkner was waiting outside, and I knew, even though I was never *numero uno* on his friends list, he'd stop her. Two against one. Better odds.

"You can't do that," she repeated. "You have to use this stuff first." My mother handed me a bottle of something called OxiClean. "It'll get those grass stains out of your clothes. What were you doing, anyway? Playing baseball in the mud or something? And my Lord, what happened to your arms? You're all scratched up. Did you get in a fight?" She looked me over, her nose wrinkling up. "God, your clothes stink, too, Cooper. Take a shower, honey, before you change."

She really didn't know? Didn't remember? Had no idea how I had gotten those scratches? That slime? That smell?

Dude, I wanted to scream, you *did this.*

I dared to look at her. She was a normal-looking, American-pie, carpooling, cookie-baking mother. Wearing jeans, an untucked and neatly pressed blue cotton button-down, her blond hair no longer a mess and up in a ponytail.

The crazy glassiness was gone from her green eyes. Whatever had possessed her had passed.

Like it always did.

She'd forgotten everything that had happened earlier and had gone back to being Mom again. For now.

My breath escaped in a whoosh. "Thanks, Mom. I'll, ah, do that."

Her palm warmed my forehead. I felt five again, and for one second, my guts untwisted. "Are you feeling okay? You look pale. *And* you're doing laundry." She laughed, just a little. Enough that a window opened inside me and I wanted to trust her.

"I'm fine." I swallowed hard. "Really."

"Okay. Be sure to do your homework. And call Megan. She called here looking for you a while ago and didn't sound happy. I thought you liked her?"

I didn't answer that question. Didn't bother telling my mother that *she* was the whole reason Megan wasn't happy. *Yeah, Megan, sorry I stood you up but my mother was trying to kill me. I was a little busy trying to escape from something that was trying to eat me and climb out of a freakin' well. Next time, before I ask you out on our first fancy date, I'll check to see if my mother's got any murder plans on the menu.*

I shuffled to the side. Was Mom really normal? Or was she just pretending again?

"Sam doesn't want me going out with Megan," I said instead of the real answer.

My mother pursed her lips. "Maybe he's concerned dating will distract you from school and getting good grades."

Sam had never given a crap about my grades. He just wanted to keep me home, under his thumb. Either way, it wasn't as though an A in algebra was the most important thing going on in my life right now. I didn't reply to that one either.

"Megan is a nice girl. I'll keep talking to Sam. And you," my mother said, her face curving up into a smile, "should ask Megan to the Freshman Fall Dance in a few weeks. If you haven't already. I'm sure she's expecting to go with you."

Now my mother was giving me dating advice? It was as if she'd been switched by aliens, from the psycho in the woods to this one, the mom I remembered from before. The one I had trusted. Loved. The one I wanted to believe still existed.

"Yeah. I will."

"Good." She looked me over one more time. "Do you want me to get you the antibiotic cream and some Band-Aids for those scratches? They really do look nasty. I'd hate them to get infected."

"No, Mom, I'm . . . ah, I'm okay."

She almost looked . . . disappointed, like I'd let her down

by not allowing her do the mom thing with Neosporin. "All right, if you're sure." Her voice sounded like a sitcom mom's. I could almost believe everything was normal in this house. And could almost fool myself into thinking the afternoon had been a figment of my imagination. "Oh, Cooper? Your birthday is next week. Did you want to do anything special?"

"No, that's okay. Let's keep it quiet."

She reached out to ruffle my hair and it took everything I had not to flinch. "Yeah, maybe you're getting too big for the family thing, huh?"

"Yeah. Maybe."

"Either way, I'll make sure you have a nice birthday. Every birthday should be great, Cooper. Because you're a special child to me." Then she smiled and walked away, looking back at me one more time over her shoulder.

Something scary glittered in her eyes for a second, then disappeared.

I bit my lip so hard, I tasted blood. Then I did as she had said, taking a shower that nearly burned my skin in the basement bathroom until the slime was gone. For once, I didn't worry about how much water I used or whether my stepfather would freak about all the gallons going down the drain.

It barely made a difference. I could have emptied the entire hot-water tank, and still the smell lingered, as if the well were some kind of blackhead in my pores. I did a heavy Axe spray, then pulled on clean clothes and left the basement by the back door. When I got outside, I expected Whipple to run onto the stone terrace and jump up on me again. I'd never gone outside without finding him there, a tennis ball in his mouth.

But no dog. I called him, but he didn't come. Maybe he was still pouting from earlier.

But another part of me knew there was more. He'd gotten a whiff of whatever was in the well and it had scared him, too.

I wasn't going back there. Wasn't going within five hundred feet of the well. Ever again.

"She's all right now," I said when I met up with Faulkner on the deck.

"What do you mean, 'all right'? You said she tried to kill you earlier." Faulkner waved toward the house, his movements panicked. He ran a hand through his hair, paced a few steps around me. "This is *Mom* we're talking about, Coop. Our *mother,* not some serial killer who just got paroled. Maybe she's demented or doing crystal meth or something. What the hell is going on? When did this start?"

What answer did he want from me? The whole thing was

way too Jerry Springer. I needed time to think, to get my head around it all.

"You wouldn't believe me if I told you," I said for the second time that day.

"You know, you're a real pain in the ass." He shook his head. "Why won't you just tell me why our mother was throwing you down that well, like you were a quarter she was making a wish on?"

I didn't want to talk about this. Talking about it meant all of this was real. I didn't want it to be real, because then I would have to believe that *thing* was real, too. "I'm going to deal with this myself, Faulkner."

Faulkner snorted. "Right. Now you're going to go all Clint Eastwood? If there's something I should know, dude, spill it."

I inhaled and caught the scent of the well still on me, like bad B.O. No amount of Axe could cover it up.

What the hell was down there?

My throat choked up again. Suddenly I wasn't the high school freshman who had felt like he could have conquered the world twenty-four hours ago. I was a scared kid who needed someone to come along and slay the dragon.

Preferably someone bigger who would believe me—

And not tell me I was crazy.

If Faulkner believed me, well, it sucked and it helped, all

at once. It helped, because it meant I didn't need to go see Dr. Feelgood and get the extra-long armed jacket and a lifetime supply of Haldol. But it sucked because it meant I wasn't nuts and my mother was, indeed, trying to kill me.

Normal teenage boys had trouble with zits. Asking girls out. Bad grades. Not homicide.

Rotten disappointment rode in my stomach like school cafeteria fish nuggets, telling me that the same woman who had given birth to me, changed my diapers, walked me into first grade, and sat through every one of my screeching clarinet recitals wanted me dead.

Not exactly good for the old self-esteem levels.

I stopped breathing through my nose. No more smelling that thing. That was too much for now. One thing at a time.

I met my brother's blue eyes and nodded. "I don't know much," I said as we walked away from the house and down our street. Into normal American-pie land. It got easier to talk the farther we were from Mom and my stepfather's eighteen-room palace. "She started acting weird a few years ago."

"Weird how?"

"Like . . . she stopped hugging me." My face got hot. "I know, but I had just turned thirteen and I still cared about that kind of thing. Not now, though. I'm older now."

"Yeah," Faulkner said, grinning. "And just so cool."

"Shut up, dork."

He laughed. "All right, I won't make fun of your ongoing need for Mommy to tuck you in at night. What else was odd?"

"Then she started following me. Watching me."

He waved it off. "Overprotective."

"Into the bathroom? When I mowed the lawn? Sitting outside my friends' houses? It got . . . creepy. But she didn't do it all the time. Just once in a while, she'd go on these . . . binges. Then it would stop." I shrugged. As if it didn't matter. As though it had been a small thing.

But it hadn't been. And it still wasn't. The weirdness had grown even bigger.

Into something with really bad breath.

"That could be baby-of-the-family crap," Faulkner said. "Mom doesn't want to let you out of her sight and all that."

"I don't think so. It was more than that."

Faulkner raised and dropped a shoulder. No commitment from him. "You said she tried to kill you before. How?"

My face got even hotter.

What kind of kid did that make me? My own mother trying to kill me? Maybe I was some evil devil spawn and I didn't know it. Maybe she hated me. Maybe she wished she'd never had me. Maybe—

Maybe she was just crazy. Maybe there wasn't anything in that well. Nothing at all.

I swallowed. "Dude, there's a reason I don't swim in the pool anymore."

Faulkner stared at me, his jaw slack. I saw him do the mental math. "Oh. Man. Really?"

"Do I *look* like I'm lying?" Suddenly I wanted to explode, to punch him, to force him into my head, to let him know I wasn't rebelling because I wanted a later curfew. "God, Faulkner, believe me for once."

"Calm down." Faulkner put up his hands. "I mean, dude, she's never done anything like that to me. Are you sure? I mean, you didn't just, like, lose at Marco Polo or something?" He laughed.

He didn't believe me. After all that, he didn't believe me?

"But you saw it happen," I protested. "You saw what she did to me in the woods . . ."

Faulkner shook his head, clearly wanting to erase the image from his mind. "I don't know, man. I don't know what I saw. Maybe it was a trick of the light or something."

"Forget it. I don't need your help. I'll ask someone else."

For a minute, I felt like the older one, as if I'd matured ten years in the past five minutes. For someone who didn't have a license yet and needed to shave only every few days, it was a really strange feeling. "I'll see you later, Faulkner." I started to head off to the right.

"Where are you going?"

"I just need to get away from here. To have some time to think. This isn't . . ." I looked back over my shoulder at the lawn, the shrubs, the flowers and plants that had stupid unpronounceable Latin names and men hired just to take care of them. I couldn't see the well from here, though I could feel it, could sense it. Could still smell it on me.

"There's something about Mom and about everything around here that isn't right," I finished. Understatement of the year.

"What if Mom and StepScrooge Sam ask me where you are?"

That's what we'd called Sam from the beginning. He hated it, but we didn't like him much, so it seemed to be right. In the eighteen months Sam had been married to our mother, Faulkner and I had always felt like squatters in his mansion, me especially. He was hard on Faulkner, but commando on me. I didn't know why. Maybe it was the extra mouth to feed.

Every dollar Mom spent on clothes for us, every piece of food we took from the fridge, was subtracted from his mental debit card. We were banned from the vineyard, as if our being there might taint the grapes. Jumel Vineyards was some kind of superduper business success story because it was located in the middle of Maine, where apparently it wasn't so easy to grow grapes because of the cold.

Sam reminded us all the time about respecting that Jumel heritage—and staying the hell away from it. Whatever. We weren't about to breathe on his precious Concords.

We'd never liked him and gave him only as much respect as we had to. That kept our mother from calling the Dr. Phil show on us, kept Sam off our backs, and kept a roof over our heads. But Sam . . . he was a hard case, always on us for one thing or another, really anal about keeping stuff clean and picked up, and a pain in the butt about the water bill, as if Faulkner and I alone were responsible for the entire global-warming problem. The only reason the pool had even been opened was because my mother had sweet-talked him into it, so that she could work out after she hurt her knee last summer. Even then, Sam's face took on this constipated look every time he walked past the Olympic-size waste of natural resources.

The man had money—yet pinched a penny until Lincoln screamed for mercy. Some days I wished my mother had married Hannibal Lecter instead.

So we tolerated Sam, Faulkner and I, to keep the peace and took extra-long showers whenever he was at work. Just because we could.

But right now, there were bigger problems on my plate than Sam and his water-bill fetish.

"Tell them . . ." I thought for a minute. "Tell them I'm

spending the night at Joey Deluca's. Tell them we have a big research project due and I'm working on it with him. Tell them it's for English."

My English grade sucked wind. I hated the classics. Hated Shakespeare. Hated Dickens even more. Thought Pip should have been drowned with the convict in the opening scene of *Great Expectations* and saved us all the torture. I'd turned out to be a total disappointment to my English-professor father and my American-classics-loving mother, who'd named me and Faulkner after their favorite authors, me for the James Fenimore guy who'd written that thing about the Indians.

"Come on. Who's going to believe that?" Faulkner said.

"They will. They'd do anything to have me pass English."

Maybe, I hoped, she'd forget I existed for a while. Maybe she'd get into one of those moods where she sort of zoned out. And she wouldn't come looking for me. I started down the street.

"Wait." Faulkner grabbed my sleeve. "You got a cell with you?"

I shook my head. Failing English meant no perks. A cell phone had been the carrot my father had dangled in front of me for a year. Yet another reason to hate Pip. He had cost me a Motorola.

For a second, I thought Faulkner might offer me his cell,

but he just shrugged. "Well, be careful. Don't get killed or picked up by some psycho."

I looked away. I already lived with a psycho. She'd made my peanut butter and jelly sandwiches, reminded me to look both ways before crossing the street, and warned me never to talk to strangers. Strangers, it turned out, weren't the ones you had to worry about. "Yeah. I will."

Faulkner dug his hands into his back pockets. *"Adiós, amigo."*

I took in a breath. All I could smell was the faintly pine scent of my cologne. Maybe I had escaped it. Maybe I had dreamed it all. Maybe it wasn't—

Then, from far off, I heard a wailing, a low, guttural keening sound, almost like something crying. But these weren't tears of sorrow. It was as if an animal had had its prize ripped away. My heart shuddered to a stop. I swallowed, but nothing moved down my throat. Ice curled around my spine. "Did you hear that?"

Faulkner paused and looked around, then looked back at me, blank. "Hear what?"

"I think . . . I think it's looking for me." Why was this happening? Why couldn't I just go back to worrying about stupid crap like ripping out a fart just when Ms. Walker called on me in math or splitting my shorts doing a jumping jack in front of the entire freshman class? I'd give anything to be humiliated in school instead of hunted like a wounded antelope on the Sahara.

"What's looking for you?"

But I didn't answer Faulkner. The thing was screaming again, louder, angrier, more insistent. Faulkner just stared at me as if I were an idiot. "I don't hear anything. Dude, you're *muy loco.*"

But I really did hear it. In fact, I could almost *feel* it, in that kind of connection that came from being so close, as if I were within touching distance, feel it reaching for me in my head, sending out mental tentacles.

My heart skittered to a stop for one long second, then started again, hammering fast.

Soon, I knew, somehow I *knew,* it would find me. And if it couldn't drag me back itself, it would find someone to do its dirty work for it—my mother.

Next time, I might not be so lucky to have a rope and Faulkner at the top of the well. Without even bothering to say goodbye to my brother, I turned and ran.

CHAPTER 3

The boy had escaped.

He should have taken him when he'd had the chance. But no, he'd been stupid and he had paused. Anticipated.

Toyed with him.

But it had been so long, so very, very long, since he'd had any fun like that. Anything to pursue, other than the occasional rat, or a bird that lost its way and fluttered into the darkness. Some spiders, bugs. The occasional idiot human. And then there were the meals that the other one fed the creature.

None of it was the one person he needed. All the things he'd eaten up until now had given up too soon, fallen apart in fear. No fight in them. Disgusting.

They weren't *real* quarry. The boy, though, he was a challenge, the kind the creature could circle and tease, delighting in the scent of his fear, the thumping of his heart. The power of terror.

He—that human, the one with all the control—he had kept him down here, kept him under his thumb, kept him from the world. And now the creature finally had a way out, something that would give him back all that he had watched wither away. And that something had a name.

Cooper.

The boy's name rolled off his tongue—or what was left of his tongue—like candy. He said it again and again, breathing it in and out. Oh, he'd have him soon. Have him back in the well.

And next time, he wouldn't hesitate.

But until then, he had to eat. It wasn't the meal he needed, the blood that would give him freedom again—freedom to escape, to walk among the world, and finally, to exact his revenge on the one who had tortured him like a spider pinned on a board, who had raped the very land the creature loved—but it would be enough to sustain him, until he could have Cooper. And then . . .

Oh, then his old life would return. A few more days until the moon rose on the exact eve he needed, the anniversary date he had waited so long for, and then he'd climb out of this hellhole and walk among people again. Reclaim his birthright—steal it from the one who sat at *his* table, drank *his* wine, walked *his* grounds.

All the others had treated the creature with compassion. Had acknowledged his gift to them. To these lands. But not this one.

No. This one needed to pay for the way he had sneered at the creature. Thrown him a pittance of food. Thumbed his nose at the wealth the creature's sacrifice had given him. Ripped down his home, replaced it with that eyesore, then laughed, actually laughed, at the creature's pain and loss.

Vengeance would be sweet. Sweeter than the blood he would soon drink.

He concentrated, though it hurt now to do it because he was so weak, so damned weak, and then he heard sounds from above. From the world of light.

Singing. Drunken slurring.

He laughed. Vineyard workers dipping into the product again. Crouching low into himself, he poured everything into his thoughts.

Come closer. These grapes are the best, the sweetest. Taste from this vine.

The song grew louder. Shuffling of leaves. Breaking branches.

Hungry? Take one bite. Just one.

The creature pressed on his own head, his fingers sinking deep into what had once been flesh and now was as soft as moss, nails scraping at what no longer even looked like skin. He concentrated harder, sending out his thoughts and reaching his vision up and over the walls.

One man. Old, with gray hair. Skinny, slow.

The creature nearly stopped in disgust. But no, the decrepit human would have to do. For now.

He pressed again on his temples, his fingers lost inside the mush above his neck. His head pounded, stabbing pain arcing through his body, but then his telepathic power began to work, and the slime on the wall grew outward in a quickly multiplying vine, over the walls and toward his prey.

The creature saw with that third mental eye acting as the extension of his reach and then with an agonized surge of effort, his thoughts joined with the land and became physical manifestations. Became *real*. The green web reaching out, wrapping around the man's legs, yanking him down to the ground. The geezer let out a shriek of surprise. His stupid song stopped. Finally.

The creature pressed harder, and his ropelike snare twisted tighter, winding around the man's flailing legs, wrapping him into a ball like a spider's prize. Worthless creature. He had barely put up a fight.

The vines inched upward, tighter, tighter still, crushing

organs and bones in their boa-constrictor grip. With each death crunch the creature's anticipation for the meal grew. He forced the last of his mental energy out with one agonizing cry, and the man came tumbling over the wall of the well and down, down, down, in a splashing ball of crumpled skin and oozing blood.

Once a man. Now a means to an end.

Soon, the creature thought. Soon he'd have the real lifeblood he needed.

Cooper.

CHAPTER 4

There's nothing like sitting in Freshman English on a Monday morning to remind you the real world does go on. And just to make things worse, it smacks you with a book report.

"Three pages, typed and double-spaced, on the symbolism found in the play within a play in act three of *Hamlet,* by Wednesday," my father said to the class. He stood at the front of the room, wearing a tweed jacket like he was Doctor freakin' Zhivago, the tips of his fingers white with chalk and his shoes covered with dust from erasing first period's notes.

The class groaned. "Dude, your dad is like a prison warden." Joey Deluca slammed his five-subject notebook shut— the only notes in it being ones from girls—and plopped his feet on the floor, making Mike Ring's chair, where Joey's feet had been resting, shake. Mike turned and glared at Joey.

"Cooper, can't you talk to him? Tell him this is high school, not Sing Sing?"

My father put his back to us and wrote the assignment on the board with the kind of penmanship that would have made my third grade teacher shout hallelujahs. Then below that, he stacked up a bunch of bullet points we had to be sure to include in our essays. Another collective groan blew through the class.

"I'm failing my own father's class," I whispered back to Joey. "He isn't going to listen to me."

He never had. That was half the problem between my father and me.

A note slid across my desk. "From Megan," whispered Drue Macy, who was Megan's best friend. She gave me the evil girlfriend eye and turned up her nose before looking away.

I glanced over my shoulder at Megan, and my heart did that funny little flip-flop thing. It always did that when I looked at her—always had for as long as I could remember. We'd been going out for six months now, but it felt like forever. In a good way. As though she'd always been my girlfriend and always would be. I had a hundred images in my head of Megan and me together, and I couldn't imagine a day without her.

People had started calling us "CooperandMegan," as if

we were one person. It had been nice, real nice. And then yesterday, I'd made plans for a fancy dinner. At a good restaurant and everything, to celebrate our six-month anniversary. Until the well got in the way.

I unfolded the paper. Megan's small, tight writing in blue pen filling only three lines. "I waited for you yesterday. Where were you?" she wrote. "Why ask me out if you were going to stand me up? And on our anniversary, too." She'd underlined *anniversary.* Four times.

"Dude, seriously," Joey went on. "I'm supposed to go out with Lindsay Beckham tomorrow night. I don't have time for Hamlet and his screwed-up family."

I folded the paper and stuffed it into my jeans. What was I going to tell her? *Sorry, I know this was a big deal, but my mother had plans to feed me to some monster in the well in the vineyard behind our house?*

Yeah, she'd believe that. I'd have better luck telling her I'd been sucked into the mother ship.

I tipped back in my chair, pretended to stretch, and glanced at Megan out of the corner of my eye. She had her head down, her hair a velvet brown curtain swishing forward around her notebook. She was taking notes.

I'd known Megan since kindergarten. When my mother and father were still married, Megan was the cliché—the girl next door. Back then, we were friends, part of the neighborhood pack that rode bikes to the playground, traded off yards for catch and swimming, stuff like that.

But then one day, something changed. A switch turned on in my brain and I stopped noticing Megan as one of the others and noticed her as *Megan*. I started paying attention to the way she walked. Talked. To her perfume. Her hair. Her eyes. Her body. Especially her body.

Then I got nervous around her. I couldn't hang out with her, even with everyone around, without becoming the stammering idiot Hulk.

It took three months before I got Braveheart enough to do something about it and finally blurted out, "Want to meet me at the movies on Sunday night? Just you and me?"

She'd rewarded me with a yes and the most amazing smile I'd ever seen. I'd thought my life was pretty damn sweet—

Until I'd ended up at the bottom of a well instead of at Vincenzo's Italian restaurant with Megan in one of those curtained booths.

Megan quit writing and looked up. Her eyes met mine. I tried on a smile, but it didn't quite fit. Her face hardened, spelling *you're a jerk,* and she looked away.

I took out her note and scribbled, "I'm sorry. I'll explain everything later, I promise," on the bottom. I thought a minute, chewing on the end of my pen. I needed something more, but it's not as if they hand out a manual on this stuff at freshman orientation. In the end, I just underlined the "I promise," signed my name, and sent it back to Megan via Drue the carrier pigeon.

Mike leaned his head back into my space. "I got a solution," he said. It took a second for me to realize he was talking to Joey. "Pay Maria to do your paper. That's what you did with *A Midsummer Night's Dream*."

"No can do. She hates me." Joey wadded up a corner of notebook paper and finger punted it into Mike's hair.

"You're a loser." Mike brushed at his head, but the loose-leaf soccer ball stayed put.

I really didn't care about the conversation, but listening to Joey and Mike kept me from thinking about my own life—about Megan being mad at me, about the well, about how I'd spent last night sleeping in an abandoned house on the outskirts of town, seriously creeped out and awake until two in the morning. Joey hadn't been home, and Mike's mother wasn't wild about his friends showing up and having an insta-sleepover. The whole camping-out-like-a-hobo thing had sounded like a good idea. Until I did it.

My friends were about as full of depth as an empty mayonnaise jar, but they made me feel as if things were normal. As though I could walk out of this building, hitch a ride on the bus to my house, and find a chicken in the oven and my mother standing there with a smile, instead of a knife aimed at my throat.

"Why does Maria hate you?" I asked.

"Her sister. Me. Hot date." Joey put out his palms, shrugged, and grinned.

"Dawg!" Mike pivoted in his seat and raised a high-five hand. "She's, like, a senior."

"Mr. Ring!" My father's voice, full of you-will-pay-attention authority.

Mike slid down in his seat and circled back around, like a puppy caught peeing on the gardenias. "Yeah, Mr. Warner?"

"What is the significance of Hamlet's soliloquy at the beginning of act three?"

"Uh, what's a solilo-key?"

My father let out a sigh. The kind that said he wondered why he'd gone into high school education when he could have been a college professor or opted to do lab research with monkeys. Something with intelligent creatures. "Never mind." He turned to me. "Cooper?"

Every time he called on me in his class, he ended my name with this little lilt of hope, as if this time, I'd have the answer. This time, I'd have done my homework. This time, I'd make him look good. This time, I'd be the one who would show everyone that the Warner professorial gene had been passed along with a hefty dose of brains.

I glanced down at the play. We had been reading it aloud a few minutes earlier, with Joey playing Polonius, the fool. Mike had been the king, Megan had been the queen, and I had been suckered into reading Hamlet's parts while the rest of the class had put their heads on their desks and slept. I squirmed in my seat, the words blurring on the page before me. I expected to struggle for an answer, to be lost for anything intelligent.

But for some reason, this time, I heard the entire thing again in my head. The whole "to be or not to be" paragraph replayed itself, as if someone else were shouting the words at me, as though Hamlet were sitting in the chair behind mine, yelling his little speech of indecision into my ear.

"I think he's scared of dying," I said. "But he's got to make this big decision about what to do. About who to kill. And, well, you know, it's not an easy thing to do. The, ah, killing thing."

I looked up. The room was silent. I rarely said more than five words in English class if I could help it, and those were usually "Can I go to the bathroom?"

The entire class stared at me. Joey was grinning. Mike had a little thumbs-up going my way. Megan looked surprised and wore that smile I really liked on her face. But my father—

My father's jaw dropped. He swallowed, closed his mouth, then opened it again. "Go on, Cooper. Go on." He waved at me encouragingly. This big goofy grin was all over his face, and he kept pushing his glasses up on his nose.

"Well, I don't know." I shifted some more. Why had I said anything at all? Now my father would do this all the time, make me perform for the class like some kind of circus lion. I started to say I didn't know anything else, but then I heard the soliloquy continue in my head—

> *To grunt and sweat under a weary life,*
> *But that the dread of something after death,*
> *The undiscovered country from whose bourn*
> *No traveller returns, puzzles the will*
> *And makes us rather bear those ills we have*
> *Than fly to others that we know not of?*
> *Thus conscience does make cowards of us all,*
> *And thus the native hue of resolution*
> *Is sicklied o'er with the pale cast of thought,*
> *And enterprises of great pith and moment*
> *With this regard their currents turn awry,*
> *And lose the name of action.*

The words began to make some weird kind of sense. "Hamlet's tired, too. There's been this kind of burden on him for a while. He thinks these people are after him, you know? And he just wants it to be over. But he feels guilty for what he's thinking about doing. Because—"

I stopped talking. I realized why I knew Hamlet's thoughts. Why reading that soliloquy had seemed so familiar. It wasn't just because I'd happened to be wearing that "Hamlet Had Issues" T-shirt yesterday when my mother tricked me into searching for the lost dog, then caught me by my collar, hauled me across the woods, and threw me down the well, into the clutches of something . . .

Something I didn't want to think about right now.

Wearing the T-shirt had been a weird karmic coincidence.

This, though, was called identifying with the guy.

Hamlet had someone, or something, after him and knew he had to do something drastic, like murder. He had the dual problem of not wanting to pull a Tony Soprano. The age-old debate—to kill or be killed. To be or not to be—

Although mine was more to be or not to be *eaten*.

I slammed my book shut. Holy crap. No way was I going to read any more.

"What else, Cooper?" My father moved forward, his white hair sticking up in places, his tweed jacket making him look like a really tall leprechaun who had discovered the lucky jackpot right in front of him—a freshman who was paying attention. "What else do you see?"

"Nothing." I lowered my head. Stared at the "Ken Luvs Lisa 4-Eva" carved into my desk.

"You're on the right track. Tell me more."

"I said nothing," I repeated, louder. I wouldn't look up. I traced the letters with my fingernail, trying to concentrate on something else, but then as I traced, the lines in the desk started to turn color under my nail, going from the pale tan of the desk to a deep, dark green slime.

My finger caught, held in a thick glue. I tried to pull it back, but it wouldn't move. Then the smell hit me. Rotten eggs. Dead pigs. Maggots. Putrid, decaying flesh.

The slime began to spread, reaching tentacles across my desk, leapfrogging one spiny piece over another, crazy green spiders spiraling out on the laminate. I slammed my other hand down, but the slime didn't stop—it railroaded right over my hand, the black-emerald death glue holding my hand in place.

The same green, the same slime. It couldn't be. It couldn't.

But it was.

Oh God, no, not here. I opened my mouth, then closed it.

It was here. The well. In this room.

My tongue had grown thick; my mouth filled with bile. My heart thundered so loudly in my chest, I couldn't hear anything around me. The well had found me, that creature had come after me, and now it had my hands, had me pinned.

It was going to eat me right here. In room 205 of Maple Valley High School, sitting behind a wood and steel desk.

Holy crap. Holy crap.

"Cooper."

I jerked back in my chair, trying to tug my hands off my desk, but they stuck, the green slime as sticky as Spider-Man's web, as strong and interlaced as the vines that held the grapes in the vineyard. And still it continued its fast multiplication across my desk, down the legs, wrapping around, grabbing my jeans, strapping me in—

We're going for a ride, Cooper. A ride right back to the bottom. You liked it there, didn't you?

I opened my mouth to scream, to beg for help, but nothing came out.

"Cooper!"

I looked up. My father was standing in front of me.

"Are you listening to me?" he said.

I blinked, waiting for him to notice I was being attacked by this crazy ravenous monster, but no, my father just looked at me like he did every single day in English. The roaring of my pulse began to slow; other noises filtered in.

Someone snickering behind me. A cough. A crinkle of paper. Joey laughing behind his hand. "Uh . . . yeah?" I said.

I glanced down, half expecting to see myself still imprisoned by green. But no, all I saw below me was the constellation of chalk dust on my father's black dress shoes. They were scuffed on the toes, worn in some places. My father had no fashion sense, only bought new clothes when he was forced to because he had to go to a wedding or a funeral, and he wore his shoes until they fell apart. His shoelaces were fraying, the plastic caps long gone. I stared hard at those everyday shoes, part of the everyday world, because they were real. They were here.

I am not in that well. I am in my desk. In a classroom. Not in that well. Not in that well.

"Are you all right?" my father asked.

No slime. No green. My hands were my own—no prison.

But in my head, I heard the whisper of laughter. A shiver chased down my back.

"Yeah." It was still the only word I could manage.

The bell rang, and the class popped out of their seats with screeches of chairs and sneakers, one mass exodus toward the hall. I moved to go, but my father's hand on my shoulder stopped me. "Stay here. I want to talk to you."

The class emptied out fast. I watched Joey Deluca try to cozy up to Maria in the hall, but she shouted something about dumping her sister and took off down the life-skills corridor. Mike laughed his butt off and slapped Joey on the back. Megan stood in the hall waiting for me, toe-tapping the score to *Rent.*

"Dad, I have to get to class."

"I'll write you a note." My father took a seat behind his desk and gestured to the chair beside his. "Sit down."

I sent Megan a go-on-without-me wave. She gave me a frustrated headshake. My next class was PE, the only one I hated more than English because we were doing gymnastics. When you're a guy, the pommel horse and the balance beam are about the scariest things on the planet. They represent permanent damage to the most important things in life. Best to avoid them. And my father was giving me the don't-argue glare. So I sat.

Besides, I wasn't ready to face anything right now. My whole world still felt really, really weird. I glanced back at my desk. It looked just like everyone else's. I must have nodded off. Had some kind of freakish daydream.

Only, part of me knew it hadn't been a daydream.

My father took his glasses off, laid them carefully on his desk, then pinched the bridge of his nose. "What's going on with you?"

"Nothing."

"Something's wrong. Your face and arms are all scratched up; you're not yourself. You zoned out on me for a while back then. Are you sleeping all right? Your mother said you didn't come home last night."

"I spent the night at Joey's."

My father toyed with his glasses, flipping the arms back and forth and tap-tapping at the felt pad on his desk. "That's funny. Because I overheard Joey say he just came back from a weekend in Michigan with his folks."

Busted. "I, ah, went over after he got home."

My father looked as if he'd sucked down a lemon. "Tell me the truth, Cooper. I'm not an idiot."

The truth. Yeah, sure he wanted that. My father was too old, too stuck in the world of Shakespeare and Twain to believe anything like this. I didn't think he'd seen a sci-fi movie in his life. He was, as he told me often, a realist. Which meant he thought everything I did fed into my chances of getting into college.

What he wouldn't get was that right now, I was more worried about surviving to the end of the week.

"Just some stuff going on with Mom and . . ." I let my voice trail off. Let my dad fill in the blanks. He was good at that. It was why he did the crossword puzzle every day in ink.

"And your stepfather?"

I studied the chalk-dust pile on the floor beneath the board. It looked like snow. How could one man have accumulated so much chalk dust in such a short period of time? "Yeah, something like that."

"You should have come to me." My father leaned forward, his chair creaking. He tipped my chin up, as though I were still a little kid, until I looked at him. "You could have stayed at my house."

"And done what, Dad? Extra analyses of *Hamlet*?" I popped out of the chair and crossed away from him. "No thank you. Whenever I come over to your house, you don't listen to me—you just keep throwing more homework in my lap. Whoa, there's a good time, Dad."

"I'm trying to prepare you for your future, Cooper. College—"

"I don't care about college right now! I have bigger things to think about." I glanced again at my desk. Ken still luved Lisa 4-Eva. The world of room 205 was still normal.

"What, like girls?" My father's face took on this uncomfortable, screwed-up, tight look. Whenever he had to talk to me about girls, he got nervous, like from some movie out of the fifties. I wondered if he'd even dated again after he and my mother divorced.

"Yeah, whatever." Whatever it took to get him off my back.

"How are things with you and Megan?"

As if my dad really wanted to talk about my girlfriend

with me. He never had before, and he wasn't about to start now.

"Dad, I have to get to PE. You know how Mr. Clayburn gets." The dude did freak when we were late. He was bald, and his entire Q-tip head turned into one big red bulb when someone came in late or moaned about a stomachache.

But that wasn't really why I wanted to leave. I couldn't quit looking at my desk, couldn't quit checking to make sure Ken still luved Lisa. If he quit luving her and the green web of slime took over again—

I couldn't think about that.

My father pursed his lips. "Fine. Here's a note." He scribbled out a pass and handed it to me, but he didn't let go. "Promise me the next time things aren't going well at home, you'll come to me instead of running off to God knows where?"

"Yeah, sure, Dad." I took the pass, then headed to the door. I stopped and looked back. I don't know why. Maybe to see if my father was still watching me, still worrying. If he had been, maybe I would have talked to him. Maybe.

But he had his leather-bound *Complete Collected Works of Shakespeare* open and was already making notes for third period.

I'd been dismissed.

CHAPTER 5

Faulkner caught up to me outside after school. "Come on, Shelley's going to give us a ride to Mickey D's. We're getting some drive-through rehab."

"Shelley? I'd rather walk. She drives like a third-grader on a sugar high." Though the thought of some fries and a burger wasn't a bad idea, being in a car with Faulkner's girlfriend could kill me faster than all the grease from every fast food joint put together.

"She's not that bad. And besides, she just got her license back."

"That's what's wrong right there, Faulkner. *Just* got her license back. Why'd they take it away in the first place?"

"Dude, that telephone pole wasn't there the week before, and who leaves trash cans in the middle of the street?" He shook his head. "You're harsh. Give her some slack."

I grabbed Faulkner's arm. "No way. My life is already in enough danger. I'm not tempting fate by getting into Shelley's car."

"Whatever. But . . . you will be home, right?" For a second, I could almost believe Faulkner cared. Then he punched me in the arm. "Because it's your turn to take out the garbage and I'm not doing your chores. *¿Comprende?*"

"Yeah, I will." I felt like adding something smart, like "hide the knives," but I suddenly felt really tired. I had to go home at some point, though, right? I dropped onto the bottom step of the granite stairs, laid my backpack beside me, and let the human exit wave pass by.

Faulkner let out a breath. "Coop, don't worry so much. Things'll work out."

I didn't look up at him. "Yeah? How do you know?"

"I don't," Faulkner said, his gaze going to the parking lot, to the normal world that ran around us like some movie. "But they just have to."

Then he patted me on the shoulder and headed off toward Shelley's dented Mazda.

Megan.

When I thought of making the world all right, that was the first name that came to mind.

The problem?

She wasn't speaking to me.

Problem two?

I needed her anyway. And I really needed to make things right between us.

And I knew just where to find her. Back when I'd been on the football team—and therefore had a life—she'd been on the other side of the pompoms. A cliché, I know, but hey, we were freshmen. We were walking clichés. It was the only way to survive and not get pummeled by the upperclassmen.

I cut across the football field, sending a wave to the team. Trying to pretend I didn't care that they were there and I wasn't. That they were going on with ordinary lives, in padding and helmets, fighting over a brown overgrown vinyl bullet, while I tried to figure out how to save myself from a monster.

Maybe I had imagined the whole thing yesterday. That's what I kept telling myself. The farther I got from the well, the more distance I put between myself and that pit, the feeling of . . . breath, of hunger on my shoulders, running down my spine, the more I could—

No.

I couldn't fool myself. Not for long. The lie worked only for a few seconds. Like a Halloween mask. The neighbors would open the door, you'd say, "Trick or treat," and in a half second, they'd know it was Tommy from next door because he had his whiny sister beside him in her fairy princess costume. Or Jenny from down the street because her four-eyed face was peeking out of the yellow felt M&M bubble.

The rah-rah of a dozen girls in blue and white carried on the air in a coordinated wave along with the punctuation marks of pompoms. I scanned the faces, the twirling bodies, looking for Megan.

But she wasn't in the group. Wasn't spelling out the school's letters with all the passion of Fall Out Boy groupies. "You seen Megan?" I asked Rebecca Maxwell, whose heftier shoulders were holding up the enthusiasm pyramid.

"She's looking for you. And, man, she's not happy. I don't know how you could do that, Cooper. I mean, six-month anniversaries are a big—"

"What do you mean, looking for me?" I said, cutting her off. As if I needed a reminder of my screwup.

"She said she was going to your house to find you and tell you what a loser you were. Something about looking for you at the tree or—" Rebecca groaned and gave the two cheerleaders above her a glare. "Ow, Colleen. How many times did you go to the freakin' snack bar today?"

"Shut up. I'm not the only cow here." Colleen Carter shifted her weight, which only made Rebecca's face pinch into the Darth Maul mask.

"My house? The tree?" The words sank in one at a time,

like concrete blocks. But Rebecca had stopped paying attention. She and Colleen were arguing about who gave elephants a bad name.

Megan.

The tree.

Which was in the woods. By the—

Oh God. I broke into a run, air sucking into my lungs, this time ignoring the calls of my friends as I broke across the football field like a quarterback on fire, then down the school driveway, and finally onto the sidewalks of Maple Valley, rounding the corners at a skid, stone dust kicking up beneath my shoes, nearly slipping as I shredded rubber to get to Megan.

The tree was in the woods behind my house. We'd meet there sometimes because StepScrooge Sam frowned on my entertaining friends in the house. I had never wanted to go into those woods again, but now I had to get there. Fast.

Every block felt like a mile, every street as long as a runway.

Then, my street sign. My house. My driveway. I ran down the long, long length of bricks, and then, when I hit the grass, I dropped my backpack. It hit the ground with a thud.

A sickening thud, almost a premonition.

"Cooper!"

I spun around so fast, I was a human top. StepScrooge Sam stood on the deck, his arms crossed over his chest. He was dressed in his golf clothes. White shirt, plaid pants. I snorted. Hard workday for him, apparently. "What?"

"Where the hell do you think you're going?"

Whatever answer I gave would be the wrong one. I heaved in a breath, trying not to look like I was in a hurry. When StepScrooge Sam wanted to talk to you, it was *now*, no later about it. "Nowhere."

He headed down the stairs. Came up within two feet of me. "You're moving awful fast for going nowhere, mister."

I shrugged. I didn't care what he thought.

"Attitude *again*. You know how I feel about attitude."

"Sorry." Appease him now—maybe he'd shut up.

But no, his voice got louder, his face got redder, and he got closer to me. "You are an ungrateful leech in this house, Cooper. I provide the food on the table, the roof over your head, the clothes on your back, and what do you give me?"

I toed at the ground. I knew the drill. I'd heard it a hundred times before. "Nothing."

"That's right. *Nothing.* Don't you think you could do more around here? To help out?"

"Yes."

"Yes, what?"

"Yes, sir." The words escaped through gritted teeth. I

shoved my hands into my pockets so he wouldn't see them curl into fists.

"Don't you dare run off right now. Because you have chores. Your room is a disaster. The trash needs to be taken out. The garage . . ."

He went on and on, but I didn't hear him. My brain just kept repeating *Megan-Megan-Megan* like some kind of internal drum. An urgent beat to get the hell out of here and find her. Something wasn't right, I just knew it.

"I'll do it all in a little while," I said. "I promise."

"No, you'll do it now." StepScrooge Sam advanced on me, anger flaring his nostrils like a bull. "I don't have time for this crap from you. I have a business to run. On top of that, one of the workers didn't show up today and the whole place is a mess. So don't you be adding another hassle to the pile. You'll do what I say and you'll do it"—he came even closer now, his index finger like a pointer at my chest, punctuating the last few words—"when I tell you."

All of a sudden, Whipple came running out of the doggy door, hurling his little fur body down the deck stairs and into the space between us. The dog started to growl. The sound was low and guttural, as vicious as a Doberman's. StepScrooge Sam turned toward the dog, glaring, and for a second I thought he might kick Whipple. "What the—?"

"Whipple, quit that," I said. What was wrong with the

dog? He'd done that only once before, when I'd come out of the well.

For a second, I considered asking Sam about the well, but then I remembered how long-winded he could get when it came to the history of the Jumel Vineyards. I didn't have time for that now. Besides, he was probably half the reason my mother was going psycho. He made her feel forced to choose between him and her own kids. Whipple was just protecting me from the angry tones in Sam's voice.

The dog backed up, standing beside my feet, but he was still, like a statue. I glanced back at the woods. Was Megan in there? Waiting for me?

And was she okay?

"Cooper, go do your chores."

Him again. He never let up. "I will."

Sam glared at me.

"Sir." I sucked in a breath. "Seriously, though, I really gotta exercise the dog first. It won't take long. I swear."

His cell phone chirped, and he let out a curse. He studied me and the phone rang again. "How long?"

The *Megan-Megan-Megan* drumbeat kept sounding in my head, so urgent my feet started shuffling. I wanted to turn and run and not answer my stepfather, but I didn't want him to come down on me with the privileges ax. "I'll be back in ten. Sir."

My mother's car swung into the driveway. Sam looked from the Audi to me, then back again. She called to him, saying something about needing help with groceries, making the decision for him. "Ten minutes," Sam warned, flipping out his cell phone and barking a greeting to whomever was on the other end.

Just before he headed off to meet my mother, I saw Sam shoot Whipple another glower. The dog held his four-legged stiff stance, not relaxing again until Sam was gone.

I didn't care. Megan was in those woods somewhere, and I had to find her. I turned and ran, running harder and faster than I had during football practice, pushing myself further than I ever had in conditioning. I charged down the lawn, and even though it hurt after the two-mile run from school and my lungs burned like kerosene chased by fire, I pumped harder, forcing my arms back and forth like pistons, pushing my aching, screaming legs to keep charging. Nothing mattered but finding Megan. Whipple ran after me, barking like he thought this was a game of chase.

I ignored the dog and shoved into the woods. Branches grabbed at me, long, sharp wooden fingers reaching, stabbing. Roots snaked out to trip my feet, as if the forest didn't want me to find her.

I shouted her name, then tried to run faster, but my body wouldn't cooperate. My lungs and legs had had enough, and they slowed, a train running down. The dog kept pace easily, running circles around my legs, nearly tangling me. I cursed and tried to push him away with my feet, searching all the while for Megan's tall, thin frame. She wasn't near our tree, the huge, ancient oak in the center of the woods that stood taller than all the others.

No. She couldn't have. But some instinct told me, some sickened knot of dread said the worst.

I kept going, deeper and deeper into the woods. Through the trees, I could see the vineyard way off to my right. Whipple barked and jumped at my legs, bouncing off them with his front paws. "Cut it out!"

The dog kept it up. The vines tangled around me, a ropy spider web blocking my way into the cove surrounding the well.

And then, buried between the tall, thick trees, I thought I saw a flash of light blue among the greens and browns. Was it Megan's jacket?

But that flash of blue was close, too close, to the well.

What if . . .

"Megan!" I started running again, calling her name, looking, looking, looking. Not seeing anything but vines and more vines—

And then I saw her.

Standing beside the well. She was looking down into

it, her hands braced on either side of the opening. I screamed her name again.

Finally she pivoted, slow, dreamlike, as if she were in a trance. I kept yelling her name, a broken record of *Megan*s. Then she blinked and took a step away from the well, and her face began to fill with color, her eyes starting to focus. "Cooper, why are you running?"

"Couldn't . . . couldn't . . . ." Breathe, breathe . . . "Couldn't wait to . . . see you."

A smile crossed her face, but it didn't pack the usual wattage. Dimmed because she was still mad? Or dimmed because of what she'd seen in the well?

She took a couple of steps toward me and I swear the color inked up in her face. Her cheeks flushed, nearly as red as the bandanna holding her hair back. "I skipped practice." A couple more steps, and now her words became stronger, her voice louder. Like the fog was lifting. "Mrs. Parker's probably going to have a coronary, but"—Megan raised a shoulder, dropped it—"I had a personal crisis."

Meaning me. Being a jerk.

Damn. I regretted all over again standing her up, even if it hadn't been my fault. Me and Megan had a really good thing going, and the last thing I wanted to do was blow it. But what was I supposed to tell her?

She stood there, waiting, I was sure, for an explanation.

Me to make nice, play the I'm-sorry card from the loser-guy deck.

Instead I stood there like an idiot. Whipple circling me like a hawk, pausing every few seconds to bark, then jump on me. He kept looking over at Megan, as if he was worried.

She shot me the look usually reserved for Thursday's mystery-meat sandwiches. "Well?"

"I had a personal crisis, too." If there was a more stupid answer on the planet, I couldn't think of it.

Megan rolled her eyes. Apparently, she agreed. "What do you mean by that? What kind of personal crisis could *you* possibly have that would make you stand me up? I mean, we've been going out for six months, Cooper. You can talk to me. Tell me what's going on."

Yeah, about pretty much anything else I could.

"Not about this. I'm sorry, Megan."

She shook her head, disgusted with me.

I gave the well another glance. I tried not to inhale. Tried not to smell that smell again, but it was there, lurking on the fringes of my nose.

Whipple rustled in the leaves around the well, nosing at something. He barked. I looked down and saw a khaki-colored hat, the wide kind with the band around the rim. I knew only one person who wore a Grandpa hat like that.

"Hey," Megan said. "Isn't that Paolo's hat?"

Paolo was this guy who had worked at the vineyard forever. One of those guys who was everybody's friend. He'd been at Sam's house for Christmas parties and let Megan and me borrow the Mule, which was like a glorified golf cart, for joy rides when Sam wasn't looking.

"Yeah." I swallowed hard. Bent forward, picked it up. And immediately wished I hadn't.

"Oh my God." Megan pressed a hand to her mouth. "I think I'm going to be sick. That's not . . . that's not what I think it is, is it?"

"I don't think so." But I was lying and I knew it. I turned the hat away from her, so she couldn't really see it. Whatever was inside made the hat heavy in my hand. "I think, like, an animal crawled into it and died or something." Then I took a look inside, curiosity shoving common sense into a closet, and almost screamed.

I had to breathe through my mouth so I wouldn't upchuck. Because when I looked into Paolo's hat, I didn't see leaves caught on the inside. Or dirt. Or an animal.

I saw gray matter. Blood. White hairs.

Like his head had exploded in there.

I glanced at the well and couldn't even let my mind go there. No freakin' way. Impossible.

I threw the hat to the ground and backed up, way fast. Told myself I didn't know what the hell a brain looked like. That it was some decayed squirrel.

Yeah. Dead squirrel.

Or dead *guy*.

Oh my God.

Had the thing in the well done that? To Paolo? Was that what would have happened to me if—

If I hadn't escaped that day?

The knot in my stomach was so tight, I could have bounced an airplane off it. "Megan, we gotta get out of here. Now."

Megan ignored me and pivoted back toward the well. It stood three feet out of the ground, its rough stone walls covered in moss. From here, it looked as innocent as a newborn, but I knew better. "So, what's this thing? I don't think I've ever noticed it before. It's kinda cool. Looks really old." She took a few steps closer, reaching out a hand to the stone ledge that ringed the top. Whipple started barking as though he'd gone insane.

I lunged for her. "Don't touch that! Don't go near it!" I grabbed her arm, pulling her back just as she was moving to peer down into the well's inky depths.

She let out a shriek of protest and stumbled back. She gave me the Crazy Uncle Earl look—for that one guy at the family get-togethers who kept a piece of foil under his Red Sox cap just in case the aliens came calling. "Cooper, what are you doing?"

"I told you to stay away from that. It's . . . dangerous."

Yeah, like hand grenades were dangerous toys.

"I'm not two. And you're not my mother." She glared at me. "In fact, you're not my *anything*. I thought we had something going, and then you start backing off. For days, no calls. No notes. Then you make this big date, tell me it's going to be a big, fancy thing, and I get all excited, Cooper, thinking we're back to normal. Back to you and me. And what happens? You stand me up—no phone call, no nothing. *Again*." She shook her head, a glimmer in her eyes that sliced me like a knife. "Just get away from me, Cooper."

She flung off my arm and moved forward. I yanked on her sleeve again, as if she were a yo-yo. "Stop, Megan."

I didn't want her to go, but what was I going to say? How could I explain the distance I'd put between us? How my home life kept getting in the way of everything I had that was good?

"Why should I do anything you say?" Her face crumpled like a tissue, and I knew I'd hurt her. *Megan*. The one person in the world I didn't want to hurt. "What happened? Everything was fine, *we* were fine, and all of a sudden, you just cut me off. What did I do?"

The well stood a foot away from her, so close, still too close. The stench of death—those rotting pigs, maggots swarming over their bodies, feasting on the decaying skin, and for one second, the image of decaying skin became Megan's skin and I nearly barfed—almost overpowered me. I kept one eye on the well, afraid that the web of green would start climbing over the edge, reach out for Megan, drag her down there.

With Paolo?

God no. That hadn't happened. Hadn't freakin' happened. And those weren't his brains in that hat. No way. Impossible.

Yeah. Was there such a thing as being a pathological liar to yourself?

Nothing moved; nothing came crawling over the edge. And one look at Megan's face told me she didn't smell the same scent I did.

I swallowed. Just tell her, my inner voice whispered. Megan, of all people, would understand. I looked into her blue eyes, eyes the color of a spring-new sky, and started to speak—

When I heard my name.

Not even my name, really, just something that croaked two syllables out in a long, screechy whisper, the kind that sounded like nails on a chalkboard, only worse. I stumbled back a step, looking around.

Cooper.

"What's the matter?" Megan asked.

I spun in a circle. Whipple barked and backed up, his body low to the ground, a growl rumbling in his throat. "Did you hear that?"

"Hear what?"

Come on down, Cooper.

This time louder, like that guy on *The Price Is Right*. Inviting me to play the game.

"That voice." But even as I asked her and the whisper built in volume, I knew.

Knew it was only in my head. Knew it was meant only for me to hear.

I looked at the well. Felt everything inside me fall to my gut with a sickening realization.

Come back. Bring her with you. Paolo's already here. We'll have a party.

There *was* something in that well. And it wanted me. What was worse . . . it wanted Megan, too.

Megan's eyes were wide, her face pale. "Cooper. You're freaking me out. What's going on?"

"Don't touch me!" I took two more steps back, hands

going to my ears, but it did nothing to block the sound, to keep it from crying now, like a wolf on a hill.

"Cooper?" She sounded truly alarmed now.

I shut my eyes and swallowed hard, even as the voice kept calling me, its tone changing now. It was taunting me. Laughing. I had to get Megan out of here, get her away from me, because anyone who came near me was in as much danger as I was.

I kept my eyes shut because I knew I couldn't look at Megan and do this. "Megan, just leave. Get out of here, damn it. I . . . I don't ever want to see you again."

"You . . ." Her voice broke. "What? How could . . ."

But she never finished her sentence. By the time I opened my eyes, Megan was gone. Whipple scuffled forward in the leaves and pressed his little body to my legs in sympathy.

The voice had stopped calling my name, and all that was left was the trailing of its laughter in my head. I bent over, picked up a rock, and hucked it into the well.

The laughter stopped.

For now.

CHAPTER 6

Twenty-four hours later and I still had no solutions.

Megan ignored me, like I'd told her to. But still, the cold shoulder stung really badly.

I told myself it was for the best, even as everything within me hurt like hell and I missed her as if I'd had part of myself amputated. I might have ruined the best relationship I'd ever had, with the person I cared most about in the world.

Keeping her away from me was right, though, until I figured out what to do. Had a plan. A solution. Or woke up from this nightmare.

Still, it hurt. Every minute of every day. And a hundred times over, I wanted to call her, write a note, apologize. Just to see her smile again. Instead I suffered.

Faulkner was out with Shelley, at some senior yearbook planning thing, leaving me to fend for myself at home. I hadn't been able to come up with an excuse to leave and sleep somewhere else, so I stayed in on Tuesday night, figuring I'd stick to my room and lock the door if I had to. But so far, all had seemed pretty normal.

Joey showed up a little after eight. StepScrooge Sam grudgingly let him in, and only because Joey said he was there for homework help. Joey burst through my bedroom door, cursing my father's name. "Dude, you gotta help me write this paper. If I fail English this quarter, my parents will keep me on house arrest for the rest of my life."

"I thought you had a date," I said.

Joey shook his head. "Lindsay bailed on me."

"Joey, I don't want to—"

"Coop, I'm begging you here. Besides, you owe me."

"For what?"

He stared at me, face blank. Thinking. Something Joey tried not to do too often. "Uh, maybe it's the other way around. Doesn't matter. We're both failing, and you want a new cell phone, right? So you can have a link to the free world, like the rest of us?"

"Yeah."

"Then man up and let's get this paper done."

Translation: Joey would sit on my bed while I did all the work. I was in no mood for that, so I pointed at my computer. "Do a Google cruise on Hamlet and see what you get."

He shrugged. "All right. First, I gotta check my vitals. My mother's got my parental block up so high, all I can visit is Mickey Mouse."

I flopped onto my bed, picked up a Hacky Sack, and tossed it from one hand to the other, waiting while Joey ran through his MySpace page and his e-mail. I pretended to listen to Joey's rambling account of life as an online stud. Finally, he managed to stumble onto the website for the CliffsNotes. "It's got, like, four sentences on that stupid play," Joey said.

I flipped open my copy of *Hamlet* and skimmed the pages of act three. The words swam before me, a mountain of Old English gibberish. A ghost appearing before Hamlet, terrifying him and telling him someone was out to kill him. Then the play, mimicking murder. *Murder.* I didn't want to think about that. English wasn't a good alternative, but it was the only one I had right now. I ran a finger down the page, looking for something that would make sense.

"The whole play would have been a lot shorter if someone had just told Hamlet to quit whining and do something already," Joey said.

I laughed. "Yeah."

Joey read some more, clicking from site to site. "Hey, what's this supposed to mean?" he asked. "They keep mentioning this in the Google stuff. 'The lady doth protest too much.' What's the big deal about that line?"

"I think it means that the queen in the pretend play keeps on saying how innocent she is, and when you keep saying it over and over, that means you're guilty."

Joey thought for a minute. "Like when Melissa Felton kept telling me she wasn't doubling up with Eric Brown. Every time we were out somewhere, that girl was totally shoulder surfing, always looking for someone else when she should have been looking at me."

"Yeah, like that," I said, not really listening as Joey kept going on about Melissa and his broken heart. "Joey. *Joey.*"

"What?"

"Dude, we should write this paper."

"No, we should go back to my house and get buzzed. I know where there's some bonus beers from when my parents had a cookout on Labor Day. Back of the fridge in the garage. They're Heinies. My dad hates those. He'll never miss 'em."

"No. I don't feel like it."

"Dude, are you, like, dying or something?"

I just might be. "Or something." I got off the bed and switched places with Joey, who hadn't typed a word anyway.

"Man, get some sunshine. You're making *me* depressed."

"Lot on my mind, that's all. Let's get this paper done and I'll feel better."

He shrugged. "Plagiarize. It works for me."

I shook my head. "My dad has this computer program or website or something where he feeds in a few lines and knows in a minute if you copied. It's like a lie detector for papers."

"What is he, the paper police?" Joey cursed. "We actually have to *write* this thing?"

"Man up, Joey," I said, repeating his words. And for twenty minutes, I did get Joey to do that—or at least, he typed while I did all the mental lifting. We worked out two separate papers—pretty much the same ideas, just different wording. I blathered on about how the play within a play was Hamlet's way of proving guilt or innocence and helping himself make a decision, but that at the end he was no more decided than before, because when it came to family, murder was never an easy decision.

Except, apparently, in my house.

"Cooper, you're a total Einstein," Joey said, reading over the words we had on the screen. "Even I think this sounds good. An easy A, for sure." He squinted at the paper. "Well, your dad *is* grammar Hitler. Probably a B."

"Yeah." While the printer spewed out the pages with a coughing whine, I checked MySpace. I'd visit Megan's page. See what was up. Make sure she wasn't telling the world what a total loser freak-out I had been yesterday.

"Hey, I'm gonna go raid your fridge. You want anything?"

"No. I'm good." I typed in my log-in information. Joey

ducked out of my room. I waited for my page to come up. At first, it started to appear. The regular black and red punk background I'd pimped from another page filtered over the DSL.

Then, like a virus, a web of green began spreading over the red and black, inching its way past the slashes of color, slipping beneath the comments section, under my friends section. It took over my background, leaving the photos and words. What the hell?

I'd been hijacked. I cursed. I didn't have time to rebuild my page and fix the background. There were more important things on my list than this. Forget it. Let whoever had flipped me to green win for now. I clicked over to the comments, looking for Megan.

Her face appeared, flickered like a TV going bad, then—

It was gone.

Looking for someone?

A new comment. With a new picture.

Of a well.

Not just any well, but *the* well in the vineyard. The well that I'd been thrown down. The well that had tried to kill me. The same well that had very likely eaten Paolo, leaving half his brains behind like some sick little Hansel and Gretel trail for me to find.

I jerked back, the chair nearly toppling over, my feet

scrambling against the oak hardwood to keep me from going headfirst onto the floor. My mouth opened, closed. No. No. That wasn't real. I'd imagined the picture of that stone thing sitting in the middle of the woods, looking just as it had the day before, when I'd been there with Megan. I shook my head, then refocused on the computer.

The picture of the well was still there, and now it had begun to expand—no, not expand—*breathe*. The well's picture spread out and up, seemed to grow and shrink, pumping with the regular rhythm of a heartbeat. Then it tilted, going on its side to show me the yawning opening at the top.

The dark hole opened wider, like a mouth saying, *Feed me. Feed me.*

I reached out a hand but held back, not touching the screen, not touching the living, breathing—*that was impossible; a picture on a computer couldn't live, could it?*—image.

I'm here, Cooper. Missed me?

Holy mother of God.

I popped out of the chair and backed up until my knees hit the bed. I fell onto the unmade jumble of sheets and blankets, shaking. I scrambled back until my head hit the headboard, but it wasn't far enough. Not nearly far enough.

I could still see the monitor. Fingers of slime pulsed and reached, spreading across my MySpace page, first out of the image of the well, as if the mouth was spewing the slime, then over it, until every inch of the screen had been devoured.

Sweat broke out on my face, my neck, everywhere.

Leapfrogging over itself just like before in the classroom, the slime inched up the monitor screen, a twisted screen saver from hell, and then, as I watched, my jaw somewhere on my chest, the jade tentacles climbed right out of the monitor, skeletal limbs feeling for the black plastic perimeter, latching on to the edge and hauling a hunk of green out, onto the monitor stand. Up one side, then the other, then across the top, spreading, always spreading, across, down, then onto the floor, crisscrossing, knotting, strengthening, and growing, until the green was as thick as cement.

My spine became ice. My hands started to shake, the tremors spreading through me, until I'd become a human earthquake. Oh God. It was going to get me here. Grab me now. Right here, in my room. There was no running. No getting away.

Then the smell, like a stink bomb, blasted out of the screen—so bad, I *saw* it floating across the room, a yellow-green cloud of death. I cut off my breath and held it tightly, refusing to inhale, to let that cloud touch my lungs.

I had to move, but fear pinned me in place. *Move,* I told myself.

Move.

Now. It's coming.

Move, moron, move.

It's coming, it's coming, it's—

I charged off the bed and ran toward the monitor. I reached for it, wanting to smash it, kill it. But even through the web of jade, the one part I could still read were the comments, as if the well wanted me to get the message.

Come on down and see me, Cooper. I'm waiting for you. I've been waiting a long, long time.

"No! You bastard, leave me alone!" I swallowed back the chunks of fear in my throat, then tried to yank the monitor up, but it wouldn't move. The slime had become Super Glue, holding on tightly. "Let go! Let go!"

I need you, Cooper. And you need me. We're special.

"Get away from me!" In answer, the web spun off the monitor, arcing out like a loogie, spewing onto my hands. I shrieked and leaped back. God no, it wasn't going to touch me again.

I was too late. A piece had already latched on to me. I tried to pluck it off, but it stuck like tar.

And then I heard the well laugh again. It laughed like Santa Claus. A happy laugh. Friendly.

That scared me more than anything.

I clawed at my hand, trying to scrape the piece away, but

it only tightened its grip. One end spiraled outward, toward the monitor, reaching for the parental slime. It was going to connect. It was going to drag me back there. Back to the—

My bedroom door opened. I spun around and saw Joey, a bag of Doritos in one hand, two Cokes in the other. "Dude. What's wrong with you?"

"There's a . . . a . . ." I turned back, pointed at my computer. But there was nothing there. Just my normal MySpace page. A few comments from Megan from a few days ago, asking where I was.

I looked down at my hand. Plain old skin, red streaks running down the back from my fingernails scratching at it. The only sign that this had really happened. Sweat trickled down my back, spreading in a circle across my chest, and my fingers shook.

"What'd you see? A mouse?" Joey laughed at his computer pun. His *very bad* computer pun. "Man, you're all sweaty. What were you doing, pushups while I was gone?"

"Yeah, uh, pushups. Trying to stay in shape. You know, for football."

"Thought you were booted off the team."

"You never know. My dad could give me a pity A."

"Yeah, and the Dallas Cowboy cheerleaders could show up in my bedroom tonight, too." Joey shook his head. "Here. You need this more than me." He shoved the Coke at me.

I took it, popped the top, and guzzled half the soda. My stomach, empty since lunch, churned. I shot another glance at the monitor. Everything was still normal in MySpace land.

"You gonna message Megan or what? Just say you were a moron. She'll forgive you. Girls like that crap." Joey said, gesturing toward the computer. Megan's face was back on the screen. Her wide smile, big blue eyes. Tempting me to come over.

"Nah. I, ah, think I'll do it in person." I wasn't going to touch that computer again. Maybe not for the rest of my life.

Joey lay down on my bed, his hands behind his head, and looked up at the ceiling. "Dude, I got a problem."

Suddenly I just wanted him to leave. He had no idea what problems really were. It was getting harder every second to convince myself that this was all some Willy Wonka–size dream. "Joey, I don't have time for—"

He popped forward. "This is a serious problem. You're my friend. You have to listen to me. There's this girl, and, like, she won't talk to me. So I want to ask her out, but I don't want to look like a desperate loser, so . . ."

I nearly strangled him. "Did you ever think I might have something going on in my life, Joey? Something more important than your stupid love life?"

Joey's upper lip crinkled in confusion. "More important? Like what? You got cancer or something?"

"No," I said, nearly shouting now. I yanked the Hamlet papers out of the printer and dropped his three pages onto his lap. "For God's sake, stop thinking only about yourself."

Joey swung off my bed and got to his feet. "Geez. Who broke your crayons?"

"Nobody. I've had a bad day." Understatement of the year, but I couldn't tell Joey what was going on. He'd be no help, none at all. There was a reason my father had picked him to read the part of the buffoon in *Hamlet*.

"Whatever. I gotta go." He took the paper, folded it into thirds, and shoved it into his back pocket. "I'm supposed to be babysitting my little brother anyway."

"You left him home *alone?*"

"What? He's, like, nine. As long as he doesn't turn on the stove, he won't burn down the house." Joey grinned, then headed out of my room.

Yet another reason not to rely on Joey for help.

I left the door open. Just in case the computer decided to freak out again. I considered leaving, but where was I going to go?

Plus, I wasn't so sure that thing couldn't follow me. Hadn't it shown up at school?

Where was I safe?

Or was there still a possibility I was making all this up,

like when I was eleven and had a week of nightmares after I'd sneaked downstairs to watch *Saw*?

"Cooper!" StepScrooge Sam called upstairs. I knew that sound in his voice. It was the get-your-butt-down-here-and-clean-the-garage-or-do-some-other-equally-horrible-chore voice.

Great. I *so* did not need him right now. Not that I had ever needed him in my life, but now was totally not a good time.

I didn't answer him.

"Cooper, answer me!"

I flipped open my math book. Pretended I was interested in algebra. I sent another glance toward the computer. The screen saver had popped on, a roving picture of a Fender guitar. I should shut it off, but that would mean *touching* the computer and there was no way I was going near that thing again.

I heard the thud of footsteps. Before I could turn off my light and pretend to be unconscious, StepScrooge Sam stuck his obnoxious blond head into the room. "Don't you dare play dumb. I called you. Twice."

"Can't hear you," I said, cupping a hand around my ear. "I flunked my hearing test at school."

He glared at me. "Not funny, Cooper. Your mother wants you."

A chill ran down my spine. No. Not her. Don't make me go down there.

"I'm not telling you twice." He thumbed toward the hall. "Get up."

Mr. Personality clearly wasn't trying to make friends tonight. "What . . . what, ah, does she want?"

"What is this, twenty questions? Get downstairs. *Now.*" He turned and walked away.

I stared at $3x + 2y = ?$ for a long time. Looked at it until the letters and numbers blurred into nothing, until I convinced myself I was a normal freshman with a friend who was an idiot, a girlfriend—or ex-girlfriend—who hated my guts, too much homework for a Tuesday night, and a stepfather who annoyed me.

"Cooper!" I heard him shout again. He wouldn't leave me alone until I went downstairs, so I shut my algebra book and trudged down to the kitchen.

"So," StepScrooge Sam was saying to my mother, "I delivered another set of twins today. Both healthy."

"That's wonderful," my mother said. Her back was to me, her hands busy at the sink, finishing up the dishes, everything all June Cleaver again. The water was off, as she washed in one sink, then set the dishes in the other to rinse all at once.

We could have afforded a maid, could have afforded a whole fleet of maids, but once my mother married my stepfather, she stopped working and started keeping the house, to give her something to do, she said.

"Yeah, I guess it's good," StepScrooge Sam said with a sigh. He ran a hand through his blond hair. He highlighted it, which made him seem too girlie to me. Some days I wanted to tell him to just be a man and go natural.

My mother turned and faced him. "What? Did something go wrong?"

"No. Nothing."

"You seem almost . . . disappointed," she said.

I wasn't surprised. StepScrooge Sam was never happy with anything. The guy had inherited three generations of Washingtons and lived in the best house in the neighborhood, a monster of a mansion he had built a few years ago. Made money like a Coke machine from his jobs delivering babies and making wine. What he had to complain about, I didn't know, but complain he did. "It was a long day. That's all," he said.

Yeah, I'll give you a long day, I wanted to say. But I didn't. I usually tried to stay as far away from anything resembling an actual conversation with him as possible. I shifted from foot to foot. What did she want with me?

Maybe I should just leave. Hope they'd forget all about me.

"How are things at the vineyard?" my mother asked.

"We're having a rough patch. But it'll pass." He let out a long breath.

My mother ran the sprayer over the few plates and bowls in the sink, then turned off the water and dried her hands. "You should relax, Sam. Let me get you the paper, honey." She went into the den.

I took a glass out of the cabinet and crossed to the sink to pour myself some water. I turned on the faucet and let it run, testing with my finger to see if it was cold.

"Cooper, what the hell do you think you're doing?"

StepScrooge Sam again. "Replenishing my fluids."

He reached past me and shut off the faucet. "You're wasting water."

"Hey, it's not even cold."

He raised a brow. "And your point is?"

There was no arguing with him when it came to things like water usage and light bulbs. I dug in my jeans, fished out a quarter, and dropped it onto the counter. "Here. For the feed-the-faucet fund." Then I crossed to the freezer and grabbed an ice cube, plopping it into my glass.

"Quit with the attitude, Cooper," Sam hissed into my ear, the niceness he'd had with my mother gone now that we were alone. "You know the rules around here. You better show me some gratitude for all I've given you, or else—"

My mother returned to the room, and StepScrooge Sam's voice cut off like a TV losing power. She handed him the paper.

"Thanks, Laura," StepScrooge Sam said, his voice gone to candy. That's how he was—drill sergeant with me, George Clooney with her. "You've had a long day, too, sweetheart. Why don't I pour you a glass of wine? Then you go relax, put up your feet."

She sent him a smile, the same kind of smile Megan used to give me, and I had to look away. "Thanks. That'd be nice." She pushed off from the counter and gestured to me. "Cooper, let's go out on the deck. I need to talk to you."

My stomach dropped to the floor.

No way I wanted to go outside with her, but what was I going to say? *Uh, no, I'm afraid you might drag me into the woods and let that thing eat me for dessert?* I glanced at my mother, saw nothing in her eyes that read homicide, and decided to take a chance.

Because a part of me kept hoping that the other day had been some really bad dream. That all the other times had been, I don't know, some bad reaction to shellfish. I know, it was insane, but who really wants to think this is possible? Yeah, come on over, Peter Pan, and take me away.

"I'm going to go watch the game." StepScrooge Sam handed her the wine, then sent me a smile I didn't return. Just for show, in front of my mom. Jerk.

My mother stepped through the French doors and onto the wooden deck, with me following behind. The yellow bug light cast her in a weird tint, making her seem unnaturally neon. We slid into the lounge chairs, facing the manicured yard.

The well lay a thousand yards into the darkness, beyond the trees.

I tried not to think about that.

"You should go easy on Sam," my mother said. "His job is stressful."

"*His* job is stressful? He delivers babies. The woman does all the work."

My mother bit back a smile. She looked normal for a minute, and again, that whisper of hope ran through me. "Well, there's more involved in having babies than that. When you're older, you'll see."

"Mom, my life is stressful, too." Didn't she realize that? Didn't she see that *she* was part of my problem lately? "StepScrooge Sam could go easier on me. Let up on the water issues, for one."

She pursed her lips as though she'd sucked on a sunflower seed. She hated being in the middle and hated hearing us call him StepScrooge Sam. "Try to get along, please? I don't need any more tension in this house." She shook her head, pausing as if she was about to say something, then changed her mind. "Just . . . think about it, Cooper."

"Yeah. I will." I looked away, past the yard, into the dark depths beyond the trees.

"Anyway, I didn't bring you out here to talk about Sam. I have something else to tell you." She laid her wine on the table between us without taking a sip. Then she turned and sat up, facing me, her hands together tightly, as if she was about to pray. I just kept staring into the woods, half expecting that thing to come charging at me, red-eyed, long claws, casting a big net of slime to hold me down. My mother to say, *Honey, look who I invited home for tea.*

"What." It wasn't even a question.

My mother paused a long moment before she spoke. "Whipple died."

I jerked around. "*What?* When?"

"This afternoon. While you were at school. Sam came home from work and found him in the woods." She reached out a hand to me, then pulled it back, as if she wasn't sure whether she should touch me. "I'm so sorry, Cooper—I know how much you loved him. We all did."

"But . . . but . . ." And then, as if I were two or something, my eyes misted up and my stomach cramped. I realized I hadn't seen the dog all day and hadn't even noticed. Guilt nearly made me throw up. "He . . . he *died?*"

My mother nodded. She stood, took one step, then sat back down again on my lounge chair. So close now, I could smell her perfume, feel the warmth from her body. I tensed for a second when she took my hand. "I'm sorry," she said again. "I loved him, too."

We'd had that dog for twelve years. From the time I was a little kid. From before the divorce. He'd been the one mainstay in this family. I could look at him and see what used to be, before—

Before everything. Before my life became something I didn't recognize.

"How could he die? He was so healthy. I played ball with him in the yard just last week." And I had. Tossed a tennis ball with him after school for, like, fifteen minutes—why hadn't I done it for thirty, forty, fifty? If I'd known I'd never do it again, I'd have given the dog hours.

That day, he'd been fine, bounding after the stupid ball just like always, tongue lolling, tail wagging, his eyes bright and happy. Easy to please.

"He was old, honey," my mother said, her eyes soft. Her hand still held mine, tightly, securely. Like it used to when I had a bad dream and couldn't sleep. Like the day she told me she and my father were getting a divorce. Like she had my first day of school, the time I fell off my bike, the day I struck out in the championship Little League game. "Sometimes bad things just happen."

Bad things. I thought of Whipple barking outside the well, then cowering at my feet, scared of the slime. Him trying to stop me from going to the well to get Megan. Jumping on my legs, trying to—

Tell me something?

Had he been trying to protect me? Had he really known there was something bad in that well?

Oh God, and now he was dead? Guilt churned in my stomach. I popped out of the chair so fast, I toppled the wineglass, shattering it on the hard wooden deck. The pale liquid spread, seeping into the oak in a wide darkening stain. In the evening light, it looked thick and dark, and it seemed to be congealing, like blood. For a second, my heart stopped, because I thought it *was* blood. Whipple's blood. But no, that couldn't be. "No, he can't be dead. He just can't. He's always been here. *Always.*"

My mother stood but didn't reach for me. "Cooper, we can get another dog."

I turned away. Shut my eyes. Couldn't look at her. Couldn't look in those woods. "It's not the same."

"No, it's not, but . . ." She drew in a breath, and then her arms stole around my back and she leaned her head on my shoulder. "But we can pretend it is, and after a while, it will be."

"No, Mom," I said, jerking away from her. I looked out at the woods and knew that as much as I tried to forget what had happened, tried to act as if it had all been some fluke, some trick of my imagination, as much as I wanted to lean back in and accept the hug she was giving me—

I couldn't.

"It won't ever be the same again."

Then I ran down the stairs and away from the house.

I crawled through my bedroom window after eleven. I'd gone to Mike Ring's house and watched a movie I'd already seen three times. For five seconds, I'd thought maybe Mike could be a help. In between snack runs to the kitchen, I'd said something to him about how I thought maybe my mom might be losing it.

"Your mom? Dude, she's like the mom everyone wishes they had. Buck up and shut up. I'll trade you any day for my dad." Mike's dad was a raging alcoholic who showed up after school at least once a week screaming his name. He'd park the van as if he were playing bumper cars, and Mike would end up shoving him over and driving home even though Mike didn't have his license. The school had called the department-of-children cops at least twice, but Mike's mom always covered for her husband. Mike's dad, I guess, pulled it together enough to pass whatever tests they gave him. Plus, he was a cop himself, so he got away with crap the rest of the world couldn't pull, just because he had a badge. And his mom, well, she wasn't much better. Mike, I knew, lied for all of them. Told teachers and other concerned adults that life at home was just fine, never saw a beer pass the old man's lips.

I guess whatever Mike lived with was better than the great unknown of the foster-care lottery.

"Yeah, but she's been acting weird lately, Mike." I couldn't think of a good way to say, "She tried to kill me this past weekend."

"You want to see acting weird, wait for my dad to come home." Then Mike changed the subject, went back to his usual goofy self, and refused to talk about anything deeper than what Britney Spears's cup size might be.

A few minutes later, Mike's father stumbled in and started ranting at his son for something that didn't really make much sense, because his father was drunk and his speech came out in a garbled bunch of obscenities. Mike's mother woke up, the dog started barking, and World War III erupted in the living room. I bugged out of there quickly. Two parents freaking out in one day was two too many for me.

When I got home, I found a glass of milk and a couple of Oreos on my nightstand, along with a note from my mother. "I'm sorry, Cooper. I'm here if you want to talk. Love, Mom."

I was way past the age of needing cookies and milk. And I didn't want to talk. My throat closed up when I noticed the empty spot on the end of my bed where Whipple usually slept. Without bothering to change out of my jeans, I slid under the sheets and waited for sleep. My day had officially sucked.

CHAPTER 7

Hunger clawed at the creature like a thousand children without mothers. The old man had not been enough.

Not nearly enough to quiet the bone-deep gnawing in the creature's gut. He dragged himself along the bottom of the hovel that had been his home for so long, he had nearly forgotten what his first home had been like. What he had been like back when he had had a name. When people had called him Auguste.

Once, he'd been an ordinary human.

Once, he'd slept in a real house.

Once, he'd had a regular life.

Once, he'd dreamed of more, of love, of a woman—

Then one day, he'd ended up down here, and he'd become a monster. Because the land had demanded. This land, which had preserved his life, given his family their rich lives, given him his power, had also demanded a merciless sacrifice. His existence.

Auguste, now a creature of the dark, brushed a hand across the earth, and in response the ground surged upward, meeting his touch, caressing him back. Loving him, in its own way. For without him, the land would lose its energy. Its power.

He heard a sound from up above and scrambled over, mouth open, waiting to be fed.

Instead, what tumbled down were rocks. Sticks. A clod of dirt.

The creature roared in protest. This was not the agreement. Not what the others had done.

"*Earn* your food, you miserable beast," the one above said, and then walked away, footsteps fast and hurried through the woods. Angry, but touched with fear.

The creature let out a screech and scrabbled up the walls, perching on the edge of the well. The one who fed him stopped, turned, and pointed a finger at him, sneering, "Get back down there. It is not your time."

Strength left the creature's arms, and he tumbled back to the bottom, where he nursed his hatred. Soon, one day, he would walk above his dungeon again, and the one who had not appreciated his sacrifice, the one who had spat on his gift to so many generations of Jumels, would pay.

Until then, he would eat what he could. And he would wait.

A rat skittered past, and the creature reached out a clawed hand and speared the animal. A squeal pierced the air.

He laughed, watching the rat squirm and wriggle, as if it had a chance of escaping the knifelike nails that had sliced through its body. The creature sniffed the air. Ah, the scent of fear. Auguste licked his lips, or what passed for lips, then lowered his jaw and bit off the top half of the rat. Blood exploded in an arc, and he closed his eyes, sucking it off his face, his skin, pretending.

It was Cooper's blood.

Bah. It was no use. This feral animal had the bitter taste of those that lived underground, not the sweet taste of innocence. Cooper . . .

Ah, Cooper's blood would be as fresh and thick and luscious as the best wine these grapes had ever birthed. Soon, oh soon, he would have his drink, and Cooper would take his rightful place as the heir. Then the creature could climb out of this well, get back to his life again.

But what life? He had no idea anymore. Would he have the stomach, after all these years, to live like those people out there did, with furniture and pillows and blankets? Those creature comforts?

Ha. Creature comforts.

Only one thing would comfort him now. Having Cooper in his grasp. Cooper's blood dripping from his mouth, pooling in his stomach. Knowing as soon as the creature melded his soul with Cooper's, Auguste would once again live.

He didn't care about any of those mundane details, those petty things that people put such stock in. No.

When he was whole again and he could walk the earth, there was only one thing he would seek. He cast his glance toward the open hole above him and smiled.

Revenge.

The creature sucked the rest of the rat down his parched throat, feeling the animal's claws scrape their way to his gut, and knew no animal would ever fill that yawning need. He needed Cooper.

He needed him soon.

CHAPTER 8

The rest of the week went on like normal, which in some ways had me more scared than if green slime had sprouted between my toes in the shower or climbed out of the fridge when I went to fill my bowl of Cocoa Puffs. My father assigned us a research paper on *Hamlet,* apparently because he was so excited by the three-page essays we had written on act three. There were days when I seriously wondered whether I even swam in the same gene pool.

Megan acted like she and I were on different planets. Joey and Mike were the only constants. Meaning they were constant idiots, but at least I could count on something.

On Friday night, I decided it was safe to stay home since Mom and Sam were going out. I was heading for the fridge for a forage feast when I heard StepScrooge Sam's voice exploding from outside on the deck.

"What the hell is going on out there?"

I paused and peeked around the wall. He was screaming into his cell so loud, his face had turned red.

"I want some answers, and I want them now. Why the hell is production down? Those grapes taste like crap lately. If this keeps up, we're going to have to scrap the entire crop, and that is *not* acceptable." He paused a second. "What the hell do you mean, Paolo didn't show up *again* today? Where the hell is he?" Sam let out a curse. He paced the deck. "Too many people are missing work. No one can call in sick. *No one.* I don't give a crap if your mother dies or you lose an arm. Do you hear me?" He ran a hand through his hair and let out a breath. I started to sneak into the kitchen, but Sam spun on his heel and headed in there first.

Busted.

He glared at me, as if everything he was hearing were all my fault. Then he pointed at the floor.

The message was clear. I'd better glue my feet to the spot. I shifted from foot to foot, waiting. Did I really need a sandwich this badly? For this crap?

Sam gripped the phone tighter, the veins in his neck so taut that I thought for sure he'd pop one. "Don't you all know how important next week is to the vineyard? It's our two-hundredth anniversary. *Two hundred years* in business, do you hear me? Five days from now, I'm supposed to have the biggest party this place has ever seen, yet business sucks and the idiots working for me can't be bothered to show up." He paused and listened for about a half second. "No. Don't give me any more excuses. Just get this place back up and running the way it should be. *Now.*"

He slammed the phone onto the kitchen counter, then turned and glared at me again. "What the hell do you think you're doing?"

"Getting a snack."

"You had dinner. What do you need to eat again for?" He shook his head, as if he had already given up on the argument. I didn't go near the cabinet, just in case. "Your mother and I are going out tonight. I want you to sweep out the garage and clear the leaves off the deck."

I didn't want to go outside. Not at night. "I have a paper to work on."

He took a step closer. "Did I just say I wanted an argument? I don't have time for this crap from you, Cooper."

Bad mood didn't even begin to describe him. I needed a way to defuse the Sam bomb before it exploded into even worse chores. "I, ah, saw Paolo's hat in the woods," I said. Maybe a clue to the worker thing would get him off my back.

If I'd thought he'd jump up and down for joy, I was wrong.

Sam didn't move. "You saw what?"

"Paolo's hat. It was, ah, out in the woods, you know, by that old thing. That . . ." I couldn't say the word. "That water thing. What is it? The . . ."

"The well?"

I heard a whisper in the air, as if something had joined the conversation, and I wanted to back up, back away, but then it was gone. The heat kicking on, I told myself. Nothing more. "Yeah."

Sam backed up a couple steps, his hand dancing across the countertop for his cell. He picked it up, dropped it again. "Did you tell anyone else about this?"

I thought of Megan. How much Sam couldn't stand her. Decided I didn't need to add any fuel to that fire. "No."

"Then don't, you understand?" I nodded. He went on. "Paolo is a drunk who goes off on binges. He's a liability. If word gets out that he was stumbling around in the vineyard after hours, I'll be sued."

Something about that didn't sound quite right. I mean, what a guy did after work was his own deal, right? But then again, it was the boss's property. "Yeah. But . . . I thought you just said on the phone that Paolo was missing."

Sam lunged toward me. "I said he didn't show up for work. That's different. He's a drunk, did you hear me? He's home and sleeping it off, like he always does. I'm firing him the next time I see him."

Except . . . a part of me kept seeing that pile of hair and brains in the hat.

StepScrooge Sam started to walk out of the kitchen, but stopped next to me. "Don't tell anyone, you hear me, Cooper?"

"Yeah."

Then he clapped me on the shoulder. Hard. And left the room.

A shiver of uneasiness ran through me, but I shrugged it off. Paolo did like his wine. Sam could be right.

After my mother and Sam left for dinner, Faulkner came down and joined me in the theater room for a bucket of buttered pops and a rerun of a Bruce Willis flick.

"Mom made this for us. Everything's cool," Faulkner said, digging into the bowl. "Nothing's happened with you and her, right? That day was probably just some weird freak-out."

In the past few days, my mother had been normal, even extra nice, as if she knew how upset I was about the dog dying. No one had talked about Whipple again after that night, but Mom had done small things, like had my favorite box of crackers and a six-pack of Coke waiting on the counter when I got home from school. She hadn't nagged me about homework or my room or getting to bed on time. She asked me a couple more times about my birthday, but I just shrugged it off. I totally wasn't in a cake-and-ice-cream mood.

So a part of me wanted to think yeah, things were normal. Everything was cool again. The whole thing had been some weird fluke. And a part of me wondered if maybe the well, or whatever was in the well, wanted me to think that, too. Wanted me to get comfortable in my shoes again, like in the movies, when the hero stops looking over his shoulder. All week, though, I'd had this feeling, this eerie raise-the-tiny-hairs-on-my-arm feeling, that something was there, waiting, like the constant buzz of mosquitoes. I didn't know what it was—or whether I'd just seen too many *Friday the 13th* sequels.

Kind of like that moment back in the kitchen earlier tonight, when Sam and I had been talking about Paolo. A weird feeling, but not much more than that.

"Yeah. Nothing," I said.

Why didn't I tell Faulkner about the green slime from days before? Why did I keep holding that back?

Why didn't I tell him how that web had spread over my hands? Attacked my computer?

Maybe because I thought he'd think I was one drumstick short of a KFC bucket?

Faulkner hadn't believed me before and sure as heck wasn't going to believe me now, not with us all back to Candy Land life.

"Muy bueno," Faulkner said, socking me in the arm. "Guess you were just hallucinating, huh? You and your

imaginary world. 'Member when you were six and used to think you were the Hulk?"

"Yeah. Whatever." I thumbed up the volume on the remote, and Faulkner and I settled back to watch Bruce Willis mow down the bad guys. Just like a normal family.

I awoke to the sound of laughter tickling my ears, like wind.

I stirred and rolled over, brushing at my ear. Then I heard a crunch beneath me, felt something poke into my ribs. And I realized I wasn't in my bed.

Oh crap.

I froze. My muscles turned to icicles, pinning me in place. I opened one eye, then the other. Ebony black kept me blind for one long second, and then the images came into a sort of hazy focus, the kind that came not because I could suddenly see in the dark—

But because I had been here before. And knew this place too well.

Twisted vines. Tangled skinny branches. Weird, nearly transparent white grapes, the last few shriveled ones left on the vines.

Rough-hewn dark gray stones, curving upward in a circular wall, coated with a deep green moss.

I scrambled backwards like a crab, all four limbs working at once, grabbing anything I could to get back, get away—

From the well.

Oh dear God. Not again.

My heart slammed in my chest, beating against the wall of my rib cage like a prisoner wanting off death row. It took three tries, three tries of slipping and falling, my bare feet losing the battle against the Slip 'n Slide of damp earth, before I got to my feet.

Going somewhere, Cooper?

I didn't stop to wonder how I had ended up here. Who had dragged me out to the middle of the woods while I slept. Who had left me by the well. I knew those answers, even if I didn't want to check off C: MOM on the multiple-choice quiz.

I turned and ran. My breath heaved in my chest, lungs struggling to wake up, along with the rest of my body, which felt so heavy, so, so heavy, as if I'd been—

Drugged?

Impossible. She would never.

Would she?

My heart sunk, knowing that if that popcorn she had made us had been drugged, then Faulkner was probably still in the theater room, out cold. Incapable of helping me.

I tried to put on some speed, but it felt as if I were slogging through pancake syrup. My legs weighed a hundred pounds each, my feet could hardly remember the one-foot-in-front-of-the-other rule, and my arms flopped at my sides instead of pumping like pistons.

Behind me, I could hear laughter, rising and falling on the wind like the screeching of gulls. Like the chuckles of the Grim Reaper himself.

I pushed myself, trying to pretend I was the Michael Phelps of the woods, but the harder I tried to run, the harder it was to breathe, to move. The trees worked against me, branches slapping my face, twigs tripping my already clumsy steps, as if the land was on the well's side.

That was crazy. Trees didn't move. Didn't think. Didn't try to kill people.

You don't know what I'm capable of, my boy. The thing laughed again. *Now, come back, because we have something to talk about.*

"Leave me alone!" I shoved at the branches, their sharp edges poking me, jabbing, hurting. "Leave me the hell alone!"

Come back, Cooper. Now! The monster's voice again. Louder, angrier.

"Get away from me!" Whatever was in my system was starting to either wear off or be beaten back by an adrenaline-and-fear cocktail. The dark closed in around me, tight like a blanket, and I had only one thought—

Get the hell out of the woods.

I let out a shriek and pushed my body even harder, even as the fallen sticks sliced at my bare feet and the tree branches hit harder against my sides, my hips, my arms. The woods were thicker here, closing off the light from the moon. My heart slammed against my chest, and I told myself I had stopped being afraid of the dark when I was nine.

Yeah, except that that had been when I had thought there weren't any monsters in the dark. *That* had turned out to be the largest load of crap anyone told his kids.

I could feel this monster watching me, could feel him sensing me.

Somehow he knew everything I did. Somehow he saw me. And somehow—

He was chasing me right now.

I heard the thunder of footsteps first, the breaking of branches, felt the heavy thud that told me I wasn't alone in the woods and that what was running behind me sure as hell wasn't the neighbor's cat. The night coated everything with its black sightless paint, and there were only sounds.

The sounds of death coming for me.

Terror clawed up my throat, and for a second, I couldn't breathe, couldn't think. I stumbled over a log and went down, feeling the air rush past my face and knowing this was it. He was coming, and I was going back down in there.

To die.

I hit the ground with a thud, face smacking against a pile of sticks, pain blasting into my eye, my head. I rolled to the side, slapping at the nature guerrilla attack, as if getting the leaves and branches off would keep the creature off, too.

Suddenly my arm was jerked to one side and I was yanked to my feet. I opened my mouth to scream, ready to face claws and teeth and God only knew what else on the appendages of that thing, that laughing, talking *thing*.

But the scream died in my throat, crawled down to my stomach like a crab too terrified to leave its shell.

It wasn't the monster. It was worse.

"Where are you going, Cooper?" my mother asked me. She had come out here in her sweats, her hair all a mess, her makeup still on her face, smudged and looking like raccoon eyes. An eerie little smile curved up her face. "You shouldn't be out in the woods alone at night. It's dangerous."

She said the last word slowly, breaking apart the syllables like dropping eggs into a bowl. *Dane-ger-us.*

With a special emphasis on the *us.*

Her smile widened, showing all her teeth, and her eyes glittered in the dark. Her grip on my arm tightened like a blood-pressure cuff, and I knew there was no going home.

There was only going back to the well.

I opened my mouth, and this time, I didn't scream—
I howled in fear.

CHAPTER 9

She dragged me through the woods, her hand on my wrist like a vise grip. I'd never seen her move like this, marching forward as if she didn't see the trees, didn't realize it was dark out, and didn't even know I was there, stumbling behind her.

This wasn't like when I was little and I'd been caught painting the back of the house red. Then, she'd been pissed off.

Now she was someone else. Someone who didn't seem to recognize me. Or—

Give a crap about me.

Her strength was over the top, superhuman, not like Mom at all. This was the woman who had to have someone open the pickle jar, for God's sake, and now she was hauling me around as though I weighed about as much as a pillow.

I tried to dig in my heels to stop her, tried to peel her

fingers off my wrist, but she kept on, a one-way train to the final destination.

The well.

And that . . . that thing.

"Mom!"

No response. She just kept making headway into the woods.

"Mom! Stop! Ow! You're hurting me!"

She let out a grunt and started moving faster, her grip too tight like overdone handcuffs. She ran hard, the effort making her grunt like a bull. Her breath rushed fast and hot in the air between us. *In. Out. In. Out.*

"Mom! Mom!"

But she didn't hear me. She wasn't there. Whoever this was, I didn't know. From somewhere in the woods, I heard the thing in the well begin to laugh. A deep, dark belly laugh, as if this were the funniest damned thing it had ever seen. Me struggling against my mother, fighting off my own impending doom.

Now my fear turned to terror, running a constant drum of telling me to get away from her. What was I going to do, though? Beat up my own mother? Grab a stick and shove it into her, like a knife? Club her with a rock?

I still couldn't bring myself to do something like that, something that would *hurt* her.

What if . . .

What if she was still in there? And I killed her?

I couldn't do it. No matter how much I wanted to get away, I just couldn't go that far.

"Mom . . ." I cried, wishing she would stop, knowing she wouldn't. I twisted hard to the right, managing as I did to get one of my arms free, enough to grab a passing tree trunk. I wrapped myself around that sucker and held on for dear life, even as the bark scraped down my skin, surely taking off a full layer.

My mother let out a shriek of surprise. She wheeled around, her eyes shining like angry black diamonds, and stared at me, really, really pissed now, as if I were a pesky hornet with its stinger in her thumb. "Let go," she said, her voice a growl.

"No."

She yanked at my left arm, but I held tightly with the right, hugging that tree as if it were the last oak on earth. "Let go of the damned tree, Cooper."

I shook my head. "This isn't you, Mom. Snap out of it. Please."

She advanced on me, her eyes so dark, they'd become one with the night. Her mouth was open, her teeth bared. When her grip slackened slightly, I jerked my other arm out of her grasp.

She let out a screech of fury, sounding like a wounded bear. She lunged for me and I knew I had to take a chance. I skidded back, my feet slipping on the leaves, and for one horrifying second, I thought I was going to fall down, but then somehow I found some kind of traction and started pedaling backwards, my arms waving like a windmill.

My mother kept coming at me, but I had the advantage of youth and fear. I spun to the right and ducked beneath a low-hanging branch, dodging the trees—had they grown closer together or was that my imagination?—trying to get away, put some distance between us, get out of these woods, get somewhere, anywhere but here.

But then, just when I thought I was in the clear, I saw the familiar curl of green weaving a fast path ahead of me, building a network faster than I could run. As if being around my mother had given it more strength, more speed, it spread its green reach farther than in the classroom or my bedroom, into a web that now looked like giant wings, wide and welcoming.

Come on in, Cooper. I'll catch you.

I dodged to the left.

The mossy green web was there, too, its blast of evil color knitting into a wild blanket that stretched between the trees. Waiting for me to run into it, some human-size spider web.

Come here, Cooper.

"Cooper!" My mother's voice behind me, but not really hers—someone else's, something else, something deeper, darker, hoarser. "Get over here! Now!"

I ducked to the right and moved faster, even though it hurt to run. Behind me, the forest floor thundered with my mother's footfalls, the air echoing with her roars of fury. The green knitted fast but not as fast, as if the well hadn't expected me to move in that direction. I pushed hard, knowing my mother wasn't far behind me—maybe six feet? Eight?

Finally, ahead there was a break in the woods, a light—

The one on the deck.

The house.

I ran even faster than I thought I could, becoming like one of those speed demon guys who leave everyone in their dust in the Boston Marathon, pushing my fists ahead of me, breaking through the brambles now, and just as I hit the last edge of the forest, the web leaped at me with one final curl, like a long green hand reaching for me. I screamed and dove forward.

I rolled, smacking at my skin, sure that the web had gotten me, that my mother had me, the thing had me.

Nothing. Nothing had me. I caught my breath, then cupped a hand around my ear and listened. The wind carried through the trees, whistling lightly. But there was no laughter. No screaming. No roars of anger.

No sounds of anything moving. Where had she gone?

And worse . . . when would she be back? Because she would be. I had no doubt about that. The thing wanted me, and she was working for him. But why, I didn't know.

I just got to my feet, ran for the house, and raced up to my room, locking the door behind me.

I was done sleeping for the night. Maybe ever again.

CHAPTER 10

I never want to see you again, Cooper." The door slammed in my face before I could get a word out.

"Megan!" I hammered on the wood with my fist as I stood there on Sunday. I'd managed to avoid StepScrooge Sam and my mother most of the weekend by telling them I was working on a project at Joey's. But the hours had ticked by, and as it had gotten closer to the time to either go home or find somewhere else to go, I'd realized there was only one place I wanted to be. "Please. I'm sorry."

No answer.

I stared at the oak door of the home of the one girl I'd ever really cared about, and wondered if this was what love felt like—like a blow to my chest, so heavy that I couldn't hold the emotion anymore.

I dropped down and sat on her stoop. I figured if I waited long enough, she'd come out and forgive me.

I had to tell her that I'd cut her out of my life to keep her safe. And that I was on her doorstep today because I now realized that if I didn't open up to her, the one person I trusted more than anyone else, I'd go crazy. I'd run out of options, if I'd really ever had any to begin with.

I was lost. Not can't-find-my-way-home lost, but lost in the way that I didn't have anyone around I could talk to.

My father was useless. He was the professor from *Gilligan's Island*—all brains, no listening power.

My brother still didn't believe me, even after finally waking up from his popcorn-induced stupor yesterday. When I told him those kernels might have been drugged, Faulkner denied it and just said he had been really tired and needed to catch up on his rest. And today he had ditched me and headed to Shelley's.

My mother—

Well, that was a lost cause and a half.

And Sam—Sam hated me.

Joey and Mike were like the bonus clowns in a Volkswagen at the circus. Good for nothing but comic relief.

But Megan—

I don't know what it was about her. Something in her

eyes, the way she seemed to listen totally intently to me when she looked at me. I knew Megan and knew she cared. That she wasn't going to run out the back door and leave me alone.

If I could just hold on to her, for a little while, maybe I could find a way to deal with all this.

It took ten minutes before Megan opened the door again. She came outside and sat down beside me without a word. She looked out over her street, her hands draped over her bare knees, bruised a little from cheerleading, dark brown hair running down her back like a river, then drew in a breath and looked at me. "I'm supposed to still be mad at you for dumping me. All the magazines say not to talk to you for at least two weeks. To really make you suffer."

"I am suffering." I gave her a grin, hoping she'd forgive me.

It took a second, but she finally did. That was one thing about Megan. She couldn't hold a grudge if you taped it to her hand. "All right. Why are you here?"

I swallowed my pride. I didn't have time to have any. "I need help."

"With algebra? That *Hamlet* research paper? Listen, Cooper, I have—"

"My mother's trying to kill me." The words tumbled out in a rush.

Mrs. Garrett shushed Elise, saying something about it being rude to criticize family members of guests.

"Maybe it was just me." Elise laughed a little. "I *was* pretty hormonal."

"Pretty hormonal?" Megan said. "You were the Godzilla of hormones."

Elise threw a roll at her. Mrs. Garrett shushed them both. Trevor and Taylor laughed their heads off.

Mrs. Garrett rose. "I'm going to go get the pie. Megan, please make sure Cooper feels welcome. Unlike your sister." She shot Elise a don't-bash-the-stepfather glare, then headed into the kitchen.

Under the table, Megan reached for my hand and gave it a squeeze. I glanced at her. If I could keep on looking into her blue eyes, everything would work out okay. I'd be able to breathe, to make some sense out of this.

But then the screaming started again in my head, softer this time, far away, because Megan lived clear on the other side of town. I could hear that creature—*how could that thing find me here?*—looking for me, and it was mad. Royally pissed off. I could tell by the tone.

Trevor stopped buzzing long enough for me to make out what the thing was saying. I leaned back in my chair, tilting my head toward the open window.

Cooper, it rasped. Then it gained in volume, clarity. It

Okay, so maybe there are better ways to say that kind of thing. I probably shouldn't have just dropped it like a bomb. Her mouth opened and closed, like a door that wouldn't stay shut. "You're . . . you're not serious."

"It's not really my mom that's doing it. Well, at least I don't think so." As I said it, the pieces started to come together—what had happened in the woods Friday night, how something else, maybe something supernatural, had worked with her, how it had seemed to control her movements, make her stronger, meaner. "At least, I hope she's not the one in control. I know that doesn't make any sense. I think it's this thing that . . ." I paused. Okay, this was where it got weird. Where Megan could easily turn and call the white-coat police on me. "This thing, this creature, a monster or wild animal or something, that lives in that old well behind my house. The one I told you to stay away from."

Megan started to laugh. She shook her head and rose. "Cooper, next time you come over to my house and start wailing on my door in the middle of Sunday dinner, pissing off my dad, try to come up with a better story."

She started back toward her door, but I grabbed her hand. "Megan, I'm serious. I know it sounds crazy, but it's true."

"You've never been serious about anything your entire

life. Especially not me. I have to get back to dinner before my mother freaks." Then she let out a sigh and looked up at the sky before glancing at me. "Did you eat?"

I shook my head.

"Do you like roast beef?"

I didn't, but I wasn't going home for a meal that night— maybe not ever, not after what had happened Friday—so I nodded. Besides, it meant being with Megan, and that alone was reason to sign on for whatever was on the menu.

"Then come inside. Nothing makes my mother happier than feeding people."

So I went inside and sat at the Garrett dining room table with Megan, her parents, her older sister, and her twin nephews. It was so . . . ordinary, so normal, when I'd just been running from *Ripley's Believe It or Not!*

Still, no matter how hard I tried to feel like I fit in to that formal dining room with its dark cherry furniture and Oriental carpet, I couldn't forget what waited for me outside those walls.

The roast beef kept lodging in my throat, the mashed potatoes tasted like glue, and the green beans seemed to twist sideways and stick on the way down to my stomach. Trevor and Taylor, the twin motor mouths of Megan's sister, Elise, kept chattering on and on about some school play they were going to be in. "I get to play a bumblebee," Trevor said, or maybe it was Taylor. I could never keep them straight. "A run around all the flowers and say, 'Buzz, buzz,' and so away the little fly and I sing a song." He turned to m "Wanna hear it?"

Before I could say no, Trevor launched into a perf mance of something about making honey and flowers. T lor, who was apparently going to be the hummingbi joined in with a continual "hmm." I wanted to grab th both and shake them, tell those kids there were things o side this house a hell of a lot scarier than bumblebees, thi that could suck the life out of their shaggy little blond hea but I figured the Garretts wouldn't like that much.

Besides, Mrs. Garrett had said she had pie for dess Ticking her off didn't seem like a good plan.

So I kept my mouth shut, suffered through a ne ending chorus of "Buzz, buzz, buzz, hmm, hmm, hm and waited for the chocolate cream.

"Hey, Cooper, your stepfather is Sam Jumel, isn't h Elise asked.

"Yeah." Not something I liked to admit in public.

"He used to be my doctor." She made a face. "Some told me he specialized in twins, so I went to see him."

"I guess he does. I don't ask. He doesn't tell."

"I didn't like him," Elise said.

"Join the club."

had my attention now and wasn't letting go. *Come back. We have unfinished business, you and I.*

It had found me again.

Not so impossible, considering it had found me in my bedroom.

Found me in school.

But this, this was different. This was *Megan's* house. This was taking it beyond personal and bringing the battle to someone I cared about. I didn't know what to do. Should I run? Should I warn her?

I looked down at the table, sure I'd see some of that green web crawling over the linens, taking the twins' heads and melding them together, smushing them into one green mass, but no, it wasn't there.

I swallowed hard. Mrs. Garrett laid a slice of pie before me, but my appetite had run off to China. In its place was the smell of the well, the claustrophobic feeling of being there again. I could taste it in my mouth, feel the rocks against my back, the slime on my hands. I jerked away from the table, releasing Megan's hand.

It wasn't here now. But that didn't mean it wouldn't be. Soon.

"I . . . I have to go."

"But you haven't had dessert," Mrs. Garrett said.

"Thanks, but, ah, I'm full. Way full." I backed up until I

hit the sideboard so hard that the dishes rattled. The corner of the furniture piece rammed into my back, a sharp poke that felt real and solid. I slid along the edge, needing that sense of reality to help me get out of the room. My heart hammered in my chest loud enough that I was sure everyone heard it. Sure the thing could hear it, track every beat like sonar.

"Buzz, buzz, buzz," Trevor called, laughing. "He's scared of my bumblebee!"

The Garretts stared at me as though I were an escaped lunatic. Elise gave me the evil eye. Mr. Garrett frowned. He'd always thought Megan could do better, like find a bum on the street corner better. He shook his head, as if he wished he'd never wasted two bucks' worth of roast beef on my stomach, and watched me leave.

Megan rose, too, and followed me out of the dining room and down the hall toward the entryway. "What the hell was that about?"

"Megan, I have to leave." I reached for the door. The growling scream increased in volume in my head, pounding out my name like a drum, over and over again, increasing waves of taunting.

Cooper, Cooper, Cooper.

Then it began to laugh. As though it could see everything I was doing. Could feel how scared I was and thought it was funny as hell.

What was I going to do? Where was I going to go? Nowhere was safe.

My chest tightened. My legs threatened to go out from beneath me.

The truth hit me in the solar plexus like a UFC fighter. If I didn't kill it, this would never stop, not until I was dead.

"Cooper." Megan grabbed my arm. "You're white as a sheet and you're acting totally psychotic. You're freaking me out."

Cooper, you're freaking her out, the thing echoed, higher pitched, mocking Megan. *If you come back here, I'll show you something really freaky.*

"*You're* freaked out?" I leaned closer to her and lowered my voice, watching the hallway to be sure none of the Garretts stumbled upon us. "I'm the one whose mother is a raving psycho every other hour. I'm the one who has this thing that's trying to find me. It's friggin' screaming in my ear right now, Megan. I know that sounds crazy, because I'm, what, three miles away from my house? But I can hear it. I don't know how, but I can. And somehow, it has my mother wrapped around its claws or whatever the hell it has, and she wants to throw me down the well so this thing can have me for dinner. So don't talk to me about freaking out because I am as freaked out as it gets."

She blinked. "You're serious, aren't you?"

I threw up my hands. "What did I just tell you out on

the stoop? Do you think I'd make up something like this for chuckles?"

"Well . . . yeah. You've pulled some pretty big pranks before."

"This is not like gluing Mr. Spinale's ass to his seat in science class! This is bigtime scary crap." I ran a hand through my hair and drew in a breath that shook. I needed to get a grip. "Listen. I need help. And you are the smartest person I know besides Faulkner. But I can't ask him to get involved because . . ."

Megan's gaze met mine, and in that knowledge of someone who has known me since kindergarten, she finished the sentence. "Because he doesn't believe you and trying to convince him would take more time than you have."

"Yeah." In that moment, I think I loved Megan. For understanding me. For knowing me. But I couldn't think about that, because I knew if I lost my focus for one second, like I had over the past week, I'd end up in the woods again. And next time, I'd end up *in* the well instead of beside it.

"Well, I believe you." Megan leaned forward and wrapped me in a hug that smelled like cocoa butter and felt like Christmas. She held tightly for a long time, then let me go. "Give me ten minutes, and then meet me at the playground."

Our old place. My Megan.

Suddenly I could breathe again.

I nodded. Then I left, hoping I hadn't just made the biggest mistake of my life by tangling her in this mess, too.

"Do you have a plan?" Megan asked.

I'd paced for the ten minutes it had taken Megan to reach the playground across the street from my old house, the small white Cape my family had lived in for years, while my parents' marriage had seemed perfect. The two of them reading novels by a crackling fire every night, one of those scenes you'd seen in a freakin' Rockwell painting. Then on D-Day, my mother walked in, dropped the divorce bomb, and moved out.

A week later, she had moved in with Sam. Faulkner and I had never understood it. My father had never seen it coming. Sometimes I walked by this house and wondered what had gone wrong. What detour all of us had missed. I guess I was directionally challenged, because I never found it.

I turned away from the house. "Not really," I told Megan. "It's kinda hard to make a plan, considering I haven't actually seen the thing that's after me. Only . . . felt it."

"Okay." The disbelief was back in her voice. The kind that said I belonged on the closest crazy couch. "So you want me to help you wipe out some unseen creature in a well that you think is trying to murder you? A creature that is working with your mother. A woman I have met, by the way, and who made me cookies when I won the sixth grade spelling bee."

"She's not who, or what, you think." But even as I said the words, they sounded insane. It was broad daylight on a Sunday. All around us, parents were hanging with their kids. Tossing Frisbees, walking dogs, throwing balls. Normal to the nth degree.

Megan paced a few steps away, then back to me. "Why would she do that? She's your mother, Coop."

"I don't know." I sat down in the center of the seesaw. "I don't know."

Megan slid down beside me, her arm draped across my back. She put her head on my shoulder and sat there a long time, quiet. This was what I liked most about her. How she could just be there, be with me. "What happened?"

I didn't say anything for a second. Just breathed in the scent of her shampoo. Clean. Innocent. A world away from my world.

I told her about how things had started to go wrong almost two years ago. About the pool and how my mother had held my head under too long during a game of Marco Polo. About the time she'd backed the car up when I was on my bike, hitting the gas hard and slamming into the front tire of my ten-speed, knocking me to the concrete. And then about my mother telling me that Whipple had gotten lost and how she had convinced me to go into the woods with her to "look for the dog."

Really only taking me back there so she could upend me like a Coke can she was going to recycle and throw me into the well. And then about the other night and her dragging me through the woods for a return visit to the bottom of the well, except I had gotten away.

When I had finished my confession Megan stared at me, her chin on her chest. "Oh my God, Cooper." She shook her head. "Oh my God."

"Yeah, that's pretty much what I've been thinking."

"Did you tell Joey? Mike?"

"Come on, Megan. Do you really see Joey or Mike taking me seriously? Doing anything that would help? If anything, they'd get drunk, pop some popcorn, and sell front-row seats to the execution. *And* they'd play bookie on who would win." I walked away, heading through the park. I gave one of the swings a push as I went, and it arced upward with a creak of protest.

I heard Megan curse behind me. She had to be royally pissed at me to swear. It wasn't that Megan was perfect, just that she had this thing against swearing. She'd given it up for Lent one year and never picked up the habit again. It was one of the things I liked about her. She stuck to stuff. Unlike me, who had all the lasting power of a Paris Hilton relationship.

"Wait, Cooper." She did a light jog and caught up to me, grabbing my hand. "Why me? Tell me that and I'll help you."

I toed at the ground, disrupting a few stones and kicking them to the side. A few feet away from us, a family of four was heading home, the kids walking between the mom and dad. My stomach clenched, and I stared at the ground again instead of at Perfecto Family. "Because you're the only one I trust. Name another high school freshman who is going to believe there's some freakin' creature in a well telling my mother to throw me down there for its midnight snack?"

"You have a point. It is pretty unbelievable."

"Exactly. If I hadn't been down there myself, I wouldn't believe it." I looked away. Swallowed hard. "I think whatever this is that takes her over is getting stronger." Friday night reared its ugly head in my mind. "I can see it in her eyes. I can feel it in the way she looks at me, hear it in the way she talks. And in the way the thing talks to me."

"It talks to you? Like, with real words?" Megan stared at me incredulously, as if this was all still too much. "What's happening, Cooper?"

The air between us stilled. The breeze froze. Leaves stopped rustling. Birds held their chatter.

And then laughter started, but it wasn't coming from anyone in the park, but from far away, far across town.

The whisper of my name carried on a slight breeze. I felt the creature reaching for me, like fingers dancing up my spine. It was coming for me. Again.

"We have to move." I yanked Megan away from the swing set and started to run.

"What is it? Tell me, Cooper. This is weird, really, really weird."

"It's looking for me again." I ran out of the park, Megan keeping up easily because she did spring track. We circled past the elementary school, down Larch Street and over to Hill. I charged down that street, down another, a third, a fourth, running until my lungs hurt and my stomach ached and I was bent over, gasping for air, looking at Megan's face beaded with sweat. And still I could hear it in the back of my head. "I can't get away from it. I have to get in a car or on a plane or on the freakin' space shuttle."

"Or . . ." Megan paused. "Kill it."

I looked at her and decided I did love Megan. I leaned over, and without hesitating—hell, why bother hesitating with anything anymore, especially after all this?—I kissed her, not caring that both of us were sweaty and still catching our breath, that we were supposed to be over, that she had made it pretty clear that she hated me, that I had broken up with her because I thought it would be better for her. Safer.

I just grabbed her and kissed her. She tasted of chocolate and goodness and made my heart sing, my head swim. I pulled back after a moment, feeling right then as if I could float all the way to the moon. "Thank you."

"For what?" A blush filled her cheeks, that smile I loved square on her lips.

"For believing me." I put an arm around her, then turned back in the direction where my old house lay, where everything used to be normal. Megan and I stood there watching the sun set, not saying anything for a long time.

But I couldn't avoid the real world forever, and the truth knocked at my brain, moving the rest aside. "And for being here," I added, giving her shoulder a squeeze, thinking it might be the last chance I got for a long time. "I need all the help I can get right now."

CHAPTER 11

I had no real weapons. It wasn't as if I could walk into a store or go to a street corner and buy a gun. I came from white-bread America, a small town in the middle of Maine, not war-zone Detroit. Guns weren't exactly lying around and gun dealers didn't hang out on the corner of Larkspur and Bayberry.

Not to mention I had exactly twenty-seven dollars in my pocket. Enough to buy a really cool water pistol. Whoo. That'd really scare the monster.

"Okay, so you don't have a gun. You do have a knife," Megan said, pulling out the long, skinny knife I'd managed to swipe from my mother's kitchen before I met up with Megan. Three nights ago, she'd used it to make lemon chicken for dinner. Now it had turned into a weapon. One

I might have to use against her. But I couldn't think about that.

No matter how bad things got, she was still my mother.

But what if things *did* get that bad? What if I was in the woods with her again and this time couldn't get away? Could I use the knife? *Could* I stab her?

I didn't know. And honest to God, I didn't want to know.

Instead, I focused on the task at hand. "I also brought along some rope. And pepper spray. StepScrooge Sam gave it to my mother for when she goes into the city to go to the mall. On the, like, once-a-year occasion she goes by herself." I rolled my eyes. "Whatever. Like Maine is riding the crime wave."

Megan paced the living room in the abandoned house we'd holed up in, the same one I'd stayed at that first night. It had been quiet that night—a seriously freaked-out quiet, but quiet all the same in my head—so I figured this place was safe.

"Is it talking to you now?" Megan asked.

"Nah. For some reason, there's nothing from the monster when I'm here."

"Did you know the old lady that lived here?"

I shook my head.

"Her family used to live on your property, you know."

"What do you mean?"

"At the vineyard. My mom told me about it. The old lady that lived here used to do tailoring and stuff for my mom. And she said her family used to live at the vineyard. Like, her great-great-great-aunt or something grew up there."

"Huh. Small world."

"Yeah." Megan crossed to the piano that sat against the wall, so old that it looked about ready to cave in. She ran a finger over the keys, and they let out a screech of notes. She thumbed through the music on the stand. "There are names here. One of them is the old lady's. Beatrice."

"Nice name. If we have kids, we'll name our kid that."

She shot me a glare. About the kids thing or the name, I wasn't sure. I gave her a grin, to show her I was kidding.

"Here's a Victoria and a"—she moved closer to read the faded writing on the last one—"Amelia."

"Can we get back to the plan?" I said, my nerves pinging like a pinball machine.

"Sorry. What is the plan?" Megan tied her hair back in a red bandanna, looking sort of like a samurai getting ready for a battle.

"You lower me into the well. I stab it. Happy ending." I doubted it would go that smoothly. But I couldn't keep running.

This thing—whatever the hell it was—was going to follow me and find me. If it didn't climb out of the well itself—

and I had a feeling it was going to at some point—it would send its skinny green soldiers to drag me back down, and one of these days, there wouldn't be a Faulkner waiting at the top to pull me out. Or a Megan.

I'd die in the well. And that wasn't the way my future was supposed to go. Not if I had anything to do about it.

"I don't know, Cooper." Megan chewed on her fingernail. "What if I'm not strong enough to pull you back out?"

"You wrap the rope around a tree and use that for leverage. You can do it, Megan." My voice sounded a lot braver than I felt, though.

For a second, I hated myself for dragging her into this. I should have gotten someone else, like Joey or Mike, even if they were idiots. I cared too much about Megan to have her get hurt. But there was no going back now.

What choice did I have? If I called Joey, he'd just laugh his head off. Knowing him, he'd let go of the rope and leave me down there for an hour just to have something to jabber about in gym the next day.

Megan and I might be over, but she was the only one I trusted to hold on and hold tight. She looked at me, her face a strong but determined shade of pale. "You ready?"

"Yeah." I managed not to sound like a weenie when I said it, but as we walked the couple of miles back to my house and into the woods, my legs turned to jelly and I wanted to piss my pants and run like hell.

If it had been anyone but Megan next to me, I might have done just that. But a guy can't wonk out in front of his girlfriend. That's beyond pitiful. So we headed toward hell while I pretended to be brave.

CHAPTER 12

From five hundred yards away, the creature sensed the boy's approach. He halted, pouring every ounce of his strength into his olfactory glands, and turned, a centimeter at a time, as if he were an antenna tuned to one station.

Cooper Warner.

The boy approached. Coming toward . . .

The well?

This turn of events took the creature by surprise, and for one long second, his thoughts scrambled and he lost the connection to the boy. He'd thought he'd have time to get ready, to orchestrate his little surprise to lure Cooper in here. But now Cooper was coming on his own.

Before, Cooper had gone to the one place the creature refused to touch. It was too sacred, too special. She had once been there, and he would not touch it because it was the only place on this earth that reminded him of when he used to be a human. A real man.

Someone who could love and care. And—

Be loved.

But all that was over—very, very over. Now his focus was solely on the next generation.

But now Cooper was back on the creature's land. Hmm . . . perhaps he'd save his surprise for later. A treat.

The creature drew his hand across his head and scraped a long, deep wake-up call into the mushy skin.

He yowled. Yellow pus streamed onto the mossy, wet stones beneath him.

Pay attention. The boy. The boy is here.

He sent his mental vision traveling over, above, and into the air, drawing in with his lungs to pinpoint the boy's location. The earth responded, working with him, he and the land one as always, nature whispering the boy's path, translating every footfall back to the creature.

It hurt, oh it hurt so badly, to think this hard, but the boy was so close, and the temptation to use the vines and the trees to grab him, drag him down, and drink that life from him now nearly took the creature's mind away.

Now, his body urged. *Now,* the earth said. *Do it now.*

No, his mind whispered. *Wait. The time isn't right.*

Three more days. Three more days.

A rustle of leaves, footsteps approaching.

The creature began to pant, and he pressed his fingertips deeper into the spongy mass above his nearly blind eyes. In the darkness, they saw nothing, but under the control of his brain, the only thing about him that really worked anymore, they saw everything.

And here they saw not just Cooper, but the girl, too.

How nice of Cooper to bring me dinner, his body said, and his tongue, or what was left of it, came out to taste the air, to slither across what was left of his lips. *And if I save a little of her for later . . . such a sweet, sweet dessert.*

He raised his head and sniffed deeply, inhaling the air above, his chest rising and falling, hurting with the effort to draw from the world outside of his. But still, he breathed with a hunger that went deeper than any before, breathed in until he caught the scent he wanted.

Flowers and warm, sweet, innocent skin.

Her skin.

He rose, his length extending up, climbing with the vines that had become part of him so many years ago, when he had been put down here and the land had reached inside and joined his body, making them one, giving him powers he hadn't realized he could have. Powers that had made these two centuries bearable. His brain reached out, thinking, thinking, thinking.

And turned over a new idea. A way to use her. Oh yes, she would do. She would be perfect for his purposes.

Until Cooper was here.

He licked his lips. And anticipated a meal like no other.

CHAPTER 13

Light glinted off the knife in shards, like some kind of oth-erworldly thing. For a second, I could believe I was in a Manga comic or one of those prisoner dudes in *Battlefield Earth*. Anywhere but where I really was.

But only for a second. Because I knew where I was. What I was doing. And right about now, I wasn't so sure why anymore.

My guts ripped into shreds, and my heart pumped like an oil rig. I kept looking up, looking for Megan's face. She smiled back at me, sending me a you'll-be-okay message. If I focused on her, I'd be okay, be able to breathe.

And not think about what was waiting for me at the bottom.

Was that thing down there? Or could I have gotten lucky in the past few hours and it had died or left for a bigger well?

Yeah, right. The monster went and looked for better digs. *Get over the fantasy, Cooper, and get back to reality.* That thing was down there, probably waiting with an open jaw to catch me.

Kept my eyes on the bright red of the bandanna in Megan's hair, the wide blue of her eyes. She smiled and whispered, "You'll be all right. I'll be waiting."

I sure as hell hoped so. Then she disappeared, and the rope began moving again.

I inched my way down, bouncing my feet along the wall, that smell invading my lungs, my throat, my stomach, rising up inside me like a tank of vomit so thick that I felt as if I were seven years old again. I'd stayed home from school with the flu, missing the class trip to the Maine State Aquarium. I'd been really pissed off, too, because I'd wanted to see the shark tank. I remember being so sick, my mother had had to keep a bucket next to my bed.

I'd puked into it so often, my whole room smelled like a vomitorium. It took days and a whole freakin' can of Lysol to get rid of that smell.

But the well . . .

The well was like multiplying my room by ten thousand, then raising it to the power of infinity. I wanted to pinch my nose and stop breathing, but I couldn't. To pinch my nose would mean letting go of the rope—no way.

And stopping breathing—well, that went without saying. My father may have thought I was stupid, but I wasn't *that* stupid.

"You all right, Cooper?" Megan's voice, as sweet as choral music, coming down to me from above. I held on to that as tightly as I did the rope. She was the real world. Normalcy. Something to come back to at the end of this.

"Right as rain on the plain," I shouted back, my voice bouncing off the walls. Forcing myself to make a joke. Not just so she'd think I was cool, but so I could focus on something other than ralphing.

Above me, she laughed, the sound almost like coins dropping onto me. "I cannot believe you're pulling a Mr. Hedden right now."

"Hitting every stone on the way down with my *p*'s, too."

Damn, I loved the sound of her laughter, so I made another joke about our history teacher, giving it the full Elmer Fudd treatment.

Mr. Hedden had a bit of a sticky lip. Whenever he said that "rain on the plain" thing—and he said it a lot—those unlucky enough to be stuck sitting in the front row got hit by his oral. That *p* did him in every time. We'd leave history cracking up, stuttering "p-p-p" and plowing spit all over one another, forgetting every damned thing we'd just learned about the War of 1812.

Megan said something else, but I didn't hear her. I dropped another few inches, and that was enough. Enough to cut off the jokes, to send a scream racing up my throat. I caught it before it escaped and swallowed the fear. No more funny stuff now. I tugged on the rope, our signal for Megan to stop lowering me. I didn't want to descend any farther.

Because I had started to hear the thing breathe. It was here. And it was waiting for me.

Oh God.

Pull me up, I wanted to scream. *Pull me the hell up.*

But what good would that do? The thing would just come after me, or send my mother, or its green vine, and I'd be back down here again, on *its* terms, not mine.

I gripped the knife tighter, staring at the blade. I could do this. I had to.

Every meal I'd ever eaten seemed to surge up in my stomach and meet my lungs. I held the rope tighter, tugged on it again, and kept bouncing down.

I heard the thing's nails scrabbling against the bottom, the last bits of rainwater in the dried-up well splish-splashing beneath its paws or feet or whatever the hell it had. The breathing was excited, like a panting dog waiting for a bone.

I stopped moving, bracing my feet against the sides of the well, and closed my eyes. I was still ten feet above it, maybe twelve, but I couldn't move. Every one of my muscles was frozen with fear.

What the hell was I doing?

"Cooper? You okay?"

Megan's voice sounded far away. Too far.

I opened my eyes. Took in a breath. Tried another. "Yeah, fine." Liar. "Just hold on a sec."

Below me, the thing kept breathing.

Just shut up; stop breathing. Stop moving. Stop it, stop it.

But the thing didn't read those thoughts. Oh, no. It just breathed louder. Moved more. Scritch-scratch. It was pacing. Anticipating me.

Sweat coated my palms, dripped down my face. The knife slipped in my grip. I scrambled, nearly losing my hold on the rope, the knife pitching forward, my hand, my stupid hand, almost letting it go—

And then, thank God, I had the knife again.

Beneath me, I swore I heard the thing laugh. Its claws ran across the bottom of the well and I braced against the wall, my back flat.

Where was it?

Was it coming for me?

Could it climb up here?

Please, oh please, tell me it couldn't climb.

I tried to reach around into the backpack for the flashlight, but I had only two hands, and I'd been too much of an idiot to think about hanging the flashlight around my wrist so that I wouldn't need a hand to hold it. My bright idea had been to get down to the bottom first and then get the light out.

Yeah, well, Stupid clearly *was* my middle name, because I needed the light now and I couldn't get it.

I twisted, moved, grunted, then stopped.

And listened.

No more noise from below. No breathing. No scratching. Nothing. Was it gone? Or was it just . . .

Waiting? Patiently and quietly?

I pushed off from the wall and tugged on the rope again, starting to make my way farther down. The rope jerked and I bounced twice hard, the bottom of the thick rope cutting into my ass, the rough fibers chafing through my jeans. "Megan, hey, careful!"

She didn't answer.

"Megan!"

The rope kept jerking. Bracing my feet against the slimy walls, I tried to slow the movements, but the rope bounced again and yanked me down two feet at once. I looked up and saw a bright wide circle of end-of-day orange sun above. "Megan, hey! Megan!"

But all was silent and still above me.

And then, like a slow-motion movie, the end of the rope curled over the ledge and spiraled down into the well. Megan was no longer there.

Leaving me officially screwed.

I opened my mouth to scream, but it was too late. I fell like a stone to the bottom. Right into the thing's waiting, eager grip.

CHAPTER 14

In space, no one hears you scream.

I watched an old movie once that opened with that line. I was eight when I saw it and it scared the crap out of me, had me thinking aliens were going to slime through my walls and eat me alive. I remember waking up in the middle of the night, screaming my fool head off and waking up Faulkner. He threw a pillow at my head and told me if I didn't shut up he'd fart on my face.

That scream had been nothing compared to what came out of my throat now.

The thing had me, and no one was going to hear me scream.

No one was going to hear me be torn to shreds, my brains left in a little pile on the bottom of my stone coffin.

Just like Paolo.

Those piercing sounds kept coming, sounds I'd never made before and hoped I'd never make again, so loud they bounced off the walls. The scream tore at my throat, but I couldn't cut it off, couldn't stop the flood of panic that just kept telling me to get away, get out of its grip.

It was behind me, finger-claw things sinking deep into my sweatshirt. Deep enough to hurt, not deep enough to cut.

It had me. It had me. And it was going to *eat me*.

I was a wild animal, arms and legs doing an epileptic dance, which only made the thing laugh and sent my panic off the charts. My feet stumbled over something, then tangled, and I tripped, ankles jumbled together.

The vines.

Then, no. I'd gotten tangled up in my own damned rope.

I screamed louder and lashed out, my arms windmilling, but still the thing had its grip on my shoulders, its breath hot and heavy on my neck.

Smelling like death.

Pitching forward, I tried to get away, running—running where? I was in a well; where was I going to go?—scrambling, grasping at air, at nothing, at anything. And behind me, that laugh, that horrible, awful laugh, as the thing kept on clutching me like a spider on steroids.

"Where you going, Cooper?" Its rasping voice seemed to float, singsongy, like Trevor's little performance only at a super-high pitch, the kind of tone only dogs could hear. No longer in my head now but echoing in the small space, bouncing back and forth, as if it had said it a dozen times.

"Where are you going, Cooper?"

It had a voice. And now it was using it. Speaking out loud, not just inside my head. Oh, holy crap.

That must mean the thing was getting stronger. I better get my ass out of there. *Now.*

The well had gone as dark as the inside of a tomb, the sun having disappeared from above, and I couldn't see my hand in front of my face. And that meant I still couldn't see whom— or what—I was dealing with. But it was there, I knew that, because it had a grip on me like an octopus with claws.

"Let go of me!" I scraped a foot down each of my ankles, pushing the rope off, then dug into the muck with my sneakers. Now or never. Do something or become Paolo's grave buddy.

I wheeled around. The creature let out a shriek of surprise, nails skittering as it stumbled across the slippery bottom. It was the same shriek my mother had made in the woods the other night when I'd grabbed that tree.

I couldn't think about that now.

I pressed my back against the wall, then raised my right hand. A faint glimmer of silver winked back at me.

All this time, I'd had the knife in my hand, and I'd forgotten. I couldn't have been more stupid if the word had been branded on my forehead. I shifted my grip, and with the weight of that handle, I finally felt as if I had a way out.

All I had to do was stab the thing. Assuming I could find it in the dark. Get in one deep wound, and then—

Okay, getting out of the well itself would be a problem of a whole other sort, but once the thing was dead—

That's all I had to do. Make it dead before it made me dead.

"I've waited a long time to meet you, Cooper," it said.

Don't talk to me. Please don't talk to me. Its voice was like nails on a chalkboard. I pressed my free hand to my ear and tightened my relationship with the wall.

"Get away from me, freak!" I arced out with the knife and hit nothing but air. The creature had slinked away. Or was it smaller than I thought?

Had it ducked down? Decided to crawl instead?

I tried to reach around for the backpack zipper in order to get the flashlight, desperate to bring light to the fear holding me. Where was the zipper?

Where *was* it?

"We're two of a kind, you know, Cooper. We're two . . ." Its voice trailed off—because it was tired? Dying? Or just thinking?—and it began that huff-huffing again. "*Very, very* special two of a kind."

"Shut up!" I screamed, giving up on the flashlight. I slashed out again with blind circles. "I'm not anything with you. To you or about you. Just get the hell away from me before I kill you!"

It chuckled, the sound deep and throaty, an evil Santa laugh. "You can't kill me, dear Cooper. I'm the whole reason you're here. And now you're going to be my . . ." Huff-huff, closer now, and even in the inky black, I could feel it, smell it coming closer. "Be my—"

"No!" I didn't want to hear any more. I lunged for the creature as it approached, the knife raised, aiming for chest level—did it have a heart? Lungs? Whatever it had, I was going to stab it there—but all I saw in the darkness were two eyes—

Two human eyes.

Green, like mine.

Exactly like mine.

Like looking in the mirror.

For a split second, I froze, and the creature started to laugh again. "You can't hurt me, Cooper. Not *me*."

I shut my eyes, and before I could think another thought, I jabbed forward, knowing if I kept my eyes open, I'd never do it. I'd never be able to stab something that looked so much like me.

Do it.

Do it *now*.

The knife sank into something soft as Jell-O and my stomach flipped over in disgust, but still I kept going and turned my fist to the right, carving into more soft, fleshy stuff.

The creature howled in pain. Shrieked my name.

Then something clawed at my arm, scraping through the heavy fleece of my sweatshirt. There was a horrible ripping sound, fabric giving way, then flesh, and the coppery scent of blood filled the air, the thing still shrieking, jerking away from the blade, but even as we separated, I kept waving the silver knife, screaming at the thing to get away.

Then, just as quickly as it had begun, it was over.

The thing had gone.

I don't know how I knew. I just did. It was as if a part of me had left, and a whisper of relief ran through me. The heavy, thick stench of its breathing had stopped. The shrieking had cut off like a stereo ripped out of the wall. The smell had eased by tenths of a degree. I opened my eyes, half expecting to see my own eyes staring back at me.

But I found only blackness.

I swung the backpack down, dug inside for the flashlight, clicked on the beam. As soon as I'd illuminated my surroundings, I wished I hadn't.

I was standing in what looked like maybe a rodent graveyard. Tiny bones littered the floor, little skulls—those were rat heads, right?—scattered like white bowling balls all over the murky floor. But that didn't make me want to hurl. It was the bigger bones, a towering stack of them, that sat in one corner.

Human bones.

Licked, or maybe chewed, clean.

And from the size of the pile, Paolo's weren't the only bones in there. "Holy shit!"

I jumped back and hit the wall, and when I did, I dropped the flashlight. It hit the stone floor with a smack. The light sputtered for one second, then disappeared.

No, no, no. Not the light—don't go out. Don't leave me down here in—

The dark closed around me again like prison walls.

Beneath my feet, the tiny rodent skeletons crunched. I kept the knife out and ready, waving it in a wild circle. Panic clawed at my mouth, squeezed my throat, crushed my lungs. I had to get out of here. Now. Before *I* was added to that pile.

"Megan!"

No answer.

"Megan! You there?"

Silence from above.

I chanced a glance up, and as if on cue, the blanket of dark began to peel away and the late-day sun returned. What the hell?

What just happened? And where was Megan?

I kept calling for her, searching above for her face, but there was no sign of her. Not so much as a peep in response. I told myself she'd gotten scared. Run off. Run home to her parents.

Except the sickening thud in my gut told me she wasn't safe in her bed, tucked between her lilac-decorated sheets.

She was gone. And down here, a note of terror struck my heart. The creature I'd just royally pissed off was gone, too, and I had no way out.

CHAPTER 15

In the movies, the hero gets out of a sticky situation in one or two tries. He's the hero, after all, so he's smart and Mac-Gyvers a quickie solution with a broomstick and a piece of gum.

I'm no genius, so it took me a good half-hour, maybe longer, to finally get out of the well.

This time, I had the rope, which didn't do me much good without someone at the other end. But I sucked it up—had to; my other choice was to stay down there, and that was *so* not an option—and felt around in the dark corners of the well until I managed to find a big rock. I tied the rope around it and, after a lot of attempts, finally winged it out of the pit. It caught on something above—a stump, tree branch, whatever. I didn't care. It was strong enough for me to climb.

On any other day, the chances of throwing a rock twenty feet up and landing it around a tree just right so that it holds enough for me to climb out would be, like, nil. But on this day, with a creepy talking monster waiting in the wings, I was way more motivated to perfect my pitching arm, which wasn't bad but wasn't Roger Clemens's, either.

As soon as I climbed over the well's ledge, I started searching for Megan, calling her name, looking all over in the woods. By now it really was dark, and I couldn't see much. There was no trace of her. I swept the area, over and over again, looking for a footprint, anything.

"Megan!"

I listened but heard nothing. Not so much as a bird calling back. "Megan!"

A flash of red in a shrub caught my eye and I stumbled toward it, going down on my knees, my heart lurching hard, sure for a second that the color was blood, then seeing right away that it was the bandanna she'd been wearing in her hair. Torn, caught in the briars.

No Megan. On the ground, I found her small Maglite. She wouldn't have left that behind, would she have?

Not unless—

I wouldn't think about that.

I got to my feet and spun around. *"Megan!"* No answer. *"Megan!"* The yellow light from the beam bounced off the ground, the shrubs, the trees, showing me everything but her heart-shaped face. *"Megan!"*

I ran back toward the well. I didn't watch where I was going, and my feet tangled in the rope I'd used to pull myself out of that pit. I fell to the ground, the flashlight bouncing out of my grip and spinning away. When it stopped, the circle of light illuminated the rock I had tied on to the end of the rope.

Not a rock at all.

I was half standing when I stopped, my brain taking in what lay three feet away, one horrible detail after another. Something hard and white. Round, smooth. Two small openings, one large, all three staring at me, as if to say—

What are you, a freakin' idiot? You didn't realize you attached your rope to a—

Skull.

Oh God. A skull. An honest to God dead man's head.

I screamed. Let out a string of curses that would have fried my grandmother's hair. I backed up so fast, I fell on my butt again and scrambled like a crab, the flashlight rolling away into the leaves. I kept going until I hit a tree, and I screamed again because for a second I thought the tree's branches were the monster reaching out again for me.

Megan gone. Talking monster in the well trying to grab me. And now a dead man's skull at my feet.

Maybe it was Paolo's skull?

God no, don't let that be Paolo. Tell me I didn't take Paolo's head and use it as a personal baseball to help me climb out of the well.

Everything in my gut lurched upward. I puked until there was nothing left to heave, and then I heaved air.

"I'm sorry, Paolo," I whispered. "I'm so sorry."

Paolo's empty eye sockets stared back at me. I lunged for the flashlight and turned it off. The skull went away, but the night invaded twice as thick and dark. Okay, not a good plan. I flicked the bulb back on, turning the beam away from the skull.

Breathe, Cooper, I told myself. *Breathe and think.*

I did just that for a good five seconds. It was just a skull. I'd seen them in science class a hundred times. In fact, we had a whole skeleton in Mr. Spinale's room. Called him Mr. Body, dressed him up for Halloween, threw a red hat on him for Christmas. That's all this was, another Mr. Body.

Yeah, one that might be someone I knew. One that had been eaten by the monster. That could be me next. Or worse—

Megan.

I breathed some more. Refocused again. Beside me, Megan's bandanna sat in a tiny, sad, crumpled pile. I stuffed it into my backpack and headed out of the woods. She wasn't here, or if she was, I couldn't find her.

Something had happened to Megan. I knew it.

I booked it for the house, sneaking into the basement, thanking God for small favors like an unlocked basement door and a phone extension in the second office on the lower level. My fingers shook so badly, it took three tries before I got Megan's number punched into the handset. In the space of the few seconds it took for the phone to ring on the other end, I must have whispered four hundred prayers. "Mrs. Garrett, this is Cooper—"

"Cooper!" Her voice. Panicked. I glanced at the clock on the wall and realized hours had gone by while I'd been searching.

It was after eleven o'clock at night. No wonder she had that tone.

"Thank God you called me back," Mrs. Garrett said. "I've been calling your house all night. Have you seen Megan?"

Megan hadn't gone home. Hope deflated in me like a popped balloon.

I couldn't tell Mrs. Garrett the truth. One, she'd never believe me, and two, I'd be in serious trouble. I had to buy time until I had some answers.

"She and I went for a walk after dinner," I said—not a total lie—"and then she said she was going to go back home. I think that was around . . . six." That, I thought, was about the time the rope fell into the well.

Guilt pulled a Rocky in my gut. What had I done? What had I been thinking? *I* did this. I asked for Megan's help. And now she was missing.

"She's always home by ten on a school night, *always*," Mrs. Garrett went on, "and she never called, never came home." The last three words were high-pitched, every parent's worst nightmare.

I hated myself for being responsible for that sound in Mrs. Garrett's voice. But what was I going to tell her?

I didn't know what had happened, not really. Megan could be okay. She could, in fact, be out looking for *me* right now. Except a part of me knew Megan's disappearance was wrapped up inside the creature and the well.

I leaned against the wall, my head pounding. All I kept seeing was that skull, then Megan's face, her trusting eyes, so ready to help me.

God, what if that monster *did* have her?

I pictured it breathing down her neck, its slime all over Megan's peach-soft skin, and I wanted to puke but couldn't. There was nothing inside me. Nothing but fear.

"Call us if you see her," Mrs. Garrett said, her voice shaking, tears heavy in her words. "Or hear from her. This isn't like Megan at all. In fact, as soon as I hang up with you, I'm going to call the police."

"I will, Mrs. Garrett." I hung up the phone, then slid down against the desk and dropped my head onto my knees. Oh God.

Megan, Megan, Megan.

What had I just done?

Had I just sent Megan to—

Her death?

CHAPTER 16

They hung up colored posters with Megan's picture, organized search parties, sent cops crawling through town, and had reporters talking to everyone from the mailman to Megan's third grade teacher, people popping out opinions like Pez.

I was dragged down to the police station early Monday morning, hours after the missing-persons report was filed. Held there for six hours and questioned by Mike's dad, the cop assigned to the case. He slammed his hand on the metal table so hard, I thought he was going to leave a dent or break a bone. "I know you did it, Cooper. I know you killed her. Just admit it and we can all go home."

"I didn't do anything." I glared at Sergeant Ring, a balding guy in his late fifties whose belt wasn't doing a very good job of keeping his gut in check.

Guilt twisted a tightening rope around my intestines.

Had I killed her? *Had* I led her to that thing and let it eat her, like it had Paolo? *Had* I done this?

That's all I kept thinking about, all that kept running through my mind.

Oh God, *Megan*.

"Tell me where she went," Sergeant Ring said.

"I don't know, I told you."

"Bullshit." Sergeant Ring leaned forward, shifting his belt under his gut, as if the donuts got top priority. His breath reeked of stale beer; his eyes were red and bleary. Even I recognized the hangover in him. "I know you're dating her. That makes you bad guy number one. Maybe I should lock you up."

"Not a chance. I watch *CSI* and *Law & Order*," I said, ready to be out of there so I could look for Megan myself. I couldn't trust these guys. For one, Ring was a total alcoholic. He could barely raise his own kid and crashed his car into his front porch last summer. Why would I think he could find Megan? For another, the whole well-and-creature story was completely unbelievable—and at this point, I didn't even know for sure that's what was responsible.

But since she'd been gone, there had been no slime and no calling from the well—and to be honest, that was more worrisome than this cop's threats. "You can't hold me without a good reason. And all you have is guesses about nothing."

Sergeant Ring leaned in even closer, so close I could tell

he needed a Mento as much as he needed a bigger belt. "I'll give you nothing, punk. *Tell me where she is.*"

The door opened, and a young, skinny cop walked in, like a "before" picture of Mike's dad. "His parents are back. This time with their lawyer."

Sergeant Ring cursed. Foiled again by the ambulance chasers. "I'll be watching you," he said, wagging a finger in my face, "wherever you go, whatever you do. You forget to tie your shoelace in gym, I'll be taking pictures. You order an extra milk at lunch and forget to pay for it, I'll arrest you for stealing. I'm going to be your new best friend, Cooper."

I had fifty smart remarks I could have sent back but didn't. This guy thought I'd killed my girlfriend or, at the very least, helped her run away. If I talked back, he'd keep me longer. All I wanted was to go look for Megan. I knew exactly where to start my search.

All these hours, the well had been silent.

Why?

Was I too far away? Or was the creature busy with Megan?

Or—and this was the option I prayed for more than anything—had I wounded the beast so badly that it was dying in some crusty corner and thus was unable to do anything but moan and shrivel away?

When I got out of the room, the lawyer kept asking me

if I'd said anything. StepScrooge Sam just glared at me, as if I'd ruined his whole day. I probably had. Whatever.

My mother stood next to Sam, very quiet. Mad? Wishing I was heading off to juvie? I couldn't tell. She said one word total—"Here?"—when they told her to sign some paper so I could be released. That was it.

The lawyer walked us out, said goodbye on the steps, and told us he'd be in touch later, and the three of us headed off to the car.

Like a big happy family.

Or a Photoshopped image of one, anyway.

No one said anything until the car was in gear and Step-Scrooge Sam had it cruising to about forty. "Where the hell is Megan?"

"If I knew, would I be here?" I slammed back against the rear seat and wished he'd shut the hell up.

"Watch your tone, young man," Sam said, his voice so low, it could have been a Doberman's growl. "Do you know what that vampire attorney is costing me? Just to keep your ass out of jail? Show your gratitude."

I bit my lip. I did a lot of that whenever I was around Sam. Lucky Faulkner—the older one, only a year away from college.

"Some cops came to the house when you were being

questioned," Sam informed me. "They wanted to search the grounds. I told them to get the hell off my property."

"Why did you do that?" I asked, alarmed.

"They didn't have a warrant, Cooper," Sam snapped. "Don't you know better than to let the police in without a warrant?"

I did know that—of course I did. But part of me hoped that someone other than me, with the means to help Megan, would find her. And that couldn't happen if StepScrooge Sam wouldn't even let anyone search the property.

"Besides," Sam said, "it's not like they would find anything, right?" He seemed to be challenging me to disagree with him.

But I couldn't. After a full day of protesting my innocence, I was too tired to fight with Sam. "Right," I said weakly.

"When we get home, I have a list of things waiting for you to do. There are consequences to your behavior, Cooper. And your attitude."

After what I'd just been through, what did he expect me to be, all sunshine and smiles?

"And if you step out of line," Sam continued, "there will be rule enforcement."

I knew what that meant. It was code, understood between just him and me, for privilege yanking. The last time I'd "stepped out of line," which to Sam was going to a party without permission, I'd spent three days in my room.

Ate my meals in my room.

Did my homework in my room.

Never left it, except to go to school and to piss.

And when the three days were over, Sam left me a note. A detailed list of yard chores involving shovels and rakes—crap they'd do on a chain gang—keeping me busy for another three days.

"Are you hearing me, Cooper?" Sam asked now.

"Yeah."

My mother sat in the passenger's seat, stiff as a mannequin, silent. What had happened to her? Not just with the whole trying-to-kill-me thing, but to her in general? She used to be the mom who would rush in and soothe the waters whenever my brother or I had a bad day or crappy report card. Try to make everyone happy with a joke or a silly song or a package of cookies. Now she'd become about as warm and fuzzy as one of those Easter Island stone dudes.

"When you get home, Cooper. No delays," Sam said.

In the rearview mirror, I saw cold, hard eyes that were looking at the road and not at me. "Dude, the cops just verbally pounded me. My girlfriend is missing. I've had a really shitty day. And you want me to do my *chores?*"

Sam braked so hard, my head almost popped off. "Just because you've had a bad day does *not* mean you can do whatever the hell you want. I work hard to keep this family together and the last thing I need is for you to pull this crap." Sam stared at the steering wheel in front of him as if he were trying to burn a hole through it. "Do you understand?"

"Jeez, fine, whatever. Take a chill pill." Whatever it took to keep Sam happy, that's what I was going to say. I wanted him to get the car moving again, get me back to the house. Faulkner and I had one cardinal rule—Don't Piss Sam Off. Break it, and your life sucked. Considering my life already sucked as bad as it could right now, I wasn't about to make things worse.

Besides, I was yessing Sam only to shut him up. As soon as I escaped the four-door prison of his Beamer, screw the chore list—I was going to go looking for Megan.

Finally, Sam swung into our driveway, still yakking about chores. I said yeah about sixty times, hopped out of the car, and tried to run inside, but Sam blocked my way. "What did I say?" His eyes glittered in the porch light.

"Chores."

"Priorities, Cooper. Priorities."

My mother had already gone inside. It was just me and Sam. "Finding my girlfriend is my only priority."

"She'll be fine."

Why was he so convinced? Did he know something I didn't? Suspicion mounted inside me, but I didn't dare question him. I knew what kind of punishment Sam would exact, and I didn't need that right now. I needed freedom, and pissing him off wouldn't give me a pass.

Sam closed in tighter. "You are only thinking about yourself and your little world. You don't know a damned thing about sacrifice, do you?"

"Uh, no." Was that the answer he wanted?

"I've spent my life building this business. My practice. I've put everything I have into all of this." He waved at the house, the massive testament to Jumel success he'd built a few years ago in place of the old stone house that used to be there. "And *you* are not going to ruin it, Cooper. *Do you understand me?*"

Did he know what was going on in this house? In the woods? Was he choosing to ignore it all? Or was he part of it? I tried to look in his eyes and see some kind of answer, but all I saw was annoyance.

I nodded again. What the hell did Sam have against me?

"You are going to do your part for this family, Cooper." He jabbed a finger at my chest, sharp and hard. "And you aren't going to screw it up, is that clear, Cooper? I'm tired of your shit."

"I'm not doing anything. I just want to find Megan."

"Let the cops handle that. *You* have other priorities." Sam's finger became a knife, sinking deeper into my chest, hurting. "You better remember them, because all you've done lately is make everything around here worse."

"Don't blame me for your problems." I jerked back, away from him. "You're not my father."

A smile spread across Sam's face, the smile that I hated, the one I wanted to smack off his lips. But if I did that, I knew I'd bring an even bigger can of crap into my life. Sam had a way of making things more miserable than anyone could stand by taking away privileges and doling them out in dribbles. "Oh, Cooper, I'm something so much better than your father. I don't bury my nose in books and lose myself in ancient, dead poets. I'm not some wimp who can't get out of the way of my chalkboard and claim my place at the head of my family. I'm a *man*, Cooper, unlike your father, which means I take control and I keep it."

I backed up another step. I'd hated Sam since the day my mother introduced him to us, but now I despised him. He'd never dissed my father like this before. "Watch what you say about my father."

"He's not here. And I am." Sam chuckled. "And so are you. Stuck together, aren't we? For better or worse, our little family."

"You're not my family." I spun toward the steps. Sam grabbed my arm.

"I'm more of a father to you than your father will ever be." He dipped his face in so close to mine, I saw the hairs inside his nose. "And don't you forget it."

CHAPTER 17

Sometimes at night, he could still hear his brother's voice.

The screaming. The cries.

But most of all, the screaming.

Auguste curled into the corner and pressed his fingers into his ears, trying to block out sounds that were two centuries old, that no longer existed in this world, only in his head. Yet he could hear them as if it were yesterday, as if Gerard were here again.

I have no choice, Auguste. No choice.

And then he'd shoved him and sent Auguste down, down, down, into this fetid pit. To pay the price the land had demanded.

Auguste screamed and buried his head in the dirt, but still the memories came. He begged for peace, sinking his fingers into the earth, pleading with it to free him from the images, but no, they replayed again and again, a warning.

Because today he had dared to think of himself. He had been selfish instead of selfless. He had gotten impatient and crawled to the top, thinking he could take a peek, just one look at what he would have in a few short days—

And the land had swooped in with a reminder, like the backhanded slaps his father had given him when he'd stolen a cookie before dinner. *Remember why you are here and how you got here.*

And who made you pay this price.

Oh, he remembered. God help him, yes, he remembered. And that was his personal pain, the agony that seeped the strength from his bones.

He'd been fifteen.

In love with Amelia Wescott, the stable master's daughter, who'd lived then in a little cottage at the back of the vineyard.

And completely, utterly unaware of the sinister gift that lurked within the vines that curled around the well. He didn't know when Gerard had found the grapes or if he'd been led here, called by the same siren song that Auguste later used to draw in the others. All he'd seen in those days was his twin brother acting different. Acting odd.

Acting . . . violent.

Their father, Edmond, ignoring it all. Trying to cultivate the wild vineyard he had purchased less than a year before. Reaping his profits, then turning around to spend them on more. More women to replace the wife he'd lost weeks after they had moved there, as if that could have filled the hole in his heart. More house to hold the things he had bought. More of everything but time for his sons.

One of whom was busy trying to kill the other. While the land, the precious land treasured by Edmond Jumel, helped.

The creature crawled deeper into the depths of his hovel, seeking darkness, escape. But there was no getting away from his memories, not now.

The vines reached out and grabbed him, holding him in place, just as they had all those years ago. The earth rose up and blanketed his body until he became one with the dank, moist, loamy surface below him. The smell invaded his nostrils; particles drifted into his ears, then down his throat, gagging him.

You will remember, Auguste. You must.

Why? he asked—no, begged.

Because this is what you must do to Cooper. It's time the chosen one took your place.

And so he suffered the agony again, the memory replaying it as real as the day it had happened.

He'd been in the stables, about to mount one of the horses and ride over to Amelia's house, his mind only on seeing her blue eyes again, holding her to his chest, knowing the sweet taste of her lips. One foot in the stirrup, one leg rising to swing over the saddle, when he'd been yanked back, onto the hard wooden floor of the barn, then out onto the lawn before he could react.

He'd looked up into a face he recognized and eyes he didn't. "Gerard! What are you doing? Release me!"

Gerard grunted and started to move faster.

Auguste scratched and fought, dug in his heels, tried to twist away, but Gerard kept going, his strength superhuman. They reached the woods, and the fear crawled up Auguste's throat and escaped in a scream that no one heard. He reached for a tree, held tightly, and then—

Gerard said something Auguste couldn't understand, and the tree bent down, as if bowing to Gerard's will, and Auguste's grip slid off. Gerard started running, not caring that his brother banged along at his feet like a sack of potatoes. Every tree root, every rock Auguste reached for, became as supple as a blade of grass.

"Gerard, stop! Please, I beg of you, stop!"

The odd language continued, and so did his brother's furious pace. He had become something other than himself, something with a sinister heart. Auguste could feel it telegraphed in the way his brother ran, the sounds he made, the stony determination in his face. Auguste begged, screamed, cried, to no avail.

And then they reached the well.

Gerard dragged Auguste up by the hair, planting him on the ledge like a sacrifice. Auguste twisted to the right, his riding boots digging for purchase against the soft earth, and then he could feel Gerard's grip loosening, and he thought, *Run now, run—*

Suddenly the vines that curled around the well began to move and grow, like fingers reaching up. Reaching for him.

He opened his mouth to scream again, but before a sound escaped, the vines leaped forward and pinned him in place. One vine curled its grip around his throat and pressed until his windpipe was nearly flattened. Dots swam in front of his eyes and he knew, he knew . . .

He was going to die.

"You are the gift," Gerard whispered in his ear. "The gift he has been waiting for."

What was Gerard talking about? What did he mean?

"You must stay here, brother, and wait for the next one. He will come, at the ordained time, and then you will be free. This is the price Father paid when he bought the land,

and now you, Auguste, must pay it for our family. If you don't stay here, this land will die. And all who live on it will die, too."

Auguste's eyes widened and his heart clenched as tightly as his windpipe.

Gerard nodded. "Yes, even her."

Amelia.

"You're insane," he whispered. But a part of him heard the truth in Gerard's words. There had been whispers in town among the workers, about why such luscious, profitable grapes grew on this inhospitable land, why the rains fell on these acres and not others. Why the previous owners had had so many years of wealth, but then the old man who lived here had gone insane and sold the land to Edmond for pennies on the dollar. The land was cursed, some said. Blessed, others said.

Magic, his father said.

"No, I'm not." Gerard shook his head, his eyes shining in the moonlight above. "I've drunk from this vine, and I know the truth now. This land has to have its sacrifice to continue giving its gift of riches and life."

"Sac—sacrifice?" Auguste tried to scramble back, but there was nowhere to go. The vines held fast, held him against the well.

"You, my brother." Gerard picked up Auguste's feet and

turned his brother around until he was bent over the yawning ink-black cavity of the well. Auguste inhaled a smell unlike any other.

The smell of death.

"This is a gift," Gerard insisted, just before giving his brother the final shove into the depths of the well. He screamed an apology—a cascade of apologies—but it was too late. The choices had been made. The gift given.

But it was a gift Auguste hadn't asked for. Or wanted.

One Auguste had now waited two hundred years to give to someone else.

CHAPTER 18

I didn't bother to sleep after I got home from the police station. When Sam got called to the hospital, I headed into the woods. I shouted down the well several times.

Nothing.

I slept in the abandoned house that night, hoping Megan might show up there, but she never did.

A few minutes before seven the next morning, I sneaked back into the house and up to my room. Just in time for Sam to knock on my door. "I'm driving you to school. You have twenty minutes."

"Good morning to you, too." Jerk.

As I got ready, I wondered why he wanted to keep such a tight leash on me. It wasn't all that unusual for him to be helicopter stepdad, hovering over my every move, but these were different circumstances. He'd come down on me extra hard yesterday when he'd handed me a list of chores that would have kept me too busy to do more than breathe. Why? So I wouldn't have time to look for Megan?

Did he think I was involved?

Or . . .

Was *he* somehow involved?

This was his land, after all. His vineyard. His woods.

Plus, he seemed to hold a special kind of hatred toward me, one I'd never really understood. I'd always figured it was because he didn't like the three-for-one package of kids that had come with my mom.

Could he have something to do with that thing in the well? If that was so, then why wasn't he the one tossing me down there? Why my mother?

That was the part I couldn't get my head around. Sam didn't like me and he had these establish-the-dominant-role issues, but he hadn't done anything homicidal. That had been all my mother's doing. Still . . .

The whole thing bugged me.

I slung my backpack over my shoulder and took one last look out the window. Somewhere in those woods was the well. And maybe Megan. One way or another, I was going to find her.

Sam didn't say a word when I got in the car. He put the Beamer in drive and squealed out of the driveway.

"Where was Mom this morning?" I asked.

"Grocery store."

"Oh." We stopped at a light and waited for a pudgy crossing guard to wave some Dora-toting kindergartners across the street. I shifted in my seat and tried to think of a good way to ask the next question. Didn't find one. So I just opened my mouth and let her fly. "What's that well in the woods for? Like, water or something?"

Sam had been about to step on the gas. He stomped on the brake instead. The car behind him laid on the horn. "Don't go near that thing. It's old. Probably dangerous."

"It, ah, looks pretty cool."

"I said don't go near it. It's Jumel property." His voice was harsh, cold. He gunned the car and the Beamer leaped forward, nearly hitting the crossing guard as she stepped off the curb again. She waved her little red stop sign at Sam, but he was already blocks away.

"But—"

Sam swiveled his gaze toward me. "Don't argue with me, Cooper. Or I'll be sure you regret it."

He stared at me, eyes like laser beams of fury. I could have cut the tension in the car with a chain saw.

I put up my hands and sat back. "Cool."

"Oh, and just so you know, Paolo came back." Sam cut his gaze to the left as he turned the car.

"Really?"

"I had to fire him for missing all that work, but yeah. He's fine."

If that was so, what the hell had been in that hat? Whose skull had that been? If not Paolo's, whose?

Sam skidded to a stop in front of my school. I got out, but before I could shut the door, he leaned toward me. "I'll be back to pick you up at the end of the day. You be here. On time."

"Don't you have to work?"

A smile curved across his face. "I'm working at home today." Then he was gone, tires squealing.

That had been weird. Not only was Sam keeping his thumb on me today, but he'd also freaked when I'd mentioned the well. Barred me from going anywhere near the thing. Because he knew about what was in there?

He had to. He'd lived there all his life. If he knew, then did he also know what was going on? And was his warning a way of protecting me—

Or keeping me from finding Megan?

By English class, I still didn't have a clue. I tossed and

turned the encounter around in my mind and got nothing. Sam had a regular raging attitude, so I couldn't be sure if it was that or if he had something else going on.

I dropped into my seat, plopped my books onto the floor, and propped my feet on Joey's chair. Joey turned around and stared at me. "What are you doing here, dude?"

I shrugged. "I'm a masochist. I like being beaten up by Shakespeare."

Joey leaned in closer. "People think you killed her, man. You need to lie low."

How could people think I had anything to do with Megan's disappearance? Didn't they know how I felt about her? How close we'd been for years, even before we'd started dating? Or was I just getting the auto had-to-be-the-boyfriend guilt-by-association thing?

"Joey, I didn't do anything," I whispered. "I don't know where Megan is."

The rest of the class filed in. People shifted away from me, sitting a row back, a row ahead. Whispers started, carrying around the room like a wave. Drue Macy glared at me and huddled in a corner with her female coven.

Mike hurried in just before the bell rang and slid into the chair beside mine. "Coop, you can tell me. Did you do it?"

"*No!* What is wrong with you guys?"

Mike shrugged. "Hey, I'm just going by what my dad said. Plus, it's all over school."

"Whatever is 'all over school,'" I parroted back with air quotes, "is not true. I had nothing to do with Megan's disappearance."

But I was lying. To them. To myself. I was the whole reason she was gone. I'd been the one to knock on her door Sunday afternoon. I'd been the one to ask her for help. I'd let her go with me to that well.

If I'd just kept my mouth shut—

She'd be sitting here right now, and none of this would be happening.

I shifted in my seat. Wished the day was over already so I could duck out of here and get back to the only thing that mattered: finding Megan.

"Sorry, Coop," Mike said after a while. "I shouldn't have said that. I know you'd never do anything to Megan. Forget my dad, too. He's a jerk."

"Thanks." It felt good to have someone in my corner. Behind me, the Drue witch-hunt kept up its whispering and pointing. Probably plotting a way to hang me after lunch.

"Plus, I know what it's like to have people think crap about you that you don't have any control over," said Mike. His face was as serious as a judge's for a second, and I knew he was talking about his father. Then Joey turned around, and Mike slipped on the goofy grin again. "Yo, moron. What do you call a blonde with a brain?"

"An endangered species?" Joey said, then laughed.

"Mr. Ring," my father thundered, glaring at Mike. "And Mr. Deluca. Do you two have something you'd like to share with the class?"

"Uh . . . no." Joey slinked down in his seat as if he could disappear.

"Good. Then open up to act five, scene one."

A mass groan ran through the class. "We're still reading this play?" Joey asked. "Why doesn't Hamlet kill himself already?"

"Because he wants to torture you just a little more, Mr. Deluca," my father deadpanned. "Why don't you read the part of First Clown?"

"Do I get to beep my nose?"

My father ignored him and assigned the other parts. Mike as Second Clown, Richard Evard as Horatio, and— surprise, surprise—me as Hamlet. I vowed never to speak up in my father's class ever again.

I tuned everything out while people started reading their lines. My gaze went to the window, my mind on the woods two miles away. I didn't even notice it was my turn until my father said, "Enter Hamlet," twice.

"Sorry." I cleared my throat, flipped forward a couple pages, and started to read. I was cool, until I got to the part where Hamlet picks up the skull.

Then I was back in the woods, holding that other skull, the one that could have been Paolo's. But it wasn't, if Sam was telling the truth. The words swam in front of my eyes, and it took a good thirty seconds before I could get my mouth moving again. "That skull had a tongue in it," I read, "and could sing once! how the knave jowls it to the ground, as if it were Cain's jaw-bone, that did the first murder! This might be the pate of a politician, which this ass now o'er-reaches; one that would circumvent God, might it not?"

Images of Paolo sprang to mind, of his crooked smile and his hat—

Oh God, that hat—

I looked down at my desk, relieved nothing green was marching across the top. I needed to get out of here. I swore, this day was never going to end.

Richard sat up in his chair and straightened his glasses. "It might, my lord." I read the response line, something about a courtier that I didn't get. I read more lines with words like *chapless* and *mazzard* that made no sense, my mind on Megan. We went on like that, with me tuning out for several minutes, until Joey piped up with a First Clown line again.

"One that was a woman, sir," he said, pausing to turn and look over his shoulder at me. "But, rest her soul, she's dead."

Several people started whispering. A few snickered. Drue let out a gasp.

I wanted to sink into the floor. But my father stood at the front of the classroom, looking at me and waiting for the next line. His face had that pinched look, as if he'd started this and wished he hadn't. Yeah, thanks, Dad. I did my part and tried to ignore everyone, ending with the line that asks the clown how long he'd been a grave maker.

But it got worse.

The clown, a.k.a. Joey, started in on lines about why Hamlet had been sent away by his mother and stepfather. "Why, because a' was mad," Joey said, then added a little cackling laugh. "A' shall recover his wits there; or if a' do not, 'tis no great matter here."

A few more lines, and then we were back to dead bodies, with me reading a piece asking the clown how long it took a man to rot. Not long, I wanted to say, when there was a flesh-eating creature waiting to lick its bones clean.

Then I was holding another imaginary skull, this time of Hamlet's court jester, Yorick. But in my head, I was seeing Paolo's skull again, and my deepest fears were telling me in a few days I might be seeing Megan's skull, and no way could

I take that. I was reading, and trying to hold on to my sanity, until I got to "Here hung those lips I have kissed I know not how oft."

That was it. My breaking point. My throat cut off. I shook my head.

The whole class went silent. Waiting for me to belt out a confession? For me to break down crying? I didn't know. I didn't care.

Then I heard it. The laughter, carrying on the breeze coming through the open window. *Better hurry, Cooper. Megan misses you. I think she's been crying.*

Megan—alive? At first I was excited, and then dread hit when I realized what that voice meant—and where she had to be.

I felt a hand on my shoulder and looked up.

My father was there. He gave me a single nod. "I think that's enough *Hamlet* for today. Take out your grammar books, please."

I guess there was more than one person in the room in my corner. It was enough to get me through the day.

CHAPTER 19

The police still hadn't gotten a search warrant for the Jumel property, but Sergeant Ring kept an eye on me as promised. He was parked in his cruiser in the cul-de-sac in front of the house. I looked out every now and then and saw him sipping from a shiny flask. As soon as dark fell and he drove away, I ran up to my room, snagging Faulkner's cell phone off the charger on the hall table as I did. He'd be pissed, but I figured if I could handle six hours in a police station, I could handle my older brother. Then I locked the door, turned on my stereo, grabbed a backpack, and started filling it.

The knife. A flashlight. A flat-head screwdriver I found in the pen holder on my desk. Megan's bandanna. I held it for a long time, then stuffed it inside.

I scanned my room, looking for . . .

Well, a monster-killing miracle. Yeah, nothing popped up. Big whoop there.

I packed a bag of Doritos I had hidden in my nightstand along with a half-empty bottle of Mountain Dew. Another Sam rule—no food in our rooms. Faulkner and I found ways around that. We called them drawers and closets.

I climbed out my bedroom window, then onto the little roof beneath. My Vans slipped on the shingles, sending one foot sliding off the edge and my heart somewhere down to my knees.

I grabbed the downspout and inched to the left, the backpack scraping against the roof. I froze, sure Sam and my mother had heard the sound.

I listened hard. I heard their voices floating up from the first floor. They were on the deck, looking out toward the woods. "Cooper seems so stressed," my mother said. "I'm sure he's worried about Megan. I can't imagine where she went to. She's not the type to run off."

"Megan's probably fine. Staying at a friend's house for a few days and all this was just an overreaction. Cooper needs to quit spending his time moping around here and get his priorities straight," Sam said.

I ducked back, plastering myself against the house. "You shouldn't be so hard on him right now," my mother responded. "Remember, he's a teenager with a lot on his mind." She sighed. "I worry about him."

That was closer to the mother I knew. The mother I remembered. The one I kept hoping was still in there. Except . . . I never knew when this one was in there or when the other one was going to come blasting out.

"Come back in, honey. I'll get you a glass of wine—" He stopped when his cell phone went off. A minute of conversation, then he was back. "Sorry, honey, but I have to go to the hospital. The Moreaux twins are ready to come into the world. Why don't you go relax, and I'll be home before you know it."

My mother let out a sigh and went inside. I heard the door shut. A breath I didn't even know I'd been holding exploded out of my lungs.

I looked down, then realized how high up the second floor was. Like, twenty feet. That's where that first-floor-cathedral-ceiling crap got you. From here, the ground looked very far away. Very hard. And very bone-breaking.

Don't look down.

Don't look down.

Shit. I'd looked.

My pulse double-timed and I tightened my grip on the downspout. Okay. How was I going to get from here—

To there?

A whole lot of break-my-back-and-kill-me distance?

I looked down again. Oh man, no way. I'd sooner risk the wrath of Sam than jump.

Then I heard the laughter. Cool and calm, as if it knew. Knew I was too chicken to make that leap.

Oh, Cooper. Are you too scared to come out and play?

It knew where I was. It knew what I was doing. Somehow it saw me. How? And why me?

Come on, Cooper, come join us. Megan's waiting, painfully waiting.

A grenade of fury detonated in my gut. I wanted to take that creature and twist its neck until it laughed itself to death. I wanted to pummel it, stomp it, stab it, just destroy it. Everything within me boiled with anger. "Don't you touch her. Don't you f—"

I'll do whatever I want. I'm in control. More laughter. *Not you.*

Megan was going to die if I didn't do something and soon. That knowledge made ice race through me, a massive Arctic front freezing every vein, every major organ.

I stood up, gritted my teeth, and jumped.

For one long second, I was tumbling into the well again, pushed by my mother to my death. I opened my mouth to scream, the terror clawing its way out of my gut and up my throat, but before the sound could escape, I landed with a hard thud and a hundred painful pokes.

In the shrubs.

For the first time since I'd moved into Castle à la Sam, I sent up a silent thanks for the megalandscaping. The man may have been a jerk, but his overage on the lawn had just saved my butt.

Literally.

I started climbing out of the shrubs, pushing off their clawing branches. The motion-sensor lights sprang to life, flooding the backyard like a watchdog on high alert. I crouched down, scanning for Sam.

Silly Cooper, he's not looking for you. I am.

I jerked back, landing farther into the shrubs. The creature laughed, as if it could see my pathetic attempt at cover. As if I were three years old and thought playing peekaboo behind a Dixie plate meant my father couldn't see me.

Then I saw the vines, the slimy, mossy spider web of green that had somehow leapfrogged across the lawn, maybe while I had been too busy being scared to jump off the roof. It zigged and zagged through the grass, under the bushes, then up and over the branches, as if it was searching, almost . . .

Sniffing.

Impossible.

But then again, what the hell had been sane about this whole thing?

I tried to back up, but the bushes were dense. Nowhere

to go. I started to climb up and over them, but the web's reach climbed, too, faster than me, its natural tentacles reaching for me like some love-crazed Jonas Brothers fan.

I pushed through the shrubs, even as they tried to scratch and claw at me. One of my Vans caught on a twig and slipped off, hanging in the thick green like a wounded soldier.

I kept going, my arms and legs working like a steam engine, climbing and clawing, until I finally hit grass, the well's vines hurdling over themselves to get to me. I spun back, reached into the shrubbery for my sneaker, and grabbed it just as one of the web things broke off from the pack and hurtled itself outward like a giant bright green kamikaze loogie. With a grunt, I threw my body back and tumbled across the grass, landing out of its reach.

For now.

I looked back at the house, sure I'd see Sam on the deck, ready to drag my ass back inside.

Instead, I saw something that scared me ten times more.

My mother, standing on the bottom step of the deck stairs, watching everything that had happened. And staring at me with an intensity bordering on painful.

Then she started walking toward me. I put on my sneaker. Everything in my brain said *run,* but my body didn't move. It was glued to the grass by the stupid half that kept hoping the whole thing was a mistake. That she was going to come out here and help me, not feed me to the lions. "Cooper," she said.

I didn't respond.

"Cooper." She got closer. Four feet away. Three feet. Now I could see her eyes and read the scary glassiness, the almost hypnotic trance.

The one I knew. Too well.

This wasn't the mom who would save me. This wasn't the mom who would tuck me into bed at night. This wasn't the mom who wanted to give me a cookie and a kiss on the cheek.

This was the mom who wanted to kill me.

My vision blurred and I shook my head, swallowing the bitter taste of betrayal. I found the sense to back up, to keep the space between us far enough that she couldn't touch me. Beneath my feet, I heard a crunch, felt the curl of the well's vines tickle at my ankles. I sidestepped, but they kept pace with me. Penned to the right and the left, and my mother in front of me.

And behind me, I felt the creature watching with its universal eye. Watching, waiting. With Megan somewhere down there, trapped and terrified.

"Come with me, Cooper." My mother put out her hand, as gently as she used to when I was a kid and she wanted me to get in the car or cross the street with her. "I'd like to introduce you to a friend."

Laughter carried on the wind. At my feet, the vines held their ground, as if waiting for orders.

"No." I shook my head some more and kept backing up, even though I couldn't see her anymore because I was crying. "No, Mom. No."

"You have to, Cooper." She advanced on me, her voice sterner now. No nonsense. The tone that used to tell me to mind my manners and not talk back. As my mother moved, the green vines twisted in and around her feet, but not as if they were catching her—more as though they were becoming part of her. She went on moving and talking, not even noticing. "You have to come. Now."

The chill in her voice and the flatness of her eyes had me seriously freaked. But it was the way the slimy vines of the well had become one with my mother that sent my terror meter over the edge. "Mom, stop, please. Please, please just stop."

She paused midstep, and for a second, that stupid bird of hope took flight in my chest again. "I wish I could," she said, her voice softer, as if there was a battle inside her and this was the voice of the real mom, trying to get out—but then her eyes glittered again, and I knew the battle was being lost. "But he needs you, Cooper. He needs you bad."

Then she lunged for me, both arms out like some twisted kind of hug. *Come to Mama.*

So I can kill you.

I spun on my heel, rubber soles slipping on the grass and knocking me to the ground. I pushed off with my hands, feeling the whisper of my mother's grip against the back of my head as I gained traction and put distance between us. I didn't look back; I didn't stop. I ran.

As if my life depended on it, because it was no freakin' cliché.

As I left the yard and headed into the woods, I heard a scream so high-pitched, it pierced my skull like an ice pick. For a second I thought it was Megan, and then I realized the sound had come from behind me and was the kind of scream that spelled seriously pissed off.

The sound rolled like a wave, then grew louder. I wheeled around and saw my mother, hauling butt across the lawn as though someone had set fire to her feet. The well's slimy web minions kept pace beside her, their range growing and spreading, as if searching the lawn for any trace of me. Any minute, she would reach me, and I had no doubt what she would do with me when she found me.

I fumbled in my pocket for Faulkner's cell phone. I ducked behind a tree and dialed the house line, praying that Sam had already left for the hospital and wouldn't pick up. One ring.

My mother, her footsteps pounding on the grass.

Two rings.

She'd made it halfway across the lawn. Now the screaming had stopped, but she seemed to be moving faster. I slid lower against the tree. And prayed.

Three rings.

She was just inside the woods now—what the hell? Did she suddenly have superhuman running powers?—and had paused to scan the trees. The vines spread out at her feet, laying a quiet, evil blanket of green across the forest floor. I sucked in a breath and wished I could disappear.

A fourth ring began, and just when I was sure the answering machine would pick up, Faulkner answered, his voice sleepy and annoyed. "What?"

"It's me, Cooper," I said.

"I know. Why do you have my cell phone?"

"I'm in the woods," I whispered. "And Mom is—" I stopped talking. She'd heard me and was moving in my direction. I flipped the phone shut, told myself I'd given Faulkner enough information, that he would believe me this time—*please, please, believe me*—and come find me, then scrambled away from the tree in what I hoped was something close to a guerrilla style.

I lay flat on the ground and wriggled through leaves and twigs, wishing I'd spent more than two years in Boy Scouts.

If I had, maybe I'd have been more prepared for something like this.

Except all the canoe trips and camping lessons in the world wouldn't have helped. They didn't exactly have How to Kill the Monster in Your Backyard 101 in the manual. And between the pledge and the snacks, they definitely didn't cover how to keep your mother from strangling you to death.

I chanced a glance over my shoulder. She seemed lost, as if she couldn't see me through the trees or as if by being low, I'd thrown her off the track. Whichever, I didn't care. I just kept wriggling, moving forward a foot at a time, with one thought on my mind now.

Megan.

I knew where she was. And I knew there was only one way to get her back. To go down there and do what I should have done the first time. Kill that thing before it killed her.

If—

And I could barely think this thought without losing my mind—

If it hadn't already.

CHAPTER 20

He could barely contain his anticipation. The boy was so close and so ready. One more day. That's all the creature had to wait. Surely he could lure Cooper down here and then hold him until tomorrow night?

The wait would make the later prize that much sweeter, after all. Blood that had sat and stewed in fear tasted oh so much better than freshly surprised blood. And Cooper would be so much more . . .

Motivated to do what needed to be done by then, too. That was what Auguste needed. A willing sacrifice. But until then . . .

He needed to eat. To keep his strength up—no, to empower his skills. The one who fed him would be angry that he had already plucked the fruit of the vineyard's humans, an act that had been forbidden. But the creature needed to expand his skills, to further his reach, if he was ever going to capture Cooper. And for that he needed more than those tiny dead human meals that *he* sent down.

All the others that had come before *him* had treated the creature well. Had thanked him for his gifts of the land, the blessings of wealth, and, most of all, his sacrifice. Had treated his home with love, respect. But not this one. This one treated the creature with disdain. With . . . hatred. For that, he would pay.

But first, the creature needed a meal. Not another old man. Bleh. That sounded as appetizing as the rats skittering at his feet. Perhaps the thing he'd been keeping in the back, his special surprise for Cooper? No, no. He'd wait. Hold it . . . use it as a draw. In case the girl wasn't enough.

No, what he wanted now was something fresh and young. Something that would let him taste *fear.* Like the girl. Or like . . .

The mother.

Once Cooper was here, she would have served her purpose, wouldn't she have? She'd been nothing but a bother anyway, fighting him every step of the way, trying to pretend she loved that pathetic Cooper.

When they both knew Cooper had been bred for a single purpose. She had merely been the womb, the carrier for the creature's spawn. How appropriate, then, that she die—

As part of his quest for life?

After all, she'd given birth to his regeneration. He would lure her down here and give her the thank-you she deserved for the gift she had given him.

Death. For his life.

CHAPTER 21

"What the hell are you doing here?"

A pair of shiny boots met my face. I stopped skulking along the edge of the woods, looking for a way out, and looked up into the mug of Sergeant Ring. I guess he hadn't knocked off for the day after all. "Nothin'."

He snorted. "Right. And I'm out here looking for alien life forms." He waved at me. "Get your ass up."

I did. I considered pulling a StepScrooge Sam and calling Sergeant Ring on the fact that he wasn't even supposed to be on the property, but I didn't want to piss him off even more. And besides, chances were he was too drunk to remember he even needed a little thing like a warrant anyway. He gestured at my back. "What's in the bag?"

Oh, crap. "Homework."

"This late?"

"I'm heading to a friend's house to work on a report. For"—I glanced down at the leaves and twigs, searching them for a believable lie, one that would keep Sergeant Ring away from my bag and me out of jail—"science."

"Why don't I believe you?"

I wanted to give him some wise remark back but knew if I did, that would make him search me, and right now I had a knife in my backpack and something even more damning—Megan's bandanna. This was not a time to do anything but be cool and polite. I tried to look around, without being too obvious, for my mother.

I didn't see her. Or hear her. Or see the well's web anywhere. Maybe the cop's showing up had scared them all off.

Or maybe they were just waiting for the cop to leave so we could all go back to that oh so fun and festive kill-or-be-killed game.

For a moment I considered fessing up and bringing him to the well, getting him to help me rescue Megan. Then I heard it. A threat that scared me more than Sam's promises of endless chores ever could.

Get him out of here, Cooper. Or you'll never see Megan again.

I gulped. "I'm sorry, sir," I said. With cops and other people's dads, I figured you could never go wrong saying *sir* a lot. "I know it looks weird and all, but I have to do this report on dirt and leaves. Mr. Spinale is really into the whole green thing. Wants us to know our world."

Sergeant Ring crossed his arms over his gut. "You weren't hiding from me?"

"I didn't even know you were there." I looked him in the eye. No lie.

He didn't believe me. At all. A preschooler could have seen that in his face. "I thought I heard someone scream back here."

"A scream?" I pretended to think. "Oh, yeah. There's this crazy bird in our woods. I don't know what it is, but it sounds like Michael Jackson on a sugar high."

Sergeant Ring let out a half laugh, half snort. "Yeah, Mike and I got one of those birds, too, up at our lake cottage. You been there before with us?"

"Uh . . . no, sir." I glanced up, as if looking for the bird. No Mom. No Faulkner, either. Had she gotten to him? Or had he somehow convinced her to go home?

And then finally, in the distance, I saw my mother and Faulkner heading to the house. Faulkner sent me a thumbs-up behind my mother's back, all while talking to her. I didn't know how he'd done it. Relief ran through me. Now all I had to do was ditch the cop and get back to looking for Megan.

"Yeah," Sergeant Ring said. "Just when you're asleep, those birds do that, and you think someone's being killed."

He laughed again as if this were the most hilarious thing that could ever happen.

Even as he acted like my best friend, he still had that "I don't trust you" gleam in his eyes. Or maybe it was a Jack Daniel's shine. I didn't know. I just had to leave. "I, ah, got to get to my friend's house. Do that report."

"For science."

"Yeah, for science." I took a step, cool as an ice cube, thinking, *Please just let me go, just let me go.* But before my foot hit the ground again, he yanked me back by the strap of my pack.

Now he'd stopped laughing. He stared hard at me. The interrogation eyes. "What do you know about your step-father's business?"

"Uh . . . nothing."

"You gotta know something. You live with him. He must talk to you."

Where was this coming from? And what did it have to do with Megan? Or me? Or heck, anything? "Seriously, I try to avoid him. The guy's a total jerk. All I know is that things aren't going well."

"Have you heard anything about the workers lately?"

Don't tell him, Cooper. Keep your mouth shut or Megan dies.

I swallowed hard. What was I supposed to say? Not the truth. Not the found-a-hat-full-of-brains-by-the-well truth, that was for sure. "I, ah, heard a couple haven't shown up for work lately."

"A couple? Try more like *six* in the past two weeks."

The pile of bones flashed in my mind again, became a pile of dead bodies.

Oh God. I wanted to hurl, but I knew if I did, I'd be puking up a pile of guilt onto the ground. "Sam, ah, hasn't said anything about six." I was nervous and rambling but still careful not to say anything that might piss off the creature and put Megan in danger. "This one guy Paolo was missing for a little while, but he came back. I heard he was, like, fired."

"You heard wrong." Sergeant Ring crossed his arms over his chest.

The tiny hairs rose on the back of my neck. I had known, deep down, that Sam had been lying about Paolo. But why? What the hell was going on around here? Sam had to know that six workers were missing. Wasn't he suspicious about a mass missing-men problem? Or did the vineyard just have majorly high turnover?

Sergeant Ring leaned in closer, his beak nearly poking out my eye. "You see anything weird around here lately?"

"What's weird?" I said.

"People acting strange. Not doing what they should." He leaned back. "Keeping secrets."

"I'm a kid. Everyone keeps secrets from me."

He harrumphed. "Maybe they do. Maybe they don't. And maybe you're just not telling me everything you know."

When was this guy going to leave me alone? Didn't he have a bar to get to? Megan was out there, and his yammering wasn't helping me find her.

"I really have to go, sir. My friends are waiting."

"Just a minute, Cooper." Mike's dad put a hand on my shoulder. The you're-not-going-anywhere move. His radio crackled, but he just turned it down, ignoring the call. "I have a few more questions for you."

I shifted my weight, hoping he'd let go.

He didn't.

"Did you know the hospital where your stepfather works is investigating him?"

Behind Mike's dad, the woods started to shift, undulating like waves. It sounded like a breeze whispering through the trees. He didn't notice.

But I did.

"Did you hear me, Cooper?"

"Huh?" My gaze stayed over his shoulder, on those woods, but it wasn't the woods—it was the greenery around them.

The sticky vines were spreading, and spreading faster than I'd ever seen them spread before. Leaping and dancing over one another, like those Chinese gymnasts at the Olympics, cartwheeling off the trees, connecting and interlocking with one another, forming not a web this time, but—

"Mr. Warner?"

Tall, thin—

"Yes, sir?"

"The hospital is looking into your stepfather's track record with deliveries. Apparently, he's lost one too many babies in the past few years." The cop shook his head. "Infant mortality. Those are the kinds of numbers they like to see go down, you know, not up."

Dead babies? Missing workers in the vineyard?

I stared at Sergeant Ring. Wished he'd say he was kidding, but he didn't. The facts stayed there. Dead babies, missing men. How was all this connected? Because it had to be—it was just too damn weird not to be.

And Sam Jumel right there in the middle of all of it.

What was up with that? What was Sam doing? I couldn't wrap my head around it, couldn't make the pieces fit together. Something was rotten in the state of Denmark, as Hamlet's friend Marcellus would say, and only a fool would go trotting around Denmark without a clue.

Behind us, the green vines had twisted and formed, knitting together from the ground up and bridging across from tree to tree, pulling off twigs and sticks, looking like hurried birds building nests. At first they looked like nothing but taller versions of what they had always been, but then they became—

A web and stick *army.*

"He's got some problems, your stepfather." The cop gave my shoulder a pat, then let me go.

"Yeah," I said, and a nervous little laugh escaped me. I took a step back. "He sure does."

And so do we, Scooby-Doo, I thought.

Because that webbed army had started to move.

The cop's radio crackled again. He ignored it a second time. "You think I'm going to go easy on you just because you're my kid's friend, Cooper? Because you've come over to my house and played Xbox a couple times?"

Behind him, the web people had taken their red-rover line three feet closer. Slide, slide, across the forest floor. Were they coming for me?

Or a Sergeant Ring appetizer?

"No, sir," was all I could manage.

He leaned forward, obtuse as a brick wall. The well's minions were now four feet away. Three and a half. Three and a quarter. "What's in the bag?"

Not good timing, five-oh. Behind him, the vine army inched forward and, I swore, crouched. Like a lion about to pounce on prey.

"I told you—homework."

"Then you won't mind if I take a look, will you?"

Yeah, I did mind. I minded, like, four years in juvie for carrying concealed. But I had more immediate worries—

Like a sneak attack from some seriously bad vine dudes who wanted to kill us both and feed us to a murdering monster.

I opened my mouth to scream at Mike's dad, to tell him to run, but run from what? A bunch of crazy grapevines? He'd think I was insane, and by the time I'd get done explaining it, he'd be dead and dragged down to the well—

And that was assuming he could even *see* the well's mercenaries. No one in my English class had seen them on the desk. Joey hadn't seen them on my computer. Faulkner probably hadn't seen them when he had lured our mother back to the house. Had Paolo seen them coming?

What if I was the only one who could see this?

Two feet away now. One and a half.

My heart threatened to explode out of my chest. Mike's dad wasn't going anywhere. And if I didn't get rid of him, I was going to watch him die right here.

That's exactly right, Cooper, the well whispered. *You'll watch him die. Maybe help me kill him. Won't that be a sweet thing for us to do together?*

And then it laughed and muttered something I couldn't hear.

As if on orders, the vine people broke apart, paper dolls becoming individuals now, their branch arms swinging up and out, reaching for both of us. I didn't need a freakin' crystal ball to know the next sixty seconds.

Their stick fingers were going to wrap around Sergeant Ring's skull, squeeze into the soft flesh, and press until his head exploded, blasting his brains outward like an overly ripe grape. He'd never pop another Bud again, never sit in Mike's living room again.

And it would be all my fault. I couldn't live with that. I couldn't watch it.

Then a thought hit me. If Sam was a part of this, there was only one place he could keep everything hidden from me, Faulkner, my mother, and the world.

"I know where my stepfather keeps his secrets," I said quickly, reaching for Sergeant Ring's sleeve, pulling him a foot closer a lot harder than I intended—or probably should have. Surprise lit his eyes. Oh crap. Don't arrest me now, dude. "It's in the winery. You know, where all the *wine* is."

The vine army took a stutter-step, as if they, too, were surprised by my move, but faster than frat boys chugging a keg they were on the move again, their arms out, their mouths—not really mouths, but something like mouths, formed out of tangles of sticks and twigs—yawning and hungry.

"Wine?" Sergeant Ring said. Apparently I was speaking his language.

"Yeah, lots of it. But we have to go now. Before Sam gets back from the hospital."

Let him go, Cooper. Let me have him. I'm hungry.

Aren't you?

Disgust rolled inside me. I wanted to scream but knew that would just make Mike's dad suspicious and he'd probably haul me off to jail. Every second he stood there seemed to drag on like an endless algebra class.

The well whispered something else I couldn't hear. Then I knew why. It was talking to them—to the vine people.

In answer, the vines reached out, and their hands just barely brushed against Sergeant Ring's back. He shifted, as if he'd felt it, but then jerked his sleeve out of my grip. "This better be about more than just some merlot, Cooper, or I'll drag you down to the station for assaulting a police officer."

"Yeah, it will be." I started walking fast, praying he'd do the same. He did.

A shriek cut through the woods. The well. Pissed I was taking its prize away. I glanced at Mike's dad, but he had no reaction on his face, no sign he'd heard anything at all.

And then, out of the corner of my eye, I saw the vine army. They had turned to one another as if they were communicating. I gripped the strap of my backpack tighter. We needed to get the hell out of the woods.

Now.

"If you want to get into the vineyard's offices, we better get a move on," I said, digging for some lies. "Like Indy Five Hundred speed. Because if Sam catches you in there, he'll shut you down in a heartbeat, and you don't want to be going to all the hassle of a search warrant, do you?"

He shot me a grin. "How much TV you watch, kid?"

I looked behind me and saw the vines had stopped their whispering.

They had broken apart, and now their twig feet were spinning, spinning, spinning, gathering speed.

I didn't bother to answer. I broke into a run and prayed he'd keep up. He let out a "hey," and then a second later, there was a thud of footsteps behind me.

Please let those be cop feet and not something else.

The creature shrieked again, sounding like twenty vultures going after a pile of roadkill. I wanted to look back, wanted to know where that evil army was, but I was afraid if I took even one second to slow down, it would be the second the well needed.

The woods crackled with activity, but I ignored the growing webs of green spinning into the trees, the whispers of hundreds of running evil grapevines-turned-army-men.

Mike's dad huffed and puffed behind me. "Cooper, this isn't a track meet. Slow down."

Fifty feet ahead of us the Jumel vineyard lay in perfect alignment. The well might be able to reach that far, but somehow I doubted it would dare send its crazy nature guys into the exposed rows of grapes. "Just a little farther."

Mike's dad grunted but kept up with me. Apparently the wine incentive was enough. Finally we hit the bright light shining over the vineyard. In my head, I heard the angry shrieks of the creature. Then it began to laugh.

Next time, Cooper. You won't win.

I glanced over my shoulder. The army of vines had locked arms again and lined the perimeter of the woods.

Waiting.

I swallowed hard. I might have gotten away this time, but I had to face them again and soon—because Megan was still in there somewhere and I would fight whatever I had to if it meant getting her back.

"Now that you've got me here, you better show me something spectacular," Mike's dad said.

We'd come in the back and now stood in the center of the bottling line, a busy room with a dumping station, a bottle cleaner, a filler, a corker, and a labeler, everything moving along a series of conveyor belts that kept whirring at a constant pace. The remaining workers—who knew better than to stop for anything short of an earthquake—barely looked up when the uniform and I walked in.

"Cooper?" Mike's dad prodded, impatient.

I'd been inside the winery only a couple of times and had barely paid attention. And I'd forgotten about one particular detail—until Sergeant Ring had started mentioning all that stuff about dead babies and missing workers.

"Over here." We headed through the production areas, past the offices, then into the fancy tasting room. A massive circular oak bar took up nearly the entire space, with wine bottles and glasses lining the mirrored wall behind it. Sam had had people in here giving the tasting room a serious spit and polish every day for a week, even though the place already shone like a prom date, all part of his perfectionist's attention to detail. There was even a hand-lettered sign on the bar that said KEEP OUT OF TASTING ROOM. READIED FOR VINEYARD'S 200TH ANNIVERSARY PARTY. ORDERS OF SAM JUMEL.

If I was caught in here, I'd be dead.

"Don't tell me you dragged me all the way back here for a wild-goose chase."

"Uh, course not." I took in a deep breath and charged forward, sliding around the bar and past the wine bottles to the side of the mirror. I wasn't even sure I was in the right place—I'd seen Sam enter this room once, when he'd had me sweeping up the winery and I had taken a break to do some sneaking around on my own. I remembered Sam had pulled open the mirror, moving the whole wall out to reveal a door. I knew if something was hidden behind a mirror, it was bound to be important. I slid my fingers along the edge.

Nothing happened.

"Cooper?"

"Give me a second." The latch had to be here somewhere. I rose on my toes, slid my fingers down again.

Nothing.

I looked at the shelves, hoping for a key. A PUSH HERE sign. Yeah, as if I'd get that lucky.

Nothing.

Mike's dad let out a long, impatient breath. *"Cooper."*

"I know, I know." Then I added, "Sir." I leaned against the mirror, my hand going to the high shelves of wine, the ones put up there just for show—the ones that dated back to the first Jumel years. My fingertips hit against one of the bottles, and it started to topple. I cursed, thinking, *Oh no, I've really done it now—Sam is going to* kill *me,* when the bottle righted itself. Then, a click.

The wall slowly swung open.

Behind it, an oak door. "This is where he keeps everything that no one is supposed to know about." I could have been wrong, but I doubted it.

Mike's dad stepped forward, tried the knob. The door opened. We both looked back, saw no one else in the tasting room, then ducked inside.

"Don't move and don't touch anything," Sergeant Ring said, pointing to a spot on the floor. "I'll do the investigating, you got it?"

I nodded and stayed where I was. I didn't know if he'd find anything, but I figured his attention was off me and thinking I'd had anything to do with Megan's disappearance, and we were away from the well's evil vine army. All around, a better situation.

Sergeant Ring wandered off to do his thing. I leaned against the wall. From here, the place spelled office. Desk, chair, a few framed awards. Nothing much. Had I been wrong?

A single tower of wine bottles sat in the corner. Wine bottles I recognized, not because I'd seen them in the tasting room, but because I *hadn't* seen them in the tasting room.

I'd seen them in the StepScrooge mansion. This was his private stash. The bottles created just for Sam—and no one else.

Wait. That wasn't right.

I thought a second, staring at those bottles, trying to figure out what bothered me about them. But I couldn't put my finger on it, so instead, I just slipped one of the bottles off the pile when Mike's dad wasn't looking and tucked it into my backpack as easily as Winona Ryder grabbing herself a pair of D&G sunglasses.

Mike's dad flipped through a few folders, then picked up two bottles of red and held them up to the light. He grinned.

He wasn't here for clues. If there was any detecting to do, I was going to have to do it. While Sergeant Ring debated between the 1989 and the 1992, I pushed off from the wall and sidled up to a small cabinet. It didn't look like much, just an old, beat-up wooden thing, the kind of cabinet sent to the office because it didn't match the house's *Better Homes & Gardens* perfecto décor. I could see my mother moving in and ordering that thing out.

Keeping my eyes on Sergeant Ring, I flicked open one of the cabinet doors. At first I didn't see anything. The lighting in the office space was kind of dim, and the cabinet was in shadows. I shuffled a step back, then looked again.

A book. Not like the latest Stephen King bestseller, but one of those old leather kind. There were some letters carved on the top that I couldn't make out, not under the dust on the cover, but it looked old. Really old.

It could have been anything. A family tree. An old Bible. A diary.

"Cooper, you think your stepdad will miss one bottle out of a thousand?"

I jerked back, away from the cabinet. "Uh . . . no. Call it evidence. You know, for DNA or whatever."

Sergeant Ring smiled. He and I, best buds again. He went back to picking the best vintage.

Before I could think twice, I reached in, swiped the leather book, and stuffed it into my backpack in one smooth move. I thought I heard a whispered *yes* as I did it, as if the creature had seen me.

No. Impossible.

Just as I got back into position against the wall, Sergeant Ring turned around. "Yeah, well, nothing here. My shift's over anyway." He clutched the bottle to his chest.

Yeah. Happy hour again. For the thousandth time, I was glad I hadn't told Mike's dad anything. He was clearly no help with anything but a corkscrew.

I wondered why Sam had hid the room behind a mirror. A secret latch. There had to be something here, maybe in that book. I couldn't be sure until I looked inside, but I wasn't going to do that in front of Sergeant Ring.

I took one last look around the room as the cop was closing the door. On the wall hung a small painting, incredibly detailed given how tiny it was, of two men standing in front of the well, back in its glory days when it had been a real working well, used, I guessed, to water the vineyard. Behind them, the old vineyard lay in neat rows, marching down the tidy acres. "Wait."

Sergeant Ring paused.

I stepped back inside the room and stood in front of the oil portrait. The colors were still Crayola bright, as if it had been created yesterday. I couldn't decipher the artist's scrawled name in the corner, but I could read the date.

1809. The year the vineyard had officially opened for business.

Beneath the painting, the names Auguste and Gerard Jumel were written in a cursive script.

Gerard Jumel. I knew that name.

It was Sam's great-great-great-times-a-gazillion-grandfather. The guy who'd taken the vineyard and made it an international sensation. He'd practically been canonized by the Jumel family for bringing them all these generations of not just money, but megawealth. He'd passed on the family secrets for the grapes, something that Sam wouldn't tell anyone except a Jumel heir.

Whatever. I didn't want in on his will anyway.

But . . . Auguste? I hadn't heard that name mentioned. Ever. Who was he?

"Not bad if you like that landscape crap," Mike's dad said

over my shoulder, gesturing toward the painting. "Though why anyone would want a painting of two guys hanging on their wall is beyond me. Tell your stepdad to get a Hot Babes on Harleys calendar. That's a real wall hanging, if you ask me."

I wasn't listening. I was staring.

At myself.

In double.

The two guys—and now I realized they weren't men at all, but teens about my age—Auguste and Gerard, standing in front of the well, were twins. And they looked exactly like me.

CHAPTER 22

The doorbell dented beneath my finger, chimes screaming for mercy, but I didn't let go. I fell against the door, panting. After I'd left the winery, grateful that Mike's dad had decided to go home and "test that wine sample," I'd booked it for my dad's house. I wanted to look for Megan, but I was too shaken up to go back in the woods right away, and besides, the vine guys were still waiting for me.

I opted for a temporary breather. A second to take all this in and figure out what it meant. What Mike's dad had told me about Sam. Those wine bottles. And now that freaky picture on the wall.

And maybe here, in the safety of the home where I'd grown up, the place where everything had once been okay, those vines wouldn't find me, wouldn't wrap around me, wouldn't drag me halfway across town and back—

"Cooper! What are you doing?" My father opened the door and stared at me, as if the alien mother ship had just dumped me on his doorstep.

"Can I . . ." I heaved in a breath—at this rate, I was going to need to cart around an oxygen tank. "Can I come in?"

"Sure, sure." He opened the door wider and waved me in. "Does your mother know where you are?"

I sure hoped not. "Of course."

A few minutes later, I was sitting on my father's worn brown leather sofa, drinking a Coke. He sat across from me, arms resting on his knees, waiting. My father did that well, sitting as quietly as a potted plant, his glasses resting on his nose, looking as though they might fall off at any second. He'd warmed up some leftover frozen pizza, the crappy diet kind, but hey, it was food, so I set it between us. We ate a bit, and then I put the Coke can on the old coffee table, the same one we'd had when I was a kid. I thought about that for a moment. Had my mother said to him, *You keep the coffee table; I'll take the kids*? "Thanks, Dad."

"When are you going to tell me?"

"Tell you what?"

"What's going on?"

"Nothing's going on. I was just thirsty and hungry. So I came by." I pointed at the empty can and started to rise. "I'm gonna grab another."

"Sit down."

He had that don't-argue-with-me tone, the one he didn't use very often. So I sat.

My father sighed. He stared at his hands for a long time, then back at me. "Talk to me, Cooper."

"About what?"

"About Megan, for one. I know you're worried. Has there been any news?"

I shook my head. Tears sprang into my eyes, but I brushed them away with the back of my fist.

"I can't imagine what that family is going through." He leaned forward. "Or you."

"I'm cool." I wasn't, but I also wasn't in any mood to talk about Megan. That would involve starting at the beginning, and I knew my dad didn't believe in fairy tales with big ugly monsters any more than Faulkner did.

"Anything I can do, you let me know."

I fiddled with my pizza. "Thanks."

"I'm here to help you. With anything." He gave me a smile. "Even your *Hamlet* paper."

"Dad, quit it. You're not supposed to help me. It's, like, a conflict of interest or something."

He chuckled. I hadn't seen him laugh in so long, I hadn't even realized he still could. The sound was . . . nice. I thought about how when all this was over, I should spend more time with my dad—outside of school. "You're right." He pretended to zip his lip and sat back. "When was the last time we did that?"

"What, talked about *Hamlet*? Try today. Second period."

"No, I meant laughed together, ate pizza, and just talked? I miss having you and your brother around all the time."

"Yeah, me too." Though my parents had joint custody, my dad had never really argued when my mother had asked for more time. He was the peacemaker, figuring if it made my mother happy, that was good enough for him.

I think he still loved her.

My father watched me for a long time, then let out another sigh. "There's more than just Megan's disappearance bugging you, Cooper. Lately, you haven't been acting like . . . yourself. You're jumpy. Forgetful. And you look like you haven't slept in a week."

I shrugged. "Things suck at home."

"How?"

The words pushed at my throat, crowding together like eleven-year-old girls outside the doors of a Hannah Montana concert. I wanted to tell him; I really did. I wanted to tell someone, someone who could help. Instead I swallowed hard and shoved the truth back to my gut. "The dog died."

My father jerked upright. "Whipple? Died? How? When?"

"I don't know. Mom said that Sam found him and . . ."

My voice trailed off. I had never asked my mother for any details about Whipple. Like where the dog was buried. Then I remembered something else that my mother had told me.

Sam . . . found him in the woods.

In the woods . . . where? By the well?

Had the creature gotten Whipple? Or had Sam?

Could Sam kill my dog? Or had he seen something kill him and just covered up the evidence? A lot of deaths circling around the name Sam lately. Two and two were beginning to add up, and I wasn't liking the total.

"And what?" my father pressed.

"And I don't know any more than that," I said, keeping my suspicions to myself. That's all they were—suspicions. I had no proof of anything.

My father's gaze narrowed. He studied me, then turned away and went to the fireplace, his back to me. "What do you think of Sam?"

The question caught me off-guard. "I don't know. I don't like him, but he's my stepfather. Kind of comes with the second marriage, doesn't it?"

"I suppose it does."

"He's been super uptight lately, too. The vineyard has this big anniversary deal coming up and business is down.

He blames everyone for that." I picked at my fingernails. "Especially me."

My father turned around and crossed his arms over his chest. "He's never really liked you, has he?"

"I dunno. I've never really liked him. We're even." I picked at my nails some more, waiting for my father to talk. But he didn't. He was like that a lot. The kind of guy who could go an hour without saying a word. I wished he'd turn on the television or the radio, anything to make noise. The clock in the hall ticked along. Still my father didn't say anything. I fidgeted on the couch. Fidgeted some more. "Why didn't you fight more to keep her?"

Oh man. Where had that come from? How had I let that one out?

It had to be the stress of the past few days. Or my blood sugar was spiking from the carbs or something.

My father didn't say anything. I studied my Vans, sure my dad was glaring at me, afraid to look. Finally, I lifted my head and checked.

Instead, I found a mixture of surprise and sadness in his eyes. He pushed off from the fireplace and came back to his chair, dropping into it with a long breath. "Your mother's known Sam a long time."

I perked up. "She has?"

He nodded. "From before you were born. He delivered you."

Disgust bubbled up inside me. It was too weird to think about that—StepScrooge Sam's being at the other end of the birth canal and seeing me pop out. "You're not serious."

"It might have started between them when she was pregnant, but I'm not sure."

I pulled childhood memories out of the corners of my mind, shuffled them, dealt them out, and revisited them. My parents on vacation, holding hands, kissing, laughing together. My mother waiting by the door for my father to get home from parent-teacher conferences, tucking her hair behind her ear or checking her lipstick in the hall mirror. My father grabbing her after dinner and giving her a hug just because she had made his favorite meatloaf.

And then one day, things changed, as fast as I could snap my fingers. She stopped waiting by the door and left TV dinners on the counter with a note. My father stopped smiling when he came home and just headed for the den, burying himself in essay corrections instead of his family. The next thing Faulkner and I knew, we were living in Sam's mansion and my father was alone.

"No, Dad, I don't think it started then. She was happy when we were kids. She loved you."

It was as if a flower had bloomed on my father's face.

Hope exploded across his features, brightening his smile, his eyes. He came to life in a way I hadn't seen in a year and a half. "You . . . you really think so?"

"Yeah, Dad," I said quietly, the two of us connecting across the wooden floor, not with a touch but because we both missed the days of meatloaf and mashed potatoes. "I do."

He held that look for one more moment, and then he rose and went back to the fireplace. "Either way, it's too late now. She married *him*."

"Yeah."

He sighed. "Yeah."

I got to my feet. "I'm gonna get another Coke."

My father didn't say anything, so I went into the kitchen and grabbed a soda from the fridge. I dug through my father's cabinets and came up pretty empty in the junk-food haul. My dad's cholesterol check had come back high a couple months ago, and he'd gone all health commando in his kitchen.

"Dad, you got any Doritos? Chips? Anything good?"

"Check the basement. Oh, and Cooper, when you're down there, get that box by the stairs. Your mother asked me to bring a few things over to the house. I might as well send them home with you. That way I don't have to go . . . well, over there. And see them."

I headed down there, not just for food, but to get away from the brick of sadness upstairs. My father was clearly holding a Good Old Days vigil, and I didn't need that. Not now. I had enough trouble with Right This Minute.

One lone bag of Lay's sat on the shelf in the basement, stuffed behind enough canned peaches to feed Ethiopia. I grabbed the red bag, then tossed it on top of the cardboard box by the stairs. The box was filled with a jumble of old school papers, a couple of dusty soccer awards for Faulkner and me, and, tucked in the side, a purplish paper with the state of Maine seal at the top.

In the kitchen, I put the box on the table. My dad was at the sink, filling a glass. I was about to open the chips when I noticed the purple paper again. And the words stamped across the top.

RECORD OF BIRTH. Beneath that, my name typed into the first box.

I tugged out the paper and gave it a skim. Father's name, mother's name, place of birth, address at time of birth—nothing I didn't already know.

I was about to put it back when one word grabbed me. *Plurality.*

"Cooper?" my dad said, coming up behind me.

But I barely heard him.

Beside *plurality,* the word *TWIN* was bolded. From the sex answer before it, where *Male* was bolded, I put together that *twin* was the checked answer.

Plurality? Twin?

As in, more than one of me?

I spun around and stared at my father. "Dad?"

He saw what I had in my hands, then nodded. "We should have told you a long time ago. Your mother thought it would upset you to know when you were little, and then as the years passed, it just seemed like we could never find the right time."

I glanced down at the paper again. "I'm a twin? I have a . . . ?"

"Brother." My father put a hand on my shoulder. "But he died at birth. Stillborn. I'm sorry."

That word came back to me: *TWIN*.

"But how . . . ? I . . ." I couldn't get a full sentence out. My mind tried to wrap itself around the information and kept failing.

Shouldn't I have felt something? Had some inkling of a connection? Wasn't that what they were always saying on the Discovery Channel, that people who had a twin that died at birth always felt this missing half? But then again, my life in the past couple years had been far from normal—and heck, in the past few months it had been close to Hollyweird—so I could have had all kinds of absent-twin feelings and been so wrapped up in all this other crap that I'd missed them, like a zit on the back of my elbow.

"It was strange," my father mused, looking at the birth certificate. "Twins never ran in the family. We were so surprised—pleasantly surprised—when we heard your mom was carrying two boys."

I sank into a chair. My father sat opposite me and took off his glasses. He swiped at his face, but all that did was deepen the lines under his eyes. My father seemed to have aged fifteen years in the past two minutes.

"Poor kid. He never had a chance," my father said.

The whole thing didn't seem real. Couldn't seem to sink in. I tried to digest it, to imagine another me, and I just . . . Couldn't.

Tears filled my father's eyes. I'd never seen him cry, not even when my mother moved out of our house, not when my grandmother died, not once. He was what people called stoic. Some people thought he was cold, but I knew better. He just wasn't comfortable around people. Give him a book, and he was as happy as a hot dog in a roll. Put him in a crowd, and he clammed right up.

He let out a breath that shook like a tree in a storm, then lifted his gaze to meet mine. "Let me tell you something, Cooper. You lose a kid—I don't care how or when—you never get over it."

I glanced down at my birth certificate, staring at the four

letters of *TWIN*. There had been another me, another half to me, and it had died.

And I'd never known.

But one other person, besides my parents, had known, had been there, had been there and held that baby. And had never said a word.

Sam.

Why? Why the big secret?

"I'm sorry," I said. To my dad. To myself. And to the brother who hadn't even had a chance to breathe. Then it finally hit me, and I felt a loss so hard, it seemed as if a part of me had been left behind, as if I'd forgotten something vital in a store somewhere, something so important, and I couldn't ever get it back.

I wanted to cry. For something I'd never seen, never held, never known. Only knew I could never have, because it was too late.

"I'm sorry, Dad," I said again, softer this time.

"I'm sorry, too." My father reached across the table, wrapped a hand around my neck, and drew me into his sweater. It scratched my face a little.

But I didn't mind.

CHAPTER 23

As soon as my father went to bed, I went up to my old room, shut the door, and upended the backpack onto my bed. Before I went after that thing and got Megan, I wanted to see if anything I'd grabbed today would give me more ammunition. I needed to know more about what I was dealing with.

The wine bottle rolled to the side. I let it go and reached for the book. I brushed off a thick layer of dust, revealing a cursive *GMJ* on the front.

It didn't take a rocket scientist to put that together with the painting I'd seen in the office. Gerard Jumel. Something *M* for his middle name. I turned the leather cover and the first yellowed page. The paper nearly crumpled in my hands. But there, in ink faded by age, were the words *Journal of Gerard Jumel.*

A chill ran up my spine. Was it just that these were the words of a guy who was dead? Or of a guy who was in that picture in Sam's office?

Or was it that a part of me knew, somehow, this was all wrapped up together?

I hesitated, then turned the next page. The first entry was dated October 10, 1808. The words were hard to read—the old ink grayed over the years, the pages as fragile as autumn leaves. But I could make out most of it.

> *The new property Father bought is ripe for farming. There are grapes everywhere. The old man here before us let it go to weeds. It will be a good year before we can open the winery. Must get back to work.*

Gerard must have been working for a while, because the next entry was months later:

> *Sad day. Found Ma's dead body near the woods. Looks like she fell in a sinkhole, though we haven't seen any of those hereabout before. Also strange—her body was covered in vines. A mysterious death. But we must go on without her.*

There were many entries after that detailing the family's grief over the loss of the mother and their determination to make a go of it on the land nonetheless. Then this:

> *Found an old well at the back of the property. The grapes by the well are the sweetest yet.*

He'd eaten those grapes? I wouldn't have touched anything near that thing, but then again, maybe he hadn't seen what I'd seen.

An entry a few days later stopped me cold.

> *Hearing a voice calling my name. It seems to follow me everywhere I go. And always, it brings me back to that well.*

I even found out about the origin of the painting I had seen in Sam's secret room:

> *Father seems drawn to the well, too. Had a portrait painted of me and Auguste standing in front of it. Says it is the heart of the Jumel vineyard.*

Gerard wrote for weeks, months, about the voice, trying to figure out what it was. As freaked about it as I was. It was weird, seeing some two-hundred-years-ago teenager the same age I was going through the same thing.

But that meant the thing in the well was—

Two hundred years old? That was impossible. Like legends-of-Bigfoot impossible.

I gulped and turned the page.

Voice is getting more urgent. Told me this land has taken Mama and will take the rest of us, too, if we don't make a proper sacrifice soon.

I kept going, skimming now, looking for more information. I didn't find anything until October 1, 1809.

It has told me something I find abhorrent but know I must do. Auguste must be sacrificed.

Sacrificed? As in, thrown down there?

Just like me?

I slammed the book shut and sat back against the bed.

That meant Sam's great-great-great-great-relatives had been in the same situation as I was. Someone trying to toss

Auguste down the well. Someone who was supposed to love him. Someone being controlled by that *thing*.

But how? And why?

I started to open the book again when another fact hit me. If Sam had had this book all along, then he knew everything. He knew about the well. He knew about the creature. He knew what it could do.

Did he also know what it was doing to my mother? To me?

I flipped the pages back to where I'd left off and found more written by Gerard on October 8. His handwriting had grown more and more sloppy, his sentences choppier, as if the thing taking over his mind had also made it harder for him to concentrate.

Land needs him. Every two hundred years it asks one thing. Sacrifice. With Auguste, the . . . land gives back. Lets us . . . live.

Lets them live?

Fear snaked through me. What would happen to my mother, my brother, if this "sacrifice" didn't happen? If I didn't do what the creature wanted? Would they . . .

Die?

I turned another page. October 9, 1809.

Will use Auguste's love for Amelia . . . make him see
why . . . must do this.

Amelia. The name rang a bell in my head, and then I remembered. Megan had said the old lady that used to live in the abandoned house, her family had grown up on the vineyard property. Had Amelia—with her piano and sheet music—been that thing's girlfriend?

Oh God, *Megan.*

I turned to the last entry.

Today, Auguste . . . the sacrifice.

October 10.

The anniversary of Jumel Vineyards. Two hundred years of business.

My birthday.

The day of the sacrifice.

Now I knew what all this was leading up to. Why I was still alive, and why I had to stay that way.

I had one day left. One day until I was going down there. If I'd had any doubts before who the sacrificial lamb was in this little scenario, I didn't have them now. It was me. I'd become this generation's Auguste.

Part of me wanted to run, to head for the nearest train

out of here, but another side knew I had to stay and deal. So I went back to the journal.

Gerard had skipped a few spaces, then started writing again, clearer, more concrete, as if now he was fine.

> *It is done. And someday, Auguste will thank me. For saving them. For saving him. When he has paid the price demanded, the chosen one will take his place. And then Auguste will walk the earth again, living the life of an immortal.*

That thing would get *out* once I was dead? Walk around? Be free? Forever?

No way. No way. That would not happen—over my dead body.

Damn. That might be true.

I turned the rest of the pages, looking for a clue, an answer as to how to kill the thing, but found nothing. No solutions. All I knew was that I was next on the list.

The chosen one.

Why? Why me? I wasn't anyone special. Cooper Warner, ordinary high school freshman, who didn't even have good enough grades to stay on the football team.

Apparently that didn't matter. I was going to become the next monster in the well. Happy birthday.

I'd never felt more lost or out of control.

I put down the book. The wine bottle rolled across the bed. I picked it up. It lay heavy in my palm, the golden liquid inside seeming to almost . . .

Shimmer.

What was it with this wine? Sam had once told me, when I'd dared to go near a bottle, that it was his and his alone. That all vineyards had a special owner's-only brew. Something the owner kept under lock and key, drank only on special occasions.

I turned the bottle over and over in my palm, thinking, remembering Sam uncorking, pouring a glass. Freaking out completely when I had pretended to take a sip from my mother's glass once, then Sam at the dinner table, reaching for the bottle of red and leaving the white for my mother—

The truth hit me. So hard, I nearly fell over.

I pulled Faulkner's cell out of my pocket. The thing was almost out of juice, though, so I had only a second. I called the house.

Faulkner picked up on the first ring. "Dude, thanks for getting Mom out of the woods today," I said. "You saved my life."

"Coop, thank God."

He sounded glad to talk to me. What was up with that?

"Listen, I have something to tell you." I cupped my hand

around the receiver. Even though I was still in my old room, I didn't want to chance waking up my father. Explaining all this weirdness to him—a man who thought the answer to any problem could be found in a book—would only make things worse. "Don't let Mom drink that wine—you know, *the* wine. Sam's special crap. There's something in there that's . . . I don't know, making her act the way she is." I wanted to tell him about the journal and the grapes, but I figured if he hadn't believed me before, he really wasn't going to believe me now, not until I could show him the journal.

"I can't do that," Faulkner said, and his voice shook on the last two words, shook like San Francisco after an earthquake. "It's . . ."

The phone hummed. "What? It's what?"

He started to breathe heavily, and I wasn't sure, but I think he might have been crying. "It's too late, Cooper. Oh, man it's too late. For all of us."

Then the phone went dead. And Faulkner was gone.

Empty.

The StepScrooge Sam mansion stood empty in a way that went beyond no people being there. The rooms echoed. They smelled musty, as if—

As if the well had been here.

Night hung heavy behind me, our street silent as a tomb.

I could feel the ticking of a mental clock. I had only until my birthday to get rid of this thing if I wanted to live. And if there was any chance Megan was still alive, I had just that long to find her.

I stepped inside, flicked on the lights, and started to look for my brother. Except even with all the lights on, the house still felt dark. Heavy. Ominous. "Faulkner? Hey, Faulk. Don't play any games, dude. It's not funny."

But there was no answer.

"Faulkner!"

I opened every door, dread multiplying with each knob I turned. But he wasn't behind any of the six-panel oak doors. He wasn't in the kitchen. The bathroom. The laundry room. I stopped at the entrance to the basement and decided to hold that for later. Instead, I turned to make my way upstairs.

And stopped. Swallowed my breath.

One of the well's evil vine men. Waiting for me at the top of the stairs.

If this thing was now outside the woods and inside the house, it must mean the creature had gotten stronger. Because the day was getting closer for the sacrifice? Because the thing was getting more anxious? Either way, it didn't look good for me.

My legs nearly went out from under me, but I grabbed

the banister and told myself it was just a bunch of sticks. I could take a bunch of sticks. I could beat this thing. I had to.

Because this wasn't just about me anymore or saving my own skin.

It was about Megan. And Faulkner. And my mother.

"You don't scare me!" I screamed. I could lie to it and myself.

The vine-and-twig man opened its stick mouth and laughed.

"I'm coming up there!" I swiped one of my mother's megasize candlesticks from the hall table, then started up the stairs. Still holding on to the banister, because if I didn't, my legs weren't going to climb.

The thing waved its arms and clapped its hands, like a baseball catcher waiting for me to send him a fastball.

Were there others in the house?

Oh God, what if there were a hundred? What if it had gotten the whole damned vineyard to turn into those things and they had taken over the whole house and they were coming to get me and take me back to the well and I was going to die before I could rescue Megan and find Faulkner and—

Get a grip, Cooper. Get a grip or you will *die.*

At the top of the stairs, the vine-and-stick man rocked on its heels and kept swinging its arms, laughing some more.

Waiting. Like this was the funniest, most entertaining thing to happen in weeks.

Like it was all a game.

I raised the candlestick higher—that sucker was heavy, made of some kind of metal that needed polishing all the time—and picked up the pace. Five steps away now. Four. I could see its eyes were made of grapes—grapes so shiny, they almost had irises in them. When I was three steps away, it crouched, then pointed to its chin, as if saying, *Go ahead, take your best shot.*

When I'd been five, my father had signed me up for Little League. I had hated him for doing it. He'd dragged me down to practice, kicking and screaming.

But once I was there, I found out I liked baseball. I made some friends—Joey and Mike, for starters—and stuck with the league until high school. I had a hell of a batting average and a pretty decent pitching arm. Coach Harding had already talked to me about trying out this spring for the varsity baseball team at Maple Valley High.

I knew that.

I didn't think the vine guy did.

And I wasn't in a sharing kind of mood right now. When I was one step away, I paused, shifted my feet to widen my stance, then let go of the banister. I waited until the stick guy started laughing again. God, I hated that laugh, and I let that hate boil into a fury that I could control, a rage that I could feel travel down my arm, burn into my fist.

I curled my grip tightly around the makeshift bat, raised it onto my shoulder, then swung, hard and even. *"Shut up!"*

The candlestick bat connected with the side of its head, smacking into the twig figure, solid enough to kill a guy. Its nature head exploded into pieces, bursting like a cartoon sun, and it stumbled back. I started to move forward, to finish the job, when the pieces of its head began to lift up from the floor and started to swirl in a circle, then—to my horror—knit themselves back together.

It laughed again and said something I couldn't understand. Even though the words had made no sense to me, I knew what they had meant. It could have been speaking Mandarin and it wouldn't have mattered, because its words were spoken in the language of the playground.

The roar of a bully. The taunting you-think-that-hurt dare.

It started toward me again and I raised the candlestick and swung harder this time.

"Get back!"

Again, its head erupted in a starburst, then zipped back together, as if it was the Road Runner, down for only a second.

"Get away, you freak!" I took another swing and another,

this time hitting it in the legs and the arms, but then at one point the candlestick just went *through* its legs. I took a step back, stunned. "What the hell?"

It laughed again, then reached forward and swung at my head with the branches of its arms. I ducked. It swung again, this time lower, faster. Faster than me.

The blow hit me squarely in the gut, blasting my breath out of my lungs and sending me flying down the stairs, somersaulting like an Olympic gymnast, except with a dismount that sent me landing on my wrist.

I screamed. The twig thing yowled and danced at the top of the stairs.

I cradled my wrist against my chest and tested it, gingerly moving it back and forth. It hurt like hell, but it moved, so it wasn't broken. A sprain. A bad one. Either way, I didn't have time for the pain.

I needed a way past that thing to make sure my brother wasn't upstairs somewhere, trapped. I picked up the candlestick again, in my other hand, and realized there was no way I could hit it using my left arm. For one, my lefty batting average was zero. For another, hitting the thing hadn't gotten me anywhere. This one didn't have the green webbing that had coated my school desk and my computer, but it had the regeneration abilities of a starfish on steroids.

Then I saw what had been sitting next to the candlestick on the hall table and knew another way to take out a vine man. I ran back upstairs again.

It was still laughing when I reached the top of the steps. I stood in front of it, raised the candlestick again.

"Yeah, real funny, isn't it? Everyone wants to be Jon Stewart. Why not try torch singer for a career!" Then with my right hand, I flicked my mother's Bic lighter. I brought the candlestick together with the lighter, then thrust both at the vine-and-twig guy. My wrist screamed in agony, but not as loudly as the stick man did.

Because I knew one other thing this vine guy didn't know.

Dry grapevines go up like kindling when you light them on fire. Without the web coating, he was as dry as paper. In seconds, he was toast.

So were the hall drapes, but I figured I'd deal with those later.

I headed down the hall, lit candle in one hand, lighter in the other, opening the rest of the doors and calling for Faulkner. No more vine guys up there.

But no Faulkner, either. Or Mom. Or Sam.

Night carpeted the yard. A few lights ringed the back, accenting Sam's ridiculous plants, painting his pretty landscaping picture, and giving me just enough light to see there weren't any vine guys on the lawn, either, thank God.

But what if they were in the woods? Just waiting for me to leave the house?

I stopped at the last door in the hall, the one that led to the attic. I turned, ran for my room, opened my closet, and tore it apart until I found the binoculars in the small storage bin in the back, left over from a camping trip with my dad last summer. He'd bought them for me in case I had wanted to look for birds.

I'd used them to scan for girls on the beach at the lake down the road.

But now I took them up the stairs to the attic and used them to look out the tiny window facing the woods.

At first all I saw were trees and more trees. Then the trees parted, like curtains. They wanted to show me something?

The well.

No. Someone *at* the well. A tall, lean figure. From here, I couldn't tell if it was a man or a woman. The night sky kept me from discerning much. Too tall to be Megan or Faulkner. Too skinny to be Sergeant Ring.

One of the vineyard workers, maybe? Or Sam? My mother?

The person was holding something close to his or her

chest. I leaned forward in the window but couldn't make out what it was. Then the person raised up the bundle, held it for a long second, and let go.

The blanket unfurled—small, white, square, the kind they used in hospitals. Whatever had been wrapped in it dropped into the well.

So hungry. So hungry. Give me more.

I scrambled back from the window, the binoculars crashing to the floor. One of the lenses cracked. My breath panted in and out and I ducked down, even though it was impossible for whoever was at the well to see me back here.

What the hell had I just seen? And heard?

Someone *feeding* that creature?

Oh my God. Oh my God.

Oh. My. God.

I crawled back, poked my head over the window ledge, then dragged the binoculars up and took another look. The figure had turned and paused in the woods, as if the person was listening, the blanket tucked under one arm.

I focused the binoculars again just as the clouds shifted past the moon, and a shaft of light fell onto the woods and revealed the person.

Sam.

In his doctor scrubs.

With dark crimson stains down the front.

I fought the urge to hurl. I knew now for sure what that bundle had been. Sergeant Ring's words came back to me.

The hospital is looking into your stepfather's track record with deliveries . . . Infant mortality . . .

Was that because he'd been feeding that thing . . .

Babies? The ones that died when he was delivering them?

Like my twin brother?

My stomach rolled and pitched, and I had to look away again for a second. When I turned back to the window, Sam was gone.

Instead, I saw Faulkner, sitting at the base of the well, slumped over. Someone had tied him in place, leaving him there, waiting to be sacrificed, like that kid Isaac in the Bible.

CHAPTER 24

The creature dragged his body across the well's bottom and screamed his fury. Again, the one who fed him had come, and again, he'd done almost nothing to repay Auguste for all he had given him. No gratitude. Nothing but disdain, hatred.

All these generations of wealth he had lain at the feet of Jumels—

And for what?

For these measly meals. Dead little nothings of humans. He kicked at the latest offering and roared another outrage.

Yes, the one who fed him, whose "generosity" the creature depended upon, had let him eat another meal tonight, as a way to build his strength for the battle yet to come, but he was tired of these ridiculous trifles to eat.

He needed older twins. That was the meat that gave him

power. Those on the edge of puberty, their lifeblood peaking at its highest—

Those were the ones that fed him best.

And yet, this Jumel fed the creature smaller bites, to keep him subdued. Under his thumb.

The generations who had come before had understood the creature. They had fed Auguste well, had tended to his needs. They'd sent down whole cows, pairs of pigs, and plenty of the right-aged humans, never making him hunt on his own.

They had tended to his home, knowing the arrangement, knowing one day Auguste would rise up from the depths of hell and be restored to life, would want to see the place he had missed for so long. See the little cottage on the edge of the vineyard, the one that had once held his heart.

So Auguste had given back. He had made the grapes grow. Had made Gerard, then Gerard's son, and then grandson, and now great-great-great-grandson, wealthy beyond their wildest dreams.

But this one had been cruel. Withholding food for days at a time. Taunting Auguste with names and words. But worst of all, he had ripped down the house. Used machines to tear it apart, limb by limb. He had shredded Amelia's cottage, had called it an eyesore. And in its place, he'd built a gaudy testament to hubris. Auguste had roared his outrage, but it hadn't mattered.

So Auguste had wreaked his vengeance on the land, drying the grapes on the vine. Reminding him whose blood this vineyard really lived on. By whose sacrifice the grapes continued to grow. Without Auguste, all this would die.

And so, too, would the Jumels.

Two hundred years ago, Gerard had pushed him down here and Auguste had stayed. So Amelia could live. And as his skin and body gave way from human to creature, he had stayed, waiting for the day when the chosen one would come and take his place.

An heir created from Auguste's own seed, sacrificed on the two-hundredth anniversary.

Auguste had only one regret, something he hadn't known until after he'd been down here and learned the rest of the story from the land, which spoke to him. Their mother had been called to bring the sacrifice, and then, when she'd refused to give up her son—

She'd been taken, as an incentive for Gerard. Their mother, the unwitting accomplice to the horrific bargain their father had received on the vineyard. Too late, Gerard had realized why his father had gotten such a good price on the land. Make the sacrifice, he'd been told, and continue the legacy, or every grape would die on the vine. And every person living there would die. If only she could have been saved, too. But that—

That was in the past. It was time for living now. *Auguste's* time.

Now Auguste would give Cooper the same choice. Either go down into the well to fulfill the land's destiny or those he loved would pay, and pay dearly.

Setting Auguste free, finally, from this cursed existence to walk the earth.

Cooper's transformation wouldn't take long. And if he struggled, well, that would only add to the excitement. He had to understand he was part of a bigger plan. A lifetime of plans.

When Cooper was in his rightful place, Auguste would finally be strong enough. Strong enough to seek justice.

CHAPTER 25

I grabbed my still-loaded backpack, throwing in the Bic lighter, then ran downstairs, past the smoldering embers of the vine guy, stomping on what was left of its head as I went. "Take that, stick man."

It turned to dust under my foot. Round one to Cooper Warner.

At least I had a way to beat those things. Now I just had to save my brother, find my girlfriend, and avoid my homicidal mother, maniacal stepfather, and a man-eating monster. Piece of cake. Right.

I ran out of there and into the woods. As soon as I hit the trees, the woods came to life, vines springing up around me, dropping down off the branches, curling in like hands reaching for my arms, my legs.

The creature was here, and he was letting me know that this time, he wasn't going to let me go.

The trees crackled with movement. A vine lifted the back of my hair and tickled at my neck. I yelped and leaped away, smacking at it. From farther in the woods, the creature began to laugh.

Just saying hello, Cooper. You're taking long enough to get here. Poor Faulkner's about done. And I don't like to play with tired toys.

"Leave my brother alone!" I pulled out the knife, raised it in my hand like a caveman trying to threaten a *T. rex.* My wrist twinged.

I'd never be able to stab the thing with my wrist like that. I needed to brace that sprain. I dug in the pack again and found Megan's bandanna.

I'd see her wear it again. And I'd see her smile again. No matter what.

"Megan," I whispered, and then I spun the bandanna tightly around my wrist, weaving it between my thumb and fingers like a flexible bandage. I picked up the knife and gave it a swing, then a jab. The sprain still hurt, but less than before. And best of all, I could hold the knife and use it.

Before I started off again, I loaded up my pack with whatever rocks I could see from the faint light cast by the moon, yanking them up before the vines could reach out and grab me. The rocks weren't much as weapons went, but then again, I wasn't much as heroes went, either.

All the while the creature laughed and laughed. I ignored him, letting my hatred build. One more weapon, I figured. My pack slammed against my back as I ran, rocks pinging my kidneys. I'd be paying for that later.

If I had a later.

The woods snapped and popped like a thousand bowls of Rice Krispies. The vine army ran with me, hell's cross-country team. And all the while, the creature lay at the bottom of that well, panting in anticipation.

I could feel him now. Feel his breathing. Feel it as if he were part of me.

Come closer, Cooper. Hurry now. We're waiting for you.

Every breath I took drew in the scent of the well. It was as if the slime, the muck, and the putrid air were clawing their way into my lungs. I tried to breathe through my mouth instead, but the smell stuck to my clothes, my skin, me.

The creature was stronger now. So strong—

Maybe too strong.

Would he get me before I got him? And keep me down there forever?

Would I turn into him?

No. I couldn't think that. Wouldn't. *Concentrate, Cooper,* I told myself. *Concentrate.*

Finally, I rounded the last tree and skidded to a halt a few feet from Faulkner. He was still slumped over, his body seeming pale, thinner. He wore only a T-shirt and jeans, his feet bare, his arms useless, tied to his sides so he could lift his hands only a few inches. He didn't move. I prayed for him to breathe, for him to flinch, blink. Anything.

Was he . . . dead?

God, please, no. Not my brother. Maybe we didn't always get along, barely tolerated each other some days. But we were brothers, and when it counted—

It *counted.*

I bent down, reached out, then drew back, afraid to touch him, in case . . .

"Faulkner?"

He moaned, then lifted his head, his limp and stringy hair swinging across his face. His eyes were glassy, his lips barely moving. Had he been drugged? "Cooper?"

Not dead. Relief ran over me like a tidal wave.

I scrambled to his side and reached for the rope binding him to the well. The knots were tight, tied by Hercules himself, I swore. "Are you okay?"

"Don't." He waved a hand at me. "Don't . . . untie me."

"We have to get you out of here." I glanced around, but

for now, the vine army stuck to the shadows as far as I could tell in the inky blackness. They had merged with the woods, their spiny bodies forming a second phalanx with the trees. Watching me. Watching Faulkner.

"We have to move fast," I said, jerking at the ropes, but they held fast. Too tight, too thick—it didn't even feel like real rope or regular knots. What the hell? If I could get the knife under the ropes, maybe that would do it.

Faulkner reached up a shaky hand and grabbed my left wrist. "It's . . . too . . . late."

The clouds shifted away from the moon, and a shaft of light dropped down over us. And over what really held him in place. It wasn't just ropes.

Vines covered Faulkner from head to toe, weaving in and out of every exposed inch of his body like an afghan of green. They wrapped in and around the ropes that were already there. They'd interlocked across his chest, crawled under his neck, and leapfrogged their way over his head, tugging down again in a macabre green veil. They laced over his legs, under his knees, then back over the stone wall. He was a cockroach pinned to the well's science lab.

No, no, *no*. Not him, too. The thing wanted only me. I was the sacrifice; I was the one who was supposed to go down there and stay.

What was happening?

I clawed at the vines, trying to loosen them, but they barely moved. "Who did this to you? Who would tie you to this thing and leave you here?"

"Mom did it," he said, his voice so weak, I had to lean in to hear him. Faulkner waited for our gazes to connect across an impossible, ridiculous, horrible situation. "To save *you*. And me."

I cursed. "But you're dying! How could she do this to you?"

"You don't understand." His words were a whisper. "The thing caught me first. She . . . stopped . . ." That was all he said.

I stared at Faulkner. Had I heard him right? "What?"

Was he crazy? Maybe he'd been given something that had gone to his brain.

No response. Faulkner's head dropped to his chest and he zoned out. He was drained, as if everything vital had been sucked out of him.

The vine army still hung on the fringes, watching. Hyenas on the prairie. Waiting for the lions to finish their kill so they could scoop up the entrails. I glared at them, then turned back to my brother. "Faulkner. You okay?"

He didn't move.

I shook him. "Stay with me, dude. I'm going to get you out of here."

He roused a little, and then his eyes met mine, and in his gaze I saw the last thing I'd ever expected to see in my older, stronger wise-ass brother.

Resignation.

"Just leave me," he said. "Run. Fa . . . fast"—he took in a breath, let it out—"as you can."

"I can't. I won't." I started sawing at the vines with the knife, ripping at them with my other hand, trying to yank them away from his arms, but as soon as I hacked off one piece, it grew back. What the—? I cut another. It came back. A third. It reappeared almost instantly. "I'm getting you out of here, Faulkner."

Somehow.

He grabbed my wrist, the one with the bandage this time, and I had to stop cutting because it hurt so badly. I bit my lip so I wouldn't scream in pain. "They are going to *kill* you, Cooper." He breathed in and out, clearly beat, as ready to quit as I had ever seen him, and it scared me, scared me worse than anything so far had, because Faulkner was the older one, the one who never got scared, never gave up, never did anything but grin and make a joke. *"Run."*

And his hand dropped away, as if that had been all he had had in him.

The knife shook in my hand so badly that I almost cut him, but I went back to sawing. Still the vines kept coming back, twice as fast each time, doubling their grip on my brother. It was as if the vines kept trying to drag him down there. But the ropes held Faulkner securely in place above— out of the vines' total control. Could he be telling the truth about our mother trying to help us? I had no time to decide. I had to get him out of there. *Now.* "I. Won't. Leave. You."

"You have—" Then the vines pulled taut, cutting off his words. Faulkner's head jerked back, as if he were a puppet and the puppet master had yanked his prize toy into line. Faulkner's eyes glazed over and his mouth dropped open.

"Of course you'll leave," Faulkner said in a voice that wasn't his own, a dark, menacing, low growl that came from somewhere below him. "Because your real family is down here, Cooper."

I scrambled backwards. "Faulkner?"

"He's gone, Cooper," said the thing inside my brother, singsongy. Teasing, thinking this whole thing was just oh so funny, a real Jay Leno now. He grinned at me. "Too bad you didn't even get to say goodbye. That's two brothers you've lost in one lifetime." He tsk-tsked. "Such terrible luck."

The creature had invaded my brother, had taken over something I loved. Okay, so maybe I had never told Faulkner I loved him, but he *was* my brother and I did. And now the thing was playing me. Faulkner wasn't gone. No way. He was too young. Too strong. Too . . .

Alive.

The thing lied. That's what he did. Just to mess with my head.

Except Faulkner wasn't moving, and his eyes were blank, and his skin was starting to pale. I stared at the left side of his chest, through a small triangle in the vines. I didn't see a single twitch of activity. *Move,* I screamed in my head. *Move up, move down. Make your heart beat, Faulkner.*

Nothing happened. Nothing moved.

Move! Breathe!

Nothing.

I leaped forward and clawed at the vines around my brother's neck, but they had him in a maximum-security collar.

"Poor Cooper," the thing said through Faulkner's mouth. All words. No breath. "Poor, poor Cooper."

"Shut up!" I screamed at the face that was my brother—and wasn't.

He just laughed.

Tears stung my eyes but I refused to let them fall. Refused to let that thing know he had gotten to me. Because as soon as the creature knew that, he won.

I pounded on Faulkner's chest, pushing at his heart, willing it to beat.

No movement. No ticking of life.

Nothing.

"Do you want your brother back?" the thing said. "You can have him, and we can all be together, be a happy little family. Just say the words, Cooper, and come with me. I'll take care of you. *Forever.*" The vines released, as if the creature was saying, *Look, my hands are off; he's all yours.* "Now all you have to do is untie the rope, Cooper, and let Faulkner go. And then come down here with me. Then everything will be fine again. Everyone will live."

Then he laughed.

Was he lying again, or was there still a way to save Faulkner? I couldn't take the chance, I decided. I had to try. I reached for the rope and started in on the first knot. "Hold on, Faulkner, I'll—"

Then I stopped.

The vines hovered over my fingers, dancing in the air, waiting. For what? If the creature was really letting Faulkner go, why were the vines still there? And why had my mother tied Faulkner up? What did she know that I didn't?

Was she protecting us? Or working for the creature?

I looked at my brother again. The idiot light finally came on and I understood. Faulkner had been the goat for the *Tyrannosaurus rex* that lived twenty feet down below, in some sicko *Jurassic Park—The Well Edition.*

My mother had known the creature had been trying to

take over Faulkner's body and use him to get to me, like the other creature had used Gerard, turning brother against brother. She had tied Faulkner up to stop him; she had stopped him before he could eat the grapes. Before he, too, could turn into what she had become. Before Faulkner could do to me what Gerard had done to Auguste.

When it mattered, my mother had come through. For Faulkner and me. There was . . .

Hope.

But if my family was ever going to have a normal life again, was ever going to go back to meatloaf and mashed potatoes, that thing had to die.

I leaned in and whispered into Faulkner's ears. "Faulkner, I'm coming back to get you. Hang on."

"Oh, how sweet," the thing mocked. "Now *let me go.*"

I moved back, eyeing that thing inside my brother. The same thing that had turned Gerard against Auguste. "I'm not untying anything. Go to hell, you bastard!"

The body that used to hold Faulkner leaned forward and turned, its mouth open, trying to snap at me. "Cooper!"

I scrambled back, dropping the knife. The body strained at the ropes, clearly frustrated by the ties that bound and held its prize out of its total control. The vines reached with the body, working in concert, like a spider web swinging with the spider trying hard, trying to overpower the other knots. The ropes nearly broke, but then no, they held fast. The creature let out a scream like a wounded animal. I thought for sure it would do some crazy ten-foot-bite thing and take my head off. *"Let me go!"*

"Never!" I shouted. The thing inside Faulkner stopped, breathing heavily as though it had passed out. Had Faulkner's body given out? Or was the creature lying in wait?

I was so afraid, I couldn't breathe. I should do what Faulkner had said.

Run.

Go back to my father's house. Call Sergeant Ring, hope he was sober enough to deal with this. Let someone else, someone with a gun or a nuclear bomb to drop down onto that thing, handle this.

I started to push away, keeping my body low to the ground, praying I wouldn't awaken the creature again. Or the army of vine guys. Or whatever other surprises that creature had in store for me.

Then a whisper, carrying up from the bottom of the well. "Cooper, is that you?"

I froze. Was that . . .

Megan's voice?

I crawled closer. Stared at Faulkner's body. It had to have

been the creature, teasing me through him. Making the sound of Megan's voice.

But still, my heart didn't want to believe that. "Megan?"

"Cooper, I'm down—"

That's enough, my dear Cooper. You know where she is now. If you want her, come and get her. We'll do a little trade.

If you're brave enough, that is.

I had seen what had happened to Faulkner. What if the same thing had been done to Megan, only multiplied one hundred times? Or worse?

What if she wasn't alive and the creature was doing a total head game?

Didn't matter. Megan might be down there, and I had to get her out.

I crawled back to Faulkner, feeling the ground. My fingers finally latched on to the blade I'd dropped when the creature had freaked me out, but once they closed around the hilt of the knife, I was ready.

I stopped beside my brother one more time. Hoping for something, anything. But he never moved. I had no time to allow my emotions in, to even think about whether Faulkner was dead or alive. Right now I had to concentrate on the one person I could save. Megan.

I dug the flashlight out of the backpack, slipped it onto

my wrist, then got the rope and tied it around a tree. I took a deep breath, climbed onto the edge of the well, and braced my feet on the inside. *"Hasta luego, amigo."*

I didn't think Faulkner heard me. But it made me feel better to say it.

And then I started down.

CHAPTER 26

The stench from the well swam over me, a massive "how you doin'" coming at me hard and heavy.

Shallow breaths. *Keep going. Don't think about it.*

One foot down. Two. Three.

I flicked the flashlight's switch and the yellow beam sprang to life. The laughter died down, dwindling off to nothing, echoing for a few seconds, then ebbing away. There were a few scuffles from below, and then . . .

Not a sound.

At first, all the light showed were the slime-coated stone walls of the well, the vines climbing up the sides like a green racetrack running to Faulkner. Then I swung the light to the bottom. Half wanting to see what was coming.

And half not.

But there was nothing below me. Nothing but the reflection of the beam in the water and the white glint of the piles of bones. I swallowed back the bile in my throat. I shook my head and looked away for a second. Those guys were dead. There was nothing I could do about them now. I had to get to Megan.

I started down again. *Move. Breathe. Concentrate. Deal with the rest later.*

"Megan?"

No answer.

"Megan, I'm on my way. I'm not leaving without you." I prayed she could hear me. That she was still alive. When I was done saving Megan and Faulkner, I was going to kill that thing. Twice, if that was possible.

My Vans slipped against the side of the well, but I held tightly to the rope. My wrist ached, and I knew I was going to pay later for the damage I was doing to it. Probably never be able to play baseball again. But I didn't care.

Two more feet. Three. Four. No sounds from below. That was no comfort to me. I'd rather have heard a Dora the Explorer CD stuck on the same track than nothing.

The quiet meant one thing.

The creature was somewhere waiting. Waiting for me to arrive.

And then the showdown would start. Like in those old cowboy movies. Like in *The Matrix.* Like in *Hamlet.* Good versus evil. Me and my knife, me versus it. Someone would walk out of here, and someone would stay at the bottom.

I slid down the rest of the way and hit the floor. Water splashed up, soaking me with the scent of the well. I moved to wipe the mud off my jeans, then stopped. What if the creature was like a dog and the more I smelled like him, the less he could sense me?

I swung the flashlight around, past the piles of bones. The walls were coated with a thick, white bubbly fungus that seemed to . . . breathe. Vines covered every inch of the walls, pulsing back and forth as if they were alive. Then, spattered here and there, darker splotches.

Dried blood.

I was sure as shit never going to watch another horror movie again. I had seen more in the past few days than Wes Craven could ever dream up.

I turned away, swinging the light around the small space. And this time I found what I thought had been there all along.

A tunnel.

Nothing sophisticated, and nothing made by human tools, I saw, when I got closer. The sides of the stones were rough, broken in some places. And then, along the edges, claw marks. The tunnel had been dug by hand. Stones yanked out, torn away by fingers, rubble piled beside it, deep ten-digit grooves cut into the walls.

God. What *was* this thing?

I shuddered and ducked down into the tunnel. It was only about four feet tall and two and a half, maybe three, feet wide, like a hobbit lived here, although I knew this was no happy Tolkien creature. The flashlight beamed off the walls. I had the knife raised and ready in an unsteady grip.

One step forward. Another. Deeper into the creature's lair, knowing that I was probably walking toward my own horrible fate. The sacrifice Gerard had written about. That my mother had been trying to push me toward. That I was pretty sure Sam was wrapped up in, too.

All around me, the walls pulsed as though they had their own heartbeat. The white stuff bubbled, and the vines seemed to watch.

The well was alive.

"Megan?" I whispered.

"Cooper!" Relief sang in her voice. "Thank God, thank God, thank God!"

"Where are you?" I swung the light around, up, and down, and at first all I saw were more stones, water, mud, vines. And then two familiar blue eyes.

She was in a prison made of vines, their green webs

locked together tightly and thickly. But she looked okay. Dirty and scared, but okay. "Megan." I started to move forward.

"Stop, Cooper. He'll get you!"

The entire New England Patriots defensive line couldn't have kept me from running to Megan. I didn't care if it was a trap; I didn't care if the entire army of vine men was there or if the creature was waiting with open jaws and open arms. I charged forward, my heart somewhere in my shoes.

Just as I reached her, just as I saw her blue eyes widen and her smile begin to take over her face, something came out of nowhere and tackled me, taking me to the ground. I lunged, hands extending toward Megan, calling for her. She screamed my name, but the word died in the air as I landed in a shallow puddle of filth, the knife falling from my hand for the second time that night. I let out a curse, tried to catch the knife—and missed.

"Welcome home, Cooper," the creature screeched, his breath hot on my neck, his body heavy on mine. "I have waited so long for you. So, so long."

I tried to squirm away, but he held tightly. He smelled like death, like that rotting-bodies farm, and I knew, I knew, if I didn't get away now, I never would.

I rolled hard to the right. The creature rolled with me, his claws digging into my back. I rolled to the left, then back to the right. "Get off me, you freak!"

"Oh, you think I am a freak, Cooper? You don't understand what I am or who I am. Or what *you* are." Then he pulled back, enough that I could flip over. And with me, my flashlight flipped, too.

Big mistake. Because now I saw what I was dealing with.

As they had the first time, the eyes hit me the hardest. Green eyes, just like mine. It was like looking at myself. But that was where the similarities to anything human ended.

Those eyes were sunk into skin as pale as a dead pig's, as loose as a sheet flapping in the wind. As rotted as a forgotten orange in the back of the refrigerator. The same white bubbling foam covered his skin, as if he was molding, rotting, right before my eyes. His face seemed to be melting off his bones—if there were even any bones left on his stick-thin frame. And when he opened his mouth to laugh, I could see inside the yawning cavernous hole that should have held teeth and held instead honed points, the jaw of a shark.

He wore no clothes, and his body was hunched, like an old, old man who'd spent a lifetime living in a wheelchair. But I knew that beneath the Jell-o squishiness he had Superman strength. I had felt his grip more than once, seen what he had done to that wall. Underestimating him would be a mistake.

He reached out a hand to me—skeletal fingers that seemed as long as yardsticks, with fingernails that flexed with his every movement. Almost as if they had a life of their own. And then I saw his fingernails weren't nails at all, but vines that grew and curled, hissing in the air as they extended his reach. "Oh, Cooper, I've waited a long time for you to come *home*." He brushed at my hair and I jerked back, trying to escape the touch, but I wasn't fast enough.

When his skin met mine, a jolt of electricity ran from my head to my chest. I leaped up as if I'd been defibrillated, and then slammed back down again, water splashing on the ground beneath me. "What the—"

"Ah, yes, just as I thought." He cackled, then smiled, the shark teeth gleaming yellow in the flashlight's beam. "You felt it, too?"

"Get away!" I tried to back up, but the tunnel was small, cramped.

"Don't fight it. When it's all over, you won't even remember . . ."

I scrambled to the left, pushing off with my feet, grabbing at the vines on the walls, anything I could, searching for the knife in the water as I did.

"Cooper!" Megan screamed. "Behind you!"

I spun back, and there in the water was the glint of silver. I dug down but missed the first time. The second. Refraction of water—I'd forgotten about that. I vowed to pay more attention in science next time. When Mr. Spinale had said that that crap could one day save my life, he hadn't been kidding.

This time I shifted to the right and came up with the blade. The wooden handle, made slimy by the filthy water, slipped in my grip, but I held on. Letting go would mean losing the battle—and becoming *it*.

And I wasn't in the mood for that.

I waved the knife at the creature, coming within a centimeter of what would have been his nose if he had had one. "Back up, freak!"

The monster didn't move. He leaned forward, his green eyes boring into mine. "You don't want to do that, Cooper."

"I did it once; I'll do it again." I sounded a lot more Clint Eastwood than I felt. Because when the creature was looking at me like that, I felt—

That connection again. Almost like the electricity when the thing had touched me, but not as strong. As if he knew me. As though he could read my mind.

A smile curved across his face, exposing those shark teeth again. The grin of something that would eat you and not think twice. The knife wavered in my hand. My legs began to shake.

Stab it. In the heart. Now.

"Of course I can read your thoughts," he said. "And you don't want to stab me, Cooper. Because doing that would kill a part of you, too. It would kill this land. Ruin all that we have worked so hard for. You're a part of this, Cooper. You don't want to do this. You, my dear boy, have already lost so much."

"Stop it!" I closed my eyes. "Get out of my head!"

"Think of something else," Megan yelled. "Don't think about what you're going to do. It can't—"

The creature sprung off his two legs like a jaguar, lunging for Megan. She shrieked and shrank back against the stone walls. The vines closed around her and the dirt below her opened up, covering her legs, tightening her prison. The earth began to pulse, as if waiting for another command.

I lashed out, sinking the knife into the monster's leg. The blade sank deep, as if I'd cut into cotton candy.

An earsplitting scream ripped through the tunnel. The creature spun toward me, green eyes now red with fury. "You don't know what you're doing, Cooper," he hissed. "What a terrible mistake you're making."

He dropped to all fours and advanced on me, breathing hard, lips peeled back in a snarl, those razor teeth ready.

I threw my pack onto the ground and flipped up the nylon flap. Reached in with my left hand and rooted for a rock. But before my hand could close around a stone, the creature was laughing.

"Sticks and stones will break my bones, but none of those will kill me." He inched forward, menacing, lethal, drool spilling from his lips. "I know what you're thinking, Cooper. I know everything about you."

I tried to do what Megan had said and think of something else. But what? I was a teenage boy, for God's sake. Deep thoughts didn't exactly come with the hormonal changes.

So I thought of Megan. The first time I had met her. Kindergarten, Miss Sarah's class.

Megan, in a ponytail and a pink dress she told me her mother made her wear for the first day, plopped down beside me. "Do you like basketball?"

I shrugged. "Yeah."

"Good. You can be my friend." She handed me a package of cheese and crackers. Shot me a smile. Got out her Crayolas. Started to color a picture of a huge basketball and two kids playing hoops. And probably stole my heart right then, though I was too stupid to know it.

Megan, ponytail, pink dress, box of Crayolas.

Over and over, I repeated the thought, until that was the only image I saw in my head. The creature hesitated, watching me. Slightly confused.

Megan, ponytail, pink dress, box of Crayolas.

Then I leaped forward, the knife fisted in my right hand, and drove the blade toward the creature. My body weight hung for one second in the air, then fell forward, propelling the force of the blade even further.

Megan, ponytail, pink dress, box of Crayolas.

The silver sheath sank deep into the creature's side, slipping beneath his skin before he saw it coming. As soon as the knife met his body, I twisted to the side, pulling the blade upward as I did.

The monster screamed, the sound like a thousand lambs being slaughtered at once, like every rabbit in the world dying under a guillotine. The piercing cry went on and on, echoing in the small tunnel, the pitch so high and so loud that I was sure my ears were bleeding.

Megan had her eyes closed, tears streaming down her face. "Make it stop, make it stop! Please, just kill it. Please, please!"

I yanked the knife back, and with it came a trail of gore and thick, pale, stringy guts. I tried to fling them off, but they stuck. The creature wheeled on me, his fingers and nails now no longer vines but dagger-shaped weapons.

He roared, betrayal and shock on what features he had. "Stop fighting me, Cooper. You *must* take my place. It's your destiny."

"No! My only destiny is to kill you." I kept thinking of

Megan and crayons and pink dresses, but I could feel him trying to pry his way into my mind. He suddenly jumped, his claws sinking into my shoulders.

I screamed. A pain worse than anything I'd ever felt shot through me. The creature began to laugh and locked his gaze with mine while he sank those claws even deeper.

"Now," he breathed, and I could smell death in what escaped from his mouth, "now I live again. You, my progeny, take my place and become one with this land." Something resembling a smile curved across his face. "My blood. Child of my loins. My *resurrection.*"

His fingers went deeper, pushing past bones and into my veins, and now the electricity between us began to pulse in time with my heartbeat. I could feel myself beginning to weaken, my knees buckling, the world going black. Around my feet, the dirt began to shift and rise, coating my feet, my ankles.

His words—what had he said? They had made no sense—faded away.

"Let go, Cooper," the creature whispered so very temptingly. "Let me *live.*"

The pulses beat harder, a steady drum pounding over my thoughts, making it hard to think of anything but sleeping . . . sleeping forever. Sleeping here, letting go, just letting go . . .

I began to let the knife slip from my fingers.

"Cooper! Don't!"

Like a lifeline, Megan's voice caught me just as I wanted to give up. If I surrendered, if I let this thing win—

She would die.

Megan . . .

Pink . . .

"Cooper! Please!" Megan again.

Dress . . .

My fingers curled around the knife again, one digit at a time.

Basketball . . .

Crackers . . .

The pulsing drumbeats zapped harder, faster. The creature's eyes bored into mine, green eyes so like my own. How could that be—how could they be the same?

"Cooper, fulfill your destiny. Be what you were made to be." The creature's body-farm breath was hot against my ear. "The chosen one."

Pink . . . red . . . green . . . blue . . . crayons . . .

Megan.

Never. Let. Go.

My last finger curled around the knife's hilt, and on the next electric pulse, I sucked in a breath and let it out with a scream and a thrust. "Never!"

The blade came up and sank into the creature's chest. His eyes popped wide with surprise and he gasped. I ripped the blade to the right, then the left, then up and down, in the shape of a cross. Creating one holy mess in his chest.

He fell back, staggered three steps, then crumpled to the ground. He twitched several times, then went still.

The vines on the wall scrambled like spiders, crawling backwards, down the walls like retreating soldiers, running toward the creature. They covered him, becoming a pile that looked like someone's fall yard cleanup.

Then . . . silence. Nothing in my head. Nothing in the well.

I limped over to Megan. "You all right?"

She nodded. "You?"

"I've been better." I bent down and cut the vines that bound her in place. These didn't grow back. They simply shriveled up and died.

The thing was dead.

It was over.

Or at least, that's what I thought.

CHAPTER 27

I have a surprise for you," Megan said.

"Megan, we've got to get out of here. I'm sure that thing is dead, but . . ." I glanced at the still, silent lump on the floor. Something nagged in my stomach, something that told me there was more to all of this, something I had missed.

"You want to see this. Believe me." She tugged me farther down the tunnel, into a space even narrower and lower than where we'd been before. The creature's words kept echoing in my head. "Progeny"? "Child of my loins"? Was it possible? I was *related* to that thing?

No way. No how. No blood. It was messing with my head, nothing more. We reached a door fashioned from an old wine cask.

I shook off the thoughts and followed Megan inside the

cramped little room. I heard her surprise before I saw it. And I nearly cried. I looked at Megan, then again at what was before me. "Is it . . . really him?"

She nodded. "The monster was keeping him as"—she swallowed—"bait. In case something happened to me. I heard him telling that to someone else."

I rushed forward and broke open the wooden bars that formed the cage holding my dog. Whipple bounded into my arms, thinner, dirtier, but as overjoyed to see me as I was to see him. He licked my head, my neck, my arms, anything he could reach, his tail wagging so fast that I thought it might pop off. I held him to my chest and stroked his head. "My mother said he was dead."

"I don't know, Cooper. He was here when . . . when that thing brought me down here." She wrapped her arms around herself and shivered.

"Let's go," I said, drawing her against me with one arm. "We've been down here long enough. All of us."

Megan nodded, then brushed away her tears. "Thank you."

"For what?"

"For coming to get me."

"I'm sorry it took so long." I held her tightly and wasn't sure I could ever let her go again. "Seems I'm always late picking you up."

Megan laughed. And it was the best sound I'd ever heard.

It took us nearly an hour to get out of the well. My shoulders were shot, and Megan was weak from spending two days down there, with nothing more to eat than a granola bar she'd had in her pocket. She'd refused the creature's offer of the special grapes. Thank God.

When I finally climbed over the edge, I expected to find Faulkner's body exactly where I'd left it. He was gone. Who had taken him? My mother? Sam?

The creature might be dead, but danger possibly still lurked out there. I stood up and scanned the woods. The sun was just beginning to rise, casting everything in shades of pink. Even Megan. "Don't move," she said.

"We have to—"

She took her bandanna off my wrist and wrapped it tightly around the worst of my cuts. "Take care of you before we do anything else," she said, finishing my sentence. She gave me a light kiss on the cheek and a tender brush against the scrapes running along my arm, her face full of concern.

The vine army was gone. The woods were back to being normal woods. Maybe I'd imagined that feeling back in the well, that feeling that something was undone. The thing was dead, and Faulkner had come out of whatever coma he'd been in and had gone home. That was what I told myself, anyway.

"You sure you're all right?" Megan asked.

"Yeah, fine." I was beat up, cut to hell, and in need of a truckload of aspirin, but I had Megan back, she was safe, and that was enough. "Totally fine."

"Okay," she said. And smiled.

Megan's mother came screaming out the door when we walked up the front walk of her house. Megan made up something about getting lost in the woods, hitting her head, falling down the well, and being knocked out, and I chimed in with a little fiction about finding her. Mrs. Garrett barely heard a word we said because she was bawling so hard and hugging Megan so tightly.

We both left out the part about the homicidal creature. Megan and I figured Mrs. Garrett didn't need that in her perfect little Betty Crocker world.

"Hey, I almost forgot." Megan smiled. "Happy birthday."

"Oh, yeah." I had really done it, hadn't I? The big day had arrived, and I had killed the creature before he had taken me.

A shiver chased up my spine. I shrugged it off. I didn't have anything to worry about anymore.

Megan gave me a kiss, then drew back, her eyes dancing, the rising sun casting sparkles over her face. "See you later, Cooper."

All I could do was nod. Because my brain was completely fried after that kiss.

CHAPTER 28

I was tired. I was hungry. And all I wanted to do was go to bed, wake up, and find Faulkner at the kitchen table, throwing Cheerios at my head.

But Sam was still out there, and so was my mother. And I didn't know whether the creature's death would end everything—

Or just ramp up the game.

The farther I got from Megan's house and the closer I got to Sam's McMansion, the more uneasy I felt. As if I were on the edge of something more.

I kept telling myself to relax. There was no laughter in the air, no crazy vines springing up around me. No voices in my head. Everything was back to plain old Maple Valley.

People were walking their dogs and paperboys were delivering newspapers. All of it as ordinary as vanilla ice cream.

Faulkner was probably home in bed, snoring away, while I was stressing over nothing. Except that nothing found me slowing up as I walked home, not quite anxious to get back.

I found my father parked across the street from Sam's house. He had his hands on the steering wheel, looking as if he was trying to make a hard decision. I knocked on the window and he jumped, then opened the door and got out. "Cooper! Oh, thank God. Where have you been?" He hugged me tightly, then drew back, looking me over. "What have you been doing? You're filthy."

I let out a long sigh. "You don't want to know, Dad."

He put a hand on my shoulder and leaned down until his eyes met mine. "Yeah, Cooper, I do."

For the first time maybe ever, I got the feeling that my father was there. Really there. Ready to listen to me. Not to what I had to say about *Hamlet*. Or my English essay. But to what was going on in my life. And right now, I was so tired and so lost.

What if this wasn't over after all?

What I needed right now, more than anything, was an ally. A grownup on my side. Somebody to tell me what to do. To help me make sense of it all.

Somebody to tell me it would all be okay.

Most of all, I needed my father. Maybe I'd always needed him, but I hadn't known that until now. "It's complicated, Dad."

"That's all right, Cooper. I have time."

So we got into his car and I told him. I started at the beginning, and I kept going until I got to dropping Megan off at her house. My father didn't say a word until I stopped. I stared at the worn gray carpet of his Toyota. "That's it," I said. "I don't know where Faulkner is or if he's okay."

"He's all right. He's at my house."

I spun in my seat. Whipple, who had curled into a ball in my lap and gone to sleep, lifted his head, dropped it down again. Relief exploded in me. Faulkner was okay. He hadn't died. If my brother had been with us then, I would have hugged him, whether he liked it or not. "He is? How'd he get there?"

"Your mother brought him over early this morning. Asked me to keep him at my house for a while."

"Whoa. Back the truck up. You *talked* to her? You *saw* her?"

He nodded. "She's at my house now. She told me a lot of the same things you just did. Let me tell you, that was a lot to swallow. This is the woman I was married to for eighteen years. And she's telling me she thinks she tried to kill my child?" My father gripped the steering wheel. "It didn't go over well, but when she explained how it happened, I began to understand."

"What? You *understood?* That she *thinks* she did this?" I wanted to shake him. To scream at him, to get him to wake up and smell the truth in his life. His ex-wife was a homicidal maniac. "Dad, she did try to kill me. I was there."

"I know, Cooper. But that wasn't her. It was something acting inside her."

I let out a gust. I knew deep down it was true, but it still annoyed me that my father was defending my mother's murderous actions. I reached for the door handle, but my father stopped me.

"Cooper, listen to me. I know things between us haven't been that great, and I know I haven't been there for you like I should have. But this time, this moment, you have to listen to me."

I stopped, but I didn't let go of the door handle.

"Your mother loves you."

I shook my head. I wanted to believe that, but I'd seen different.

"That wasn't her acting like that. She's fighting whatever is inside her. You have to believe me. She wants to talk to you, so she can explain."

I snorted. "I don't want her to find me."

My father grabbed my arm. "Your mother loves you," he repeated.

I stared at the street until it blurred in front of me. "No, she doesn't."

"She does." My father kept holding on. "Come on, Cooper, you know your mother. Think back—think of all the times we've had together. The camping trips. The vacations. The game nights. That's not her acting like that. There's something else . . . something controlling her. I think it's him."

"The thing. This place. This land. It's cursed or something." The same thing that had controlled Gerard, that had whispered in his ear and had made him throw his own brother down that well.

"No." My father paused, and when he spoke again, his voice was filled with a hatred I had never heard before. *"Him."*

"Sam?" There was only one other person who would want me in that well. Whose self-interests would be served by having me become the next creature.

My father nodded slowly. Once. I got the feeling that if Sam had been there right then, my professor father might have strangled him. For ruining his marriage. For ruining his life. For ruining his family. And most of all, for trying to kill his youngest son. "This is all my fault."

"Dad, you didn't do anything."

"That's the problem. I saw this coming. Let it happen." He ran a hand through his hair. "Well, I didn't see *this,* exactly, but I saw Sam was up to no good. Your mother . . . she just wanted to leave me so badly, and I didn't want to upset her. I never wanted her to be . . ."

"Unhappy."

He looked at me and let out a sigh that sounded as if it weighed more than the whole car. "Yeah."

"That's the trouble, Dad. You never throw any rocks. Break a few windows. Get mad. *Fight.* It might do you some good."

It might have done us all some good. Might have headed this off. Kept Sam from invading our lives like a cancer.

"I tried, you know," he said. "After she first left, I was here every morning for a month."

"Here?"

"When you were at school and Sam was at work, I was here, talking to your mother. I nearly got fired because I missed so much school. I kept thinking if I argued with her enough, she'd see the light and come back, but every time I talked to her, she was . . ." He raised his hands in defeat.

"Like a cult member."

"Exactly." My father shook his head. "I don't know what it is about him. He has this . . . power over her."

"It was the wine," I said. "He gave it to her all the time,

and after she drank it, she got all weird." With Gerard, it had been the grapes, but with my mother, the wine. A special wine made from special grapes.

The monster's crop.

Wine was stronger than grapes, wasn't it? Fermented, concentrated. Maybe that's why Sam had used it. Because a mother's bond was so much harder to break.

"That makes sense," my father said. "He gave her some, you know, when she was a patient of his. Back when she first saw him, just before she got pregnant with you. Some new-patient gift or something. She drank a little of it and acted really oddly. The reaction didn't last long, but it was enough to really worry me. I dumped the wine down the drain. We had a huge fight. Your mother and I, we hardly ever fought. Every once in a while, Sam would contact her—a card, a phone call from his office—trying to get her to come back as a patient, but she never responded."

He'd been trying all that time to get her back under his thumb. But without her drinking the wine, it had been impossible.

"One day, she went back to his office for a checkup. I don't know why."

I thought back. To the weeks before this had begun. "He sent her a bottle," I recalled. "With some flowers. I was home when the delivery guy came to the door."

"I didn't know. The day I saw another bottle of that wine was"—my father looked out the window—"the day she left me for him."

Then this whole nightmare had begun. I guess I'd always been the chosen one and Sam had always known. It wasn't as if he picked me when I became an adolescent. Almost two years ago, Sam had started working on her, probably figuring he needed the extra time to keep it from being suspicious when I disappeared. If he had married my mother in September, and I disappeared a month later, the cops would have been all over him. But give him eighteen months of history with a troubled, ungrateful stepson, and he had a perfect setup for a teenage-runaway scenario. *Gee, Officer, I don't know what happened to that Cooper. We tried so hard to make him happy, and then one day, poof—he takes off.*

"Where is he now?" I asked.

"The police station. Mike's dad picked him up for questioning."

"Questioning? For what?"

"When your mother brought Faulkner to my house, she told me her story and her concerns about Sam. She also brought along something she found in the house that scared her."

It took only a second to connect the dots. The sickening

images of the night before came hurtling back. "The bloody blanket and scrubs."

My father nodded. "I don't know what he's doing, Cooper. And I don't think I want to know."

I didn't say anything. There were just some things I decided to keep to myself. My father didn't need that extra sucker punch of truth.

"I want you to come stay with me," my father said.

"I'll be . . ." I was going to say *fine,* then decided my father was right. "Let me grab some stuff and come over later. I want to see Megan again first."

My father shook his head. "I don't feel comfortable leaving you here."

"I'm not staying, Dad. Seriously, I'm stuffing a few clothes into a backpack and then booking it for Megan's."

"I'll wait, give you a ride."

I laid a hand on his arm. "Take the dog and go home to Faulkner. Make sure he's okay. I'll be fine. That thing is dead. There's nothing to worry about anymore. You said yourself that Sam is at the police station."

My father weighed that for a moment, then let out a sigh. "You're determined, aren't you?"

"Just . . . stronger today than I was before."

"All right. But if you're not at my house in an hour, I'm sending out the SWAT team."

I laughed for the first time in what felt like forever, then hugged my father. "It'll be cool. Promise."

He held me tightly, tighter than he ever had before. "I'm so glad you're safe, Faulkner's safe, and Megan's home. Now that Sam's probably going to be in custody and your mother's back to being Mom again, I think everything's going to be just fine."

"Thanks, Dad." Still, even as he hugged me . . .

I wondered. Was it safe, or did I just want to believe that? Either way, I put on a brave face when my father drew back and reassured him for the thousandth time that I'd be okay and would be at his house before he knew it.

I got out of the car. Whipple followed me, refusing to stay behind. "All right, boy, let's go," I said to him. "Last stop on the train back to normal."

Turns out I was wrong about more than one thing that day.

CHAPTER 29

A birthday cake sat on the countertop. My name had been scrawled across the top in dark red icing. That was the first sign that something was wrong.

With all the excitement of last night and this morning, my mother couldn't possibly have had time to bake me a cake for my birthday.

But someone had.

Dread curled a vise grip around my senses. I backed up, away from the cake, away from the blood-red *Cooper* written on it.

"Going somewhere?"

I spun around. Sam leaned against the doorway, as casual as a golfer waiting for a caddy. "I thought you were at the police station," I said.

"Did you learn nothing from your little stay down

there?" He pushed off from the wall and took two steps toward me. "Hire a good lawyer and they can't hold you for long."

I took a step back. At my feet, Whipple began to growl at Sam. "I'm staying at my dad's tonight."

Sam smiled, a smile that held no warmth. "Why? It's your birthday. You need to be here. With your real family."

A chill ran through the room and me. I had to get out of there. If I could distract Sam, maybe I could get out the door.

I glanced around the kitchen, looking for something, anything, that would buy me enough time to make a run for it.

Only one thing sat on the counter. I darted to the right, grabbed the cake, and threw it at Sam. The frosting exploded across his face and chest, coating him with white, then red, making him look like a clown in a really bad accident. He roared with anger, but I was already gone.

Whipple kept pace beside me as I charged down the steps of the deck and onto the lawn. It was twenty yards, maybe a little less, to the driveway and then another fifty yards to the nearest neighbor. I was younger than Sam, faster. I could outrun him.

Then I heard him outside, calling first my name, then

screaming words I didn't recognize. Speaking that same ancient, guttural language the stick man had used.

I kept running.

Then the earth shifted beneath my feet, Sam's perfectly manicured lawn pushing up in a growing hill, then opening in a yawning hole, the grass tearing into pieces on either side of my feet. I tried to jump over the crevice, but the earth grew up and out, expanding like hands that reached for my feet, my legs.

The grass fists came down on me, taking me to the ground like two cornerbacks. Whipple yelped and leaped to the side. I clawed at the edge, pushing with my feet, digging and moving, refusing to let them drag me down.

I could hear Sam running, his feet pounding against the ground. In seconds, he'd be here. And then what would happen?

Push. Now.

The grass was rising again, growing, the blades reaching for my ears, my eyes, my mouth.

With a scream, I shoved as hard as I could and broke the first of the two earthy holds on me. No time to pause, to think; I shoved again, and the second gave way. I scrambled to my feet and began to run again, brushing off still-clinging clumps of grass, their roots curling around my skin.

Sam let out another furious shout, then more of those odd words. I ducked to the left, the right, then left again, a receiver with a football dodging the opposing team, trying to think ahead of him, ahead of whatever creepy nature thing he had working for him.

The yard opened up one hole after another, grassy hands springing up, reaching for me, their green fingers coming so close that I could feel the whisper of their touch against my ankles and my calves. My chest burned, but I kept running.

I veered toward the driveway. Sam shouted another order. Suddenly, the lawn split apart, an earthquake driving a wedge right down the side. The ground shivered, and my steps faltered.

The lawn rolled up on one side, a huge wave of grass, then started toward me. There was no way I was going to make it to the driveway.

Maybe no way I was going to make it out of here at all.

I turned and ran in the only other direction left.

Toward the woods.

CHAPTER 30

Cooper . . . oh, Cooper."

Sam called my name like a mother coaxing back a runaway preschooler. I ducked lower behind the massive oak tree and tried to catch my breath without making any noise. Just a few minutes, that was all I needed, and I'd be ready to run again.

"Don't make me call on them," Sam said. "Don't make this difficult."

Call on whom? The vine men? I wasn't worried about them. I'd dug the lighter out of my backpack and had it in my hand. The knife in the opposite hand. I figured I was ready for whatever Sam was going to do.

Leaves crunched. He was close, maybe only two feet away. I slid down more. Held my breath.

"Don't say I didn't warn you," he said. Then he spoke again in that language, releasing a few short words.

For a long second, nothing happened, and I thought I was in the clear. Then the trees began to move.

They lifted up out of the ground with earsplitting crunching noises. Their roots became legs, branches became arms, and tops swung down to become heads that seemed to be scanning the woods.

Looking for me.

The oak in front of me jerked up and I scrambled back, only to find myself hitting the legs of another tree. Whipple barked, and Sam—

Sam laughed.

He called out another command. The trees turned as one and began to move toward me. Whipple went crazy, barking and circling, then took off running in the woods. I tried to run before the trees could reach me.

But I was battling impossible odds. Before I could move, the earth opened up again and began to swallow me, dragging me down, down, down, sucking me into the dirt like quicksand. Was this what had happened to Gerard and Auguste's mom? I dropped the lighter and knife, trying to fight against the dirt vacuum. I opened my mouth to scream, and a stream of dirt squirted upward, like a backwards waterfall, toward my face.

I shut my mouth, and dirt smacked against my closed lips. But it didn't give up, the brown granules building a snaking path up toward my ears, my nose—

I was going to die.

The dark, heavy blanket sucked me down, squeezing my chest so I couldn't drag in another breath. Panic engulfed me, but I couldn't move, couldn't battle the giant sucking hole filling in around me as fast as it opened up. It was up to my chest, neck, chin, then under my nose. I closed my eyes.

Sam, you win.

Just as I was about to go under, I heard a muffled scream, something that sounded like my name. I wanted to say it was too late, to let me go, but I couldn't. The dirt had walled my mouth shut.

Something charged past my head, then touched my shoulder. It latched on and began to pull. A hand, someone trying to . . .

Save me?

Survival instinct kicked in. My feet began to work, pushing against the dirt still trying hard to suck me in. I clawed with my fingers and at first felt as if I were going nowhere, and then my chin was free, my neck, my chest, my arm.

"Take my hand."

I twisted and reached. And latched on to my mother.

"Hurry," she said, her eyes wide with fear.

"How . . . ?"

She shook her head, placing a finger against her lips.

I nodded and crawled out of the hole with her help. I'd lost the lighter and knife, but it was a small price to pay for being alive.

She reached out and placed a hand on either side of my face, as if making sure I was okay. I hesitated, but then I saw she was Mom again, no craziness in her face, and I decided right then I'd trust her. She'd saved my life when she had had every opportunity to let me die.

"I called the police station," she panted. "When I heard Sam had been released I realized what he might do . . ."

She drew me in for a quick, tight hug and a kiss on my head. I swore just before she pulled away that I felt a tear drop onto my neck.

"Where is Sam?" I asked nervously.

"Sam went to get *him*," my mother whispered. "We need to run. Can you do that?"

The trees were closed in tightly, like a fence of forest. They stood still, watching, observing, maybe waiting for Sam to return and issue new orders. I could see gaps between their trunks, wide enough for us to sneak through.

"Yeah."

We squeezed through a small gap between an oak and a

maple but got only a few steps before Sam came crashing through the forest. "Where do you think you two are going?"

"Sam, leave him alone," my mother said. "Let him go."

"No can do. He was bred for this. Thanks to you, *Mom*." Sam barked out another series of orders, and we were ripped by the trees from where we stood, swung from tree to tree like rag dolls to our final destination.

The only one Sam had ever intended.

The well.

My mother and I landed in two crumpled heaps on the ground. I got to my feet, aching, hurt, but with nothing broken. My mother didn't move. Whipple came charging through the woods and nosed at her, whimpering.

"Mom?"

"She's served her purpose, Cooper. Let her go." Sam strode up to the well, grinning like he'd won the lottery, his blond hair touched by the sun behind him.

"Do something! Help her!"

"I don't need her anymore. She was the incubator for you, and now she'll let me keep my hands clean. The mother killing her own son." He laughed. "No one would ever believe the truth about what really happened to dear Cooper."

My mother moaned, and Whipple nudged her. But still she didn't get up. I wanted to go to her, to help her, but Sam reached into his jacket pocket and pulled out a switchblade. In one deft move, he depressed the button and released the blade. It gleamed in the light, evil. Menacing.

Sam took a step closer. With a noisy, shuddering crunch, the trees closed ranks, sealing off my escape. "In life, Cooper," Sam said, "we all need to make sacrifices for a higher purpose. And you, you need to sacrifice yourself so the rest of us can continue to live. We'll have a wonderful life, and so will so many more generations of Jumels. Then, in two hundred years, you'll have your turn."

I backed up, but there was nowhere to go, nowhere but into the well.

"Today is a very special day, Cooper. Today is your—" He waved his hand, meaning for me to finish the sentence.

"Birthday." I knew that, but the creature was dead. What did it matter anymore? Didn't Sam know what I'd done?

"And someone else's birthday, too." He grinned, and it sent a chill down my spine. "Not to mention, today is also the anniversary of Auguste's sacrifice. And the day he finally returns to the living."

"I killed Auguste, Sam," I said. "It's over."

Sam shook his head. "Oh, he's not dead. There's still time. As long as he has your blood before the sun goes down, the destiny can be fulfilled. All it takes to continue his legacy"—Sam advanced on me—"is for the chosen one to take his place before sundown. Go ahead, Cooper. As you can see, he's been waiting a long, long time for you." Sam pointed over my shoulder with the blade. And smiled the kind of reverent smile you gave the pope.

I turned. The monster hung over the edge of the well, his thin frame barely clinging to the stones. His skin draped off his body like loose wallpaper and his mouth hung open, slack like a thirsty dog's. A thick red gash ran down his chest, exposing the wide, yawning pus-filled hole opened by my knife the previous night. Vines cradled him in place, massive webbing keeping him upright.

He hadn't died.

He was still here.

Waiting.

For me.

I tried to step back, but branches poked into my back, shoving me forward, closer. The ground beneath my feet undulated, an ocean of dirt forcing my feet to stumble another step closer. Another.

The creature smiled, but it was a weak grin. One that said he wasn't doing so well. Those same eyes as before looked back at me, but the spark inside them had dimmed a little. In the light of day, the creature seemed ten times worse—

paler, deader. Or maybe that was only because I had wounded him so badly the night before. I hoped, at least, that was why.

Whipple circled the well, barking and yelping. My mother still lay off to the side, but I could see her stir.

"Cooper, meet your father, Auguste." Sam crossed to the creature, getting almost close enough to touch him. But not quite. Was Sam scared of the monster, too?

Wait. *Father? Had he said 'father'?* What the hell?

"This thing here, this creature," Sam went on, "has lived in this cesspool all these years so that we could live like kings. I know he's a hideous, pitiful thing to look at, but he has power. Power you can only imagine."

I shook my head, tried again to back away from this horror. From the truth I still didn't want to face. "I'm *not* related to him."

"Oh but you are," Sam said, beaming with pride, and my stomach turned over. "It's a great honor, Cooper. A great, great honor."

Maybe in Sam's sick mind. "But . . . why *me?*" I started to realize that this time, there was no way out.

I was going down there. To stay.

"Because you were made for this," Sam said, as if he were explaining to a toddler that babies came from the stork. "I had to have a blood descendant, one of Auguste's, because that's what the land demands. An heir to the creature in the well every two hundred years. It's the price we pay, and the land gives back." He looked over his shoulder at the well almost reverently.

"You go down there, then," I said. "You're a Jumel. You're so set on this." I looked behind me, but the ground and trees kept up their wall.

"You couldn't pay me enough to do that." Sam chuckled. "Besides, the power is strongest from Auguste's own progeny. I, unfortunately, am descended from Gerard. But you, my dear Cooper, come straight from Auguste."

If this wasn't so horrifying, I would have laughed. But I didn't. What the monster had said to me in the well—"child of my loins"—had been true. Auguste raised his head and smiled. "Cooper," he whispered, his voice cracking into almost nothing. Breath wheezed in and out of the pus-filled cavity in his chest. "Dear Cooper."

"I had to find a carrier for his seed," Sam went on, ignoring the labored breathing of the creature. "I tried so many women, and they all failed me. Lost the babies, those idiots. Then your mother came in one day. A little wine to help her relax—a bonus of coming to my practice, I told her—and presto, she's asleep. That was my chance to impregnate her with Auguste's children."

I needed you, Cooper. Needed you to set me free. And now

when you take my place, I live again as a man. My seed . . . for
the return of my life.

The creature had gone back to talking in my head. I knew it was because he was weaker, having been wounded by me. But that didn't stop the horror of his words. "I don't understand. How is that thing still alive? After two hundred years?"

Sam grinned. "You are what you eat, Cooper." And then he laughed, a laugh that almost made me puke. "Or maybe it's 'you eat what you are.'"

Repugnance shot through me as I realized what the creature had been eating for centuries. I thought of Sam's specialty when it came to delivering babies. *Twins.*

"Twins." I would have ralphed, but the trees had crowded in even farther, pressing me within touching distance of the creature.

"They aren't so easy to get, you know," Sam said, still keeping his distance from the creature. He gave it a wary glance every now and then. "But when you work my job, sometimes . . . accidents happen."

The bundle. The bloody blanket. "B-b-babies? More than just the one last night?"

Sam shrugged. "Not too many, Cooper. Just enough to keep Auguste alive until you turned fifteen. It's a magical age, don't you think?"

He was raving. A lunatic. I didn't think he expected an answer.

"Of course, *your* twin was vital to his existence. *Your* twin gave him the strength to survive the past fifteen years, gave him the knowledge and proof that his sentence was almost finished. It was perhaps his most important feeding. And now here we are; you're finally fifteen. In other cultures, fifteen is the age for change. For girls in Spain, it's their *quinceañera*. In the Baha'i faith, it's the year a boy becomes a man. In Japan, they have a *genpuku* ceremony for teenage boys." He tipped the knife under my chin. "But here, dear Cooper, we have a ceremony of a different sort."

"You're insane. I'm not going down there."

You will, the creature whispered. *It is your destiny.*

Sam chuckled. "It's October tenth. Two hundred years since Auguste was sent into this hell on the special and sacred ground that has fed his existence. Poor you will have to wait two hundred years for your turn to live again."

The creature reared up on the edge of the well, throwing forward what seemed like a last-ditch effort of energy, his eyes glittering. "Stop talking...and...do it now! *Give him to me!*"

Sam spun toward the monster. "Shut up, old man. I'll do what I want."

"You . . . work . . . for . . . me," the creature rasped. "I . . . am . . . your—"

"You're my meal ticket, and that means you don't need to talk," Sam said. "So shut your mouth, you stupid beast."

"Watch . . . how . . . you . . . talk to me."

Sam leaned toward Auguste. "I can talk any way I want to you. I don't even need you anymore, you hideous troll." He reached out and grabbed me by the shirt. "Cooper is the future of this vineyard, not you. As long as he's in that well, Jumel lives on. And you can just *die*."

In the creature's eyes, I saw hatred. Not for me. But for Sam.

Sam ignored it all and instead closed the gap between me and him. "You will be sacrificed today, Cooper. There's no escape. Consider yourself . . . a business expense. Just like Paolo and those babies." He laughed, then thrust me against the well. I tried to twist away, but Auguste grabbed my arms from behind. The vines twined around him and me, knitting his grip tighter. He pulled me back, exposing my neck to Sam's blade.

"Give up the fight, Cooper. Accept your destiny," the creature whispered, well water dripping from his mouth and puddling on my neck, the stench emanating off him in waves. His claws dug into my shoulders again, opening old wounds. Blood burst from my cuts like grapes being popped open.

I struggled but got nowhere. My dog bit Sam's ankles, but Sam kicked him in the head. The dog cried out. Fury blinded me. "Leave him alone!"

Sam swung the knife across. I jerked to the left, but it wasn't enough and the knife nicked my throat. Pain raced through my body and I screamed.

Auguste's web closed around my throat, cut off my breath. The world began to go black. "Stay still," the creature whispered, "and the change will be almost painless."

He lowered his head to my neck, and the vines danced up my skin, slithering along my arm, my throat, my cheek—

Just then, a burst of orange erupted around us. Flames? I couldn't tell. I heard the trees crunch and stomp, moving away. Whipple started barking. The screaming doubled. Was that me? The creature? Whipple?

"Don't stop!" Sam ordered the creature. He raised his arms back, palms out, ready to shove me down there. I tried to turn to the right to get away, but the creature's grip tightened even more and he let out a gasp, as if he was pouring every last ounce of strength into the effort to hold on to me and drag me down with him. No escape, no way out.

I saw Sam's hands coming toward me and braced myself. I closed my eyes and thought of Megan.

Ponytail.

Pink dress.

Box of Crayolas.

Blue eyes.

Her smile.

"Cooper! Run!"

I opened my eyes, and there was—

My mother. Holding the lighter I'd dropped earlier in one hand and a thick sheaf of branches in the other, the leaves aflame. She used the homemade torch to hit the trees, forcing them back. It was enough to clear a hole and let her in. Then she lunged at the monster, flames first.

Fire licked at the creature's body and he cried out, loosening his grip. At the same time, Whipple leaped onto Auguste, biting one of his arms. Auguste went to smack the dog, which gave me just enough time to jerk away from the creature.

Sam wheeled toward my mother and raised the switchblade. He screamed his hatred with a burst of expletives.

He was going to kill her.

I dove for Sam's knees, trying to tackle him as I'd tackled a dozen sophomores and juniors in football, knowing if I hit him hard and low, I'd take him down. When I plowed into him, Sam teetered backwards, staggering several steps.

But he wasn't a high schooler. He was an adult. A very angry, very determined adult, who recovered his balance and started toward my mother again. I was still on the ground, too many seconds from another tackle.

I kicked out, sending the closest thing I saw sailing under Sam's feet. He stumbled, then began to go down, tripping and falling—

Right over the skull I had left there a few days before. Way to go, Paolo.

Sam, with his arms pinwheeling, turned, reaching for someone, something to help him, but there was no one there. No one who cared. "Auguste! Grab me, you idiot!"

"I don't need *you* anymore, *you hideous troll*," the creature said, then reached for Sam and yanked him onto the edge of the well.

Sam's eyes widened in surprise, then anger. "If I die, you die!" He grabbed Auguste around the neck and plunged the knife into the creature's heart. The two of them hung there for a moment on the edge of the well, caught in the vines' hold. The creature clawed at Sam and Sam stabbed him back, each of them roaring in fury and agony, before the vines finally gave way and they both disappeared, falling down, down, down, into the inky darkness of the well.

Silence. And then the call of a bird. The flutter of wings, the scuffle of squirrels in the trees. The world slowly coming back to life in the forest.

I looked around. The trees had gone back to their places, the disruptions in the earth looking like freshly turned soil. A few branches and leaves smoldered in piles here and there, quickly becoming ashes. My mother stood beside me, breathing hard. "Are you okay, Mom?"

"Yeah. Are you?"

I nodded.

She drew me to her side and breathed in the scent of my hair, placing a soft kiss on my forehead. "I love you, Cooper," she said, her voice the one I knew, the one I remembered. "And I'm so, so sorry. For everything."

I leaned into her. This was my mom. *Really* my mom. Whipple came up beside us and pressed his body to our legs, giving his seal of approval. "I love you, too, Mom. And it's okay. It's all okay."

We stood like that for a long moment. I think one of us cried.

"Do you think that thing is gone?" my mother asked.

I took the torch she'd fashioned out of branches, feeling a hundred times more grown up than I had two weeks ago. "Let's make sure it is." I walked over to the well, lighting all the champagne-colored grapes that grew along the perimeter, then firing up the vines crawling over the edge, letting the flames carry down and into the dark depths. Then together we grabbed a second branch, lit it afire, and threw it down, watching its path. We saw the flames flicker, then go out. And we heard . . .

Nothing.

No laughing. No scratching. No movement.

Then we laid the torch to more dry autumn leaves. Just as they began to catch and turn the woods to bright orange, my mother took my hand and together, with Whipple trailing behind us, we ran home.

It was over.

CHAPTER 31

Mr. Ring." My father let out a sigh. "Tell me you have something intelligent to say."

Mike grinned. "I can tell you that, but it doesn't mean it's true, Mr. Warner."

My father rolled his eyes and went back to the chalkboard. He started writing, causing a mini snowstorm to start falling onto his shoes. "Don't forget your final papers for *Hamlet* are due tomorrow—"

Collective groan.

"And since you all loved *Hamlet* so much, I thought we'd do another Shakespearean classic for our next selection." He wrote seven letters on the board in his precise script. *"Macbeth."* Then he turned back to us and beamed, as if he'd announced we'd be reading comic books.

"Dude!" Joey said, elbowing me. "Will you talk to your

father? Get him some happy pills or something? The guy is torturing us."

I smiled. "Joey, you don't know my dad that well. He *is* happy right now. He could be a walking ad for sunshine." Lately my father had been singing in the shower, cooking pancakes in the morning, smiling on the way to school. And all because my mother was back home. Things were back to normal, which meant Faulkner barely talked to me, my parents read the paper together every night, and we all lived in the house near the playground and down the street from Megan.

It was as if the past two years had been erased. Almost, anyway. When I went to sleep at night, I could swear I still heard laughter and my name being called, but those were nightmares, and what was happening during the day was just too perfect to worry about a few leftover bad dreams.

Joey shook his head. "You are so weird lately. What has gotten into you?"

"Nothing." I traced the outline of "Ken Luvs Lisa 4-Eva" on my desk with my fingernail. They still loved each other, and that meant the world was still all right. I tugged a pencil out of my backpack, and beneath Ken's permanent declaration, I leaded one of my own.

Cooper Luvs Megan.
Forever.

"Mr. Warner?"

I popped my head up. "Yeah?"

"Do you have anything meaningful to add to this conversation?" my father asked.

I thought for a second. "Does *Macbeth* end better than *Hamlet*? I'd like to see the good guy live in this one."

My father grinned. "You have a point." He turned back to the chalkboard and swiped away the seven letters. "Let's rethink that choice, shall we?"

My eyes met my father's. He might not be my dad by blood, but heck, when had that ever counted? Where it mattered was where it mattered. In my head, in my heart. "Yeah, Dad. Let's do that."

Joey slapped me on the back, called me a hero.

He had no idea.

After class, Megan caught up to me. She slipped her hand into mine. Her touch felt right, perfect. I squeezed her hand and gave her a smile.

"Hey," she said.

"Hey." I grinned. Like an idiot. But come on, I was still a high school freshman. I hadn't exactly grown a lot of new brain cells overnight. "Megan, I need to ask you something."

She paused midstep. The red bandanna was in her hair today, and I was half tempted to reach out and touch it. "What?"

I paused. Ever since that day last week when we'd climbed out of the well, our relationship had been in a holding pattern. We'd been together—but not officially dating, as if neither of us wanted to disturb the status quo. I had avoided asking her out again because I wasn't so sure she wanted to date a guy who was related to a creature that ate people.

I mean, that's not the kind of thing you put on the family tree.

But if there was one thing the past couple of weeks had taught me, it was that life was too short and too weird to spend it not taking risks.

"Do you . . ." I paused. "Do you . . ."

She grinned and parked a fist on her hip. "Don't tell me, Cooper Warner, that you're afraid to ask me out after all you've gone through?"

"Of course I'm not afraid." But I hesitated again. Would she really want me after all this? Want to kiss me? Want to be with me?

"Well?" She arched a brow. The crowds of Maple Valley High kept moving around us in a wave. Faulkner came up behind me and bounced off my back.

On purpose. In the way only an obnoxious older brother could. *"Por favor, hermano,"* he said, then looped an arm around Shelley.

"Hey!" I said to him.

He grinned. "Check your pocket, dude. *Su padre le dio un regalo.*"

Him and the Spanish again. I was about to deport him. "What?"

He rolled his eyes. "Dad gave you a gift. Said if you flunk your *Hamlet* paper, he's taking it back. Told me to tell you that you, of all people in his class, should get Hamlet." Then he tugged Shelley closer and whispered something in her ear. She giggled and leaned into him before the two of them headed down the hall.

I dug in my back pocket, where Faulkner had reverse pickpocketed me, and pulled out a shiny new cell phone. A grin spread across my face so wide, I thought it might explode. "I never thought I'd say this, but my father is cool."

Megan smiled. "He's always been cool. Your mom, too."

"Yeah." I nodded. "They're not too bad for parents."

The warning bell rang. Megan arched a brow again, still waiting for me to get to the point.

Oh yeah, that. I had, like, thirty seconds to ask her before someone else did. "Will you go to the Freshman Fall Dance with me on Friday?" The words poured out of me in a jumble. "And be my girlfriend again?"

She grinned. "I thought you'd never ask, Cooper." Then she stood on her tiptoes and gave me a kiss. And sent my world into a tailspin.

This had to be the best day ever.

I hurried off to my next class, still thinking about Megan, not really paying attention to anything else. I headed down the hall by the front offices and nearly ran into Sergeant Ring.

"Cooper. A word?"

I ducked into the principal's office with Mike's dad while the gossip mill got busy in the hall. Seeing me get pulled into the office with a uniformed cop would be enough to keep people talking about me for a year.

"We found your stepfather," Sergeant Ring said as soon as the door shut behind us, taking a seat on the corner of Mr. Hinkley's desk. Mr. Hinkley wasn't there—probably out busting tardies. "At the bottom of the well."

"Was he . . . ?" I let the sentence trail off. The last time I saw Sam, my mother and I had called the fire department as soon as we had left his land. But by the time the firefighters arrived, it was too late. The fire had moved extremely quickly, and the entire Jumel grounds were burned to a crisp—the woods, the winery, the McMansion, everything. Strangely, the inferno hadn't spread beyond the bounds of the Jumel property. It had taken them nearly a week to sort through the rubble.

Mike's dad nodded. "We found the skeletons of his workers down there, too. Looks like he might have been responsible. He must have realized we were putting two and two together with the disappearances and leaped to his death."

"He had been acting really weird lately." Understatement of the year.

Sergeant Ring leaned in closer. Human lie detector. He stared at me for a long, long moment before drawing back. "And that well—it wasn't like a regular well. It had a tunnel in it. Very odd."

I shrugged. "I don't know. Sam never told me anything. He didn't like me much."

Sergeant Ring just nodded. He ran a hand through his hair. "Hey, that wine from your stepfather's office—it was bad or something," he said. "Tasted like crap. Made me sicker than a damned dog. I swore off drinking after that."

"Really?"

"Yeah. I had some last night, and I tell you, I don't know why people said that vineyard was so good, because that stuff was awful." He closed the gap between us, back in menacing-cop mode. "You *are* going to keep that between us, though, right?"

"Yeah, sure." Mike's dad had drunk the wine *last* night. After all of this had ended. Maybe everything had been true, and once the Jumel legacy was over, the wine spoiled, too. If it sobered up Mike's dad, hey, maybe there was one bright side to this whole thing. I toyed with the dictionary on the shelf. Tried to act cool. "Did you, ah, find anything else down there?"

"No. Just your stepfather and the skeletons of the dead babies he'd 'lost' and the six missing workers. Nothing else. I'm sorry about your stepfather." Mike's dad went on about contacting my mom for funeral arrangements or something, but I wasn't listening.

There'd been no other skeletons, no other bodies.

Meaning they hadn't found the creature.

Had he disappeared, like the vine man I'd obliterated on the stairs, when he died?

Or had he survived?

My gaze went to the window. The warm day suddenly felt cold. No one could have survived that fall, the stabbing by Sam, the fire . . .

Could he have?

But he had lasted two hundred years, when any ordinary thing would have died . . .

No, he was dead, I decided and started to turn away.

My new cell phone rang, and I dug it out of my pocket. Who could have the phone number already? Even I didn't know the number. I flipped the top and put it to my ear. "Hello?"

Silence.

"Hello?"

And then a sound started. At first I thought it was the chatter of static, the hum of a bad connection. But the noise intensified and began to grow in volume, and a chill ran down my spine.

There was only one sound like that in the world. The quiet, evil undertow of—

Laughter.

A. J. WHITTEN is a pseudonym for *New York Times* best-selling author Shirley Jump writing with her teenage daughter, Amanda. A shared love of horror movies and a desire to spice up the Shakespeare stories that are required reading in high school led to their collaboration on *The Well*. Learn more at **www.ajwhitten.com.**